DMITRY SHELEG

The Heir of an Ancient Bloodline

Remember the heroes of yesteryear!

D Sheleg

Living Ice

BOOK ONE

PUBLISHED BY MAGIC DOME BOOKS
IN COLLABORATION WITH 1C-PUBLISHING

The Heir of an Ancient Bloodline
Living Ice Book 1

Published by Magic Dome Books in collaboration
with 1C-Publishing, 2024

ISBN: 978-80-7693-508-2

This book is entirely a work of fiction. Any correlation with real people or events is coincidental.

Table of Contents:

Prologue

THE SILENCE IN THE ROOM was broken by the rhythmic, long-familiar sound of medical devices running, keeping a feeble body alive.

An ancient man lay on a hard couch and patiently waited for news. He was quite the expert at that; he'd been doing nothing else for the past fifty years. He wasn't too uncomfortable under all the pipes or in the cold air down in the cellar.

He'd managed to get used to the first of those things in his long years of being paralyzed, and he had a special relationship to the second.

On the surface, he wasn't much to look at. His emaciated skeleton was draped with thin, wrinkled skin covered in unpleasantly colored spots. Many disfigured varicose veins stood out plainly on his body. A bald head without a bit of hair, a toothless mouth, and hollow faded eyes put the finishing touches on the portrait of a man clinging to life.

Truly, no one would have recognized him now as the renowned prince of the Morozov bloodline, once a mighty warrior and mage, one of the pillars of the Nosiriansky Empire, the favorite of Empress Anastasia the Second, living out his days in the house of his son-in-law — his late daughter's husband.

From outside the door came a barely audible rustle. The door opened, and an elderly but sturdy man — who hadn't yet lost his warrior's build but no longer radiated the strength he once relied on — came silently into the room.

The ancient mage's loyal old servant was gently carrying the body of a ten-year-old boy in his arms and shedding soundless tears.

The mage's eyes widened as he understood the tragedy that had taken place. The room abruptly became colder.

Had he waited in vain for fifty years, only for all hope of reviving his bloodline to disappear? Or was there still hope?

"He killed him," the servant whispered, falling to his knees and extending his arms to show the boy's body to his master. "He killed him right after the ritual."

He shook with silent sobs.

His favorite student! Slain by the hand of his own father for not making it through the ritual testing his magical abilities! He'd turned out to be a Normal — someone with no predisposition for magic. But that was no reason for a man to kill his own little son! Besides, the power would be passed down to another generation later on. And a child with no magical abilities simply wouldn't become a very powerful mage — he could still have become a mage. In the very worst case, he could have become a warrior. It wasn't the usual path for someone from a noble house, but if there was no other, what was to be done? The old blood could have been preserved that way too. But... such thoughts were now useless... the boy was dead...

"Theophane, how long ago did this happen?" A croaking, inhuman voice filled with an otherworldly strength rang out.

The servant froze. Sweat broke out on his face, his heart pounded madly in his chest, and his hands began to tremble.

"Two minutes ago!" he whispered, swallowing the saliva that had become sticky in his mouth. "After the ritual, I took the boy and hurried straight to you!"

The old servant was frightened, very frightened, for his master had spoken for the first time in thirty years. He couldn't believe it.

"It is not too late," said the old mage thoughtfully. He commanded: "Lay Ivan down directly on my chest."

Theophane unquestioningly did as his master asked and stood still, hoping for a miracle. He understood what had to happen and gratefully bowed his head, accepting with respect and pride the great trust that the old mage was showing to him.

Not everyone would reveal to others, not even to a loyal servant, knowledge of demonic rituals. On the other hand, the old mage had no companion more loyal.

Theophane was not a narrow-minded man — he had lived through too much for such weakness. For this reason he understood that sometimes life forced such circumstances, and worse, to be necessary. In any case, he had no intention of condemning his master for wanting to save his bloodline.

The old mage placed his emaciated hand on his grandson's head and, closing his eyes, went still as ice.

The room abruptly became colder, more and more with each passing second. The walls, the floor, and the ceiling became covered in frost, then a coat of thick ice.

"Death adds years to one's life," said the old mage with a kind of madness in his voice. "Know this, Theophane! And remember that when Ivan awakens, he will not be the same as before!"

"I will remember, Master!" cried Theophane.

"Then you may go! Let me handle the rest!" The old mage's voice reverberated powerfully, and Theophane hurried from the room, not wanting to watch him perform his last ritual before death.

In truth, he couldn't have been present for it

— anyone unprepared would simply die amid the unruly magical energy.

The magic made his skin break out in goosebumps and his hair stand on end, even though he had stepped away from the door into safety. The Morozov prince was rightly regarded as one of the most powerful sorcerers in the world.

The temperature of the air in the hallway and the nearby rooms dropped even lower.

If this goes on for long, people will start to show up wondering what's happening, thought Theophane. *We can only hope that doesn't happen.*

He uttered a foul curse, checked that his weapons were still in their hidden sheaths, and stood still. As usual, this gave him confidence in his own strength.

He managed a crooked smirk. If necessary, he would spill the blood of this entire wretched household.

If he could have seen through the wall, he would have seen an elaborate, many-tiered seal made of ice surrounding the old mage and his grandson.

It burned with a ghostly blue fire and pulsed in time with the old mage's heartbeat as he worked the magic.

At a certain point, the endless stream of power rushed into the boy's body. Rekindled from the inside, it began to twitch in time with the old mage's heart too.

The pulsing flashes grew faster and faster.

The old mage's face turned white from the monstrous exertion, his frightful throbbing veins showed through even more clearly, his dry and worn teeth turned dark, his mouth opened in some kind of wild soundless scream, but he obstinately continued to put all of his strength into the ritual.

His persistence was soon rewarded.

A blinding flash from the boy's body marked the end of the ritual, and the boy — who had only been lying there on his grandfather's chest for a short while — let out a loud cough.

The seal immediately stopped its pulsating. Another instant, and the elaborate pattern of weightless crystals dissolved into the air.

Theophane, sensing that the ritual had ended, reentered the room.

The boy was breathing.

A single tear rolled down Theophane's wrinkled face, and his heart ached. He respectfully bowed to his now-lifeless master, who'd known many things that today's mages had no power to do.

He took the boy in his arms and carried him from the room. He had to get him out of the house quickly, and he had to do it without being noticed — no one could know that Ivan was alive.

No such luck. Just past the door he ran into a patrol squad — a mage and two soldiers.

"What happened here?" asked the eldest of them, a mage wearing a second-level master's degree holder's ring, shivering from the cold and emanations left behind by the magic.

A dangerous opponent, thought Theophane, calculating his odds.

"Hey! Servant! I'm talking to you!" said the mage in an irritated voice. Theophane answered quickly:

"My master is dead." He lowered his head and explained, "You are feeling the effects of his death."

"Well, look at that! The old geezer really kicked the bucket!" said one of the young soldiers in astonishment, glancing into the room.

Theophane frowned. No one dared to address a prince so disrespectfully in his presence, not even in death.

Sometimes he felt sorry for the residents of the Temnikov estate, not knowing there was a Hero-rank warrior among them, and believing that the rumors circulating about the Morozov servant were just empty tales.

Or perhaps it's a good thing, he thought. *If they knew, they wouldn't be so careless.*

"Why do you have the boy's corpse?" asked the mage, gesturing to Ivan.

"Corpse?" Theophane raised his head suspiciously. "Where did you hear that the boy was dead? I took him from the ritual hall only a few minutes ago."

The head of the family would never have started spreading the news of his own son's death, so this information couldn't have reached the public ear so quickly.

Theophane studied the patrol squad's uniforms carefully and noticed the Belov family insignia.

Why not the Temnikov insignia? he thought, puzzled. *Why is the new wife's family showing such presumptuousness in another house? What's even happening?*

The mage gave him an irritated smile.

"Where did I hear that he was dead?" he said, then promptly answered his own question: "It's not a secret to anyone. A prince has no need of a Normal in a gifted family."

The high-born can be prejudiced, but not usually to this extent! thought Theophane, suspecting foul play. *Something is wrong here.*

"Can we kill him now?" said one of the soldiers to the mage. "As we were ordered? Why are we standing here talking to him? He can't know any of this — he's just some old man."

So... this means that Ivan and the master's deaths were planned in advance? Theophane suddenly understood what the Belov family was plotting.

"Shut up!" hissed the mage to the soldier. "It was worth waiting to see if it worked, and he — "

He didn't have time to finish his sentence, because the next moment his head split from his body. Even with a second-level master's degree, neither his defensive amulets nor his fairly high rank in the magical hierarchy came to his aid. Against a legendary swordmaster trained in the school of "Steel Autumn's Death," his magical arts proved useless.

He hadn't even finished falling before both of his companions collapsed to the ground unconscious. Still alive, for now, for a good swordmaster needed "tongues" with important information. They would die after he interrogated them — their fate was decided.

The mage clearly knew more, thought Theophane calmly, taking the bodies into the room where his master had died, *but he could have made for a few unpleasant surprises. I hope these two will be enough.*

Theophane moved quickly — the cellar would soon be filled with interested parties and innocent bystanders alike, and his chance to get away from the estate in secret would be reduced to almost nothing.

He laid Ivan on the ground not too far from himself, then got to work — he clenched the younger soldier's mouth in his huge palm, then started to drive a dagger into painful spots, severing the nerves and depriving him of his ability to move with cold-blooded composure.

"Mmm..." the soldier mumbled, woken by the pain.

"You can't move now," Theophane said quietly to him. He set to wounding him with just as much cold-blooded composure, trying to make it as painful as possible without touching any vital organs. A "tongue" needed some strength left for a thoughtful discussion.

His prisoner writhed, trying to say at least a word or two, but Theophane didn't give him the chance. He continued mutilating his wounded body, waiting for the unending pain to make him desperate to speak only truth.

"I need answers," said Theophane, staring into his agonized eyes. "Answer honestly, and I'll let you live. Don't, and you'll die an awful death."

Then he took his hand away from the face of the young man, who started to babble erratically:

"I know that Morozov was supposed to die today. We were ordered to confirm it and kill his servant! That's all! I know nothing else!"

"You sure?" Theophane asked him menacingly, squeezing the soldier's mouth closed again and driving his knife into his leg.

"Mmm!" The soldier lurched upwards in pain. "We... we... we... I heard that Morozov might give you information, something about his money! That we were supposed to get his money. But the other soldiers and I didn't believe that he would trust an ordinary servant with important secrets. That's everything I know! I swear!"

Theophane looked at his prisoner's arm.

A first-level Soldier — not bad for a boy his age, he thought.

The interrogation continued.

As it turned out, Theophane had guessed correctly. Temnikov's new wife had tried to deprive the Morozovs of their rightful heir.

And all over some wretched money!

Apparently, the death of the bloodline's hope was supposed to be the last straw for the old mage living out these long years in the cellar and battling with death each day. Surely that one desire was keeping him alive — the hope of prolonging his ancient bloodline.

And it worked, Theophane realized sorrowfully. *My master is dead. Now that Belov woman will become the rightful proprietress of this estate, and slowly but surely she'll be able to eliminate the children with Morozov blood, so that her descendants will rise to the head of the Temnikov line. That witch!*

Of course, despite her caution, the lowlife hadn't taken into account the old Morozov prince's unbelievable power — and the fact that the family barely had any money!

The young soldier suddenly screamed, looking in horror at the boy — killed by his own father not long ago — standing by the wall. "He's alive again! He's alive! He's alive!"

Ivan was standing motionless, staring attentively at the soldier covered in blood and Theophane with the long knife in his hand.

I didn't even notice that he'd come to, thought Theophane in astonishment, driving his knife into the terrified soldier's eye. *No one must know that the Morozov heir is alive.*

The second soldier died without waking up — a stab to the heart ended his journey through this life. Theophane quickly wiped the blood from his knife, approached Ivan, and took him by the hand.

Ivan took one silent look at him and fainted.

He hasn't recovered yet — it's not every day one rises from the dead, thought Theophane. *Good thing he's unconscious anyway. He won't make trouble. I'll get him into a car and create a few distractions. I hope that will give us enough time to escape.*

"Farewell, Master," he said quietly aloud to the lifeless old mage, whose body was slowly but surely turning to ice. "I will raise your heir! The house of Morozov must live!"

Chapter 1

DO YOU KNOW what cold is?

No… what *real*, bone-tearing, freezing cold is? When your whole being trembles and writhes, trying to keep in at least a tiny bit of warmth. When you slowly start to lose feeling in all of your limbs, and your eyes become two frozen ice crystals. When your body naively attempts to save itself by raising the tiniest hairs, trying to create an “insulating coat” to preserve a tiny bit of heat and draw out the slow agony.

When it starts to seem like the blood in your veins has turned to *ice*, and red, sharp, chafing little crystals are being pumped straight to your heart. Your body starts to convulse, your muscles are reduced to spasms.

That is the *end!* You’ve spent all your energy on your spasming muscles, your body can’t give your brain everything it needs. Your thoughts become muddled, you start to hallucinate.

You're freezing, and you know for sure that it's over! There will be nothing else! You'll never laugh and have good times with your friends like you used to, enjoy life without a care, spend your time on interesting work, take care of your children, love your wife...

There will be nothing... nothing good, nothing bad. At this point you'd be ready to take the bad, the worst life you could imagine, if only you could remain among the living.

None of it will be there anymore — you know it, it'll all be gone, because you're dying. You're dying horrifically and torturously — you're freezing to death.

You're cold on the outside, you're cold on the inside, you are the cold.

It's like you're becoming a silent block of ice with a heart, beating weakly and very slowly, burning and longing for warmth.

You know that you want to live! LIVE! Feel! But it's too late.

Your oxygen-deprived brain sends muddled hallucinations to your fevered mind. You feel some kind of force taking hold of you, as if you're a little grain of sand, and dragging you swiftly to who knows where.

After a few moments, you suddenly feel like you're in a web of cold light.

Ice everywhere... ice and cold... they

surround you from every side and nourish you with their powerful energy. It doesn't scare you at all — after everything you've been through, you're not afraid of ice. You're intimately familiar with it.

"You have understood with your very being what piercing cold is." A strange voice calls out to you. *"From now on, you shall be the heir of the Morozov bloodline! You must be worthy!"*

You see a bright flash in your mind's eye, and you plummet into nonexistence.

* * *

Waking up wasn't fun.

The first thing I noticed when I woke up was that I'd fallen asleep in a really bad position, and clearly not anywhere I wanted to be. This was obvious from whatever I was lying on, which was way too flat and hard.

I lowered my hand and felt smooth ceramic tile.

I must've really gotten wasted if I passed out in the bathroom, I thought, a little irritated. No wonder everything hurt and I had a headache.

I wasn't a big fan of getting drunk — strike that, I was a big fan of not getting drunk. Sometimes I let myself have a little alcohol at parties, though, and only if I was in good friendly company. So waking up in a place like this in such a disgusting condition was new for me.

On the other hand, at least this would be an

interesting experience, I thought with a smirk. Now I'd know what a real hangover felt like.

In addition to the pain and the sudden nausea, memories were nagging at me. What a realistic dream… it had been so unusual and scary that my heart was pounding and didn't seem to have any intention of calming down.

As if I really died from the cold. Brr… I shuddered.

What I saw when I opened my eyes plunged me into deep, paralyzing shock.

Right in front of me, a brawny old man with a plain, creased face and a long, thick ponytail was torturing someone who was lying on the ground. He was doing it pretty professionally and with amazing skill, too.

He was holding the poor man to the ground with his huge knee, preventing him from moving. He was squeezing this poor stranger's mouth with his left hand and holding a long crooked knife in his right, using the knife skillfully to slice into his soft flesh as he tried to scream.

Oh, hell! What on earth was going on here?

The floor and walls near this butcher-looking guy were literally covered in blood, but — to my poorly timed and meaningless surprise — the old man didn't have a drop on him.

What was I thinking? Idiot! What difference did it make if he had blood on him or not? I scolded myself. I had to run away fast before he finished up with this guy and got to me.

To my embarrassment, I knew full well that I had no chance against a maniac. Even though I worked out, used to like wrestling when I was younger, and had gotten into a few dozen street fights, I knew I couldn't handle a burly, armed man. And this guy wasn't exactly young.

Despite the whole mix of vivid emotions inside of me, on the outside I was completely still. It seemed like my feelings were locked somewhere deep in my soul, like something was stifling them and not letting them escape to the outside. Like they were raging behind thick armored glass, which — unlike it usually would — was letting at least a few quiet, incoherent words through for me to hear.

Behind thick armored glass. The phrase struck me unexpectedly, and I repeated it slowly in my mind. Armored glass, armored glass... I kept repeating it, trying to prod my memory into understanding the association. Armored glass... glass... glass... or, perhaps, ice? ICE?

My head was in roaring turmoil.

I realized my headache was from the awakening of memories that had been languishing inside of me. Two lives flashed before my eyes at once: the life of a ten-year-old boy, and the life of a grown man.

The boy was named Ivan, after his renowned grandfather. He was the seventh son of the head of the Temnikov house and the heir to the Morozov bloodline.

His mother had died in labor after pouring all her strength into birthing him, allowing him to be born strong and healthy. His birth had brought hope to the Morozov line.

His mother's father, Ivan's grandfather, had conceived a daughter late into his old age, in an utterly hopeless condition, after the rest of his family had died under tragic circumstances — defending themselves against an attack from some kind of demonic army that had broken free near their family estate. So Ivan had no relatives on his mother's side.

If fate hadn't turned its back on the old man again, his new wife would have given him a son who would have undergone the initiation ritual, and he would have lived the rest of his days in peace. But she'd given him a daughter, and she'd died in childbirth. So it had fallen to the old Morozov prince not only to raise his daughter and arrange her marriage, but also to wait for the birth of grandsons.

The situation had been made even worse by an ancient magical law that stated only the seventh son of a female heir had the right to inherit in the name of her bloodline. According to the noble family code, this law had been made many centuries ago, in a time of great warriors, to prevent strong magical families from declining after the death of several heirs.

Only his immovable willpower and his desire to sustain his bloodline had kept the old mage's soul tethered to the living world. None among mortals knew how he'd done it, how he'd lasted long enough to finally see the birth of his long-awaited heir.

Ivan had been raised and educated by Theophane, a "Hero"-rank warrior who had long ago sworn his loyalty to the house of Morozov, and just as long ago been struck from the record of those living. He was the one torturing the man on the floor.

The boy Ivan's memories were as clear as they could be, but the second person's memories were superficial and incomplete. I saw fragments of someone's life as he'd grown up, gone to school, worked at a construction site, served in the army, gone to college... I remembered him studying, dating, getting married, rejoicing at the birth of his children, having a job somewhere with a lot of ice and snow...

However, most of this person's memories appeared in a bunch of incoherent forms that I didn't have the energy to decipher at the moment.

A little bit of good did come of this: my understanding of the world had changed. I was no longer a little boy blindly hoping to lead the Morozov bloodline to greatness — I had become a grown man with some solid life experience and a general knowledge of world order, used to making independent decisions and analyzing situations. I had started to think more flexibly, and I knew that the goal of life could be so much more than that.

The second person had one very unpleasant and extremely brutal memory — he remembered his own death. A terrible death from unimaginable cold, which would now be with me forever.

So what was keeping these strong feelings from spilling out? Cold? Ice? How should I describe this state of being? Did I even need to?

I realized that it was the cold saving me from flying into hysterics over the two minds inside me. Who was I — Ivan Temnikov with the mind of a grown man? Or, conversely, a fragment of a foreign soul with a little boy's memory?

I rose to my feet. Surprisingly, my body obeyed readily.

Did that mean I was Ivan? And not that man? If not, it would take me a while to get used to this new body's childlike proportions. Although I might be wrong — this was my first time doing this.

At that moment, Theophane grabbed me with his strong hands. The look in his eyes was cold and full of unbelievable cruelty. For a moment I was terrified that he would kill me, and it would all end right there...

I woke up in the back seat of a car. A Jeep (based on how it looked from the inside, at least, that was what it was) was confidently tearing down a deserted road through the night, taking us farther and farther from the Temnikov estate.

"How are you doing?" asked Theophane as soon as he noticed I was awake.

"I'm fine," I answered mechanically after a

slight pause, which was enough to examine my general state.

Theophane watched me attentively through the rearview mirror.

"That's good," he said thoughtfully and slowly. "Move up to the front seat — we need to have a serious talk."

I was a pretty skinny boy, fairly agile and well trained too, so I slipped between the two front seats of the car without difficulty. I sat in the front seat as he'd suggested and buckled my seatbelt.

I'd definitely need it, I thought for some reason. All kinds of things happened on the road — even a warrior like Theophane could run into some drunk idiot who was out driving, and no amount of battle prowess could save him from that.

A little jab of pain shot through the back of my head, like it had been stabbed with a knitting needle.

My two sets of memories were strangely interlaced, allowing me to operate freely off of one or the other.

Sitting next to Theophane, I saw him both as my wise mentor who had raised me from my early childhood and as a dangerous man who'd killed defenseless people right before my eyes. I felt like I was Ivan Temnikov, heir to the Morozov bloodline, but at the same time I knew that I was someone from another world.

Why another world? I guess because in that

world there was no such thing as mages and a lot of stuff like that.

For example, even the car we were riding in right now. It gave me a feeling of cognitive dissonance. Sure, on a technical level, cars from different worlds shouldn't be that different from each other. There was the steering wheel, here were the seats, the gearbox, the back, the glove compartment, and the speedometer! And the speedometer was in Arabic numerals, by the way! But everything looked a little off. Maybe it all came down to that.

I got another jab of pain in my head.

The car was what surprised me? What about the language I was speaking — how I was so confidently speaking Russian with him? What about the existence of magic? And ancient noble lineages? None of that surprised me? How could I sit here puzzling over how unbelievably similar the technology was between these two worlds when there were all these obvious historical and supernatural differences? Could this be the parallel world that had been written about in stories? Extremely different from ours, but at the same time unbelievably similar? Where had I heard that?

Jab to the head.

There it was again! How did I see myself? As the boy or as the man? I needed to figure it out quickly, or I'd just go out of my mind!

Theophane cleared his throat quietly,

reminding me that he was there, and all the unwanted thoughts disappeared from my mind.

I had to admit, my proximity to this cold-blooded killer frightened me a bit. Even now in a peaceful, almost home-like setting, he seemed extremely dangerous and powerful. Somewhere in my soul I felt a dark strength coming from him.

It was really strange, because Ivan would never have felt anything like this — he had great respect for his mentor. I remembered Theophane as not only a good teacher but also a merciless killer.

I wondered what he'd do if he found out there was another mind in his student's body. What made this new consciousness appear in the first place? Was it the ritual my father did? Seemed unlikely. He was only supposed to be testing whether I'd become a mage or not...

On that note, why had Theophane tortured that poor man? And why were we leaving the estate? What was going on in general? Maybe we were leaving because I'd turned out to be an "intruder?" The Temnikovs wanted to kill me, and Theophane was saving me? Entirely logical...

Or were we fleeing for another reason?

I got another sharp pain in my head, and my memory forcefully showed me new details from the grown man's life.

Interesting, I thought grimly. With all these personality quirks, wouldn't I be diagnosed with schizophrenia?

Once again, I hadn't noticed that I'd retreated into myself, but Theophane had stopped scaring me now. I felt a firm confidence that this man could never cause me any harm. Well, at the very least, not as long as he thought I was a Morozov!

"Ivan, why are you so quiet?" he asked, frowning a bit. "Usually you're more inquisitive and ask me a lot of questions. I think this is exactly the kind of situation where that habit would be very appropriate."

"I'm apprehensive about asking questions because I may get answers that disconcert me," I answered mechanically without thinking, then immediately bit my tongue.

That was a very adult sentence. It wasn't what a child would say. I had to be more careful.

Theophane frowned, and I could sense his anger — which, thank the Savior, was clearly not directed at me.

Hold on, what's this about the "Savior?" I thought involuntarily. I racked my brains. Oh, a local deity! Okay.

"In that case, ask them," said Theophane. "A warrior must look his fears in the eye."

"Is that so?" I said slowly and thoughtfully, then made up my mind. "All right. Then can you tell me what happened in Grandfather's room? Why did you kill those people? Why did we leave the estate? How did my ritual go? And where are we going?"

I hoped that his answers might give me some

idea of why I had an unexpected "intruder" in my body, and I could work out a plan of action from there.

Something in me shuddered at that thought. The cold inside me clearly told me that *I* was the "intruder."

How can this be? I thought in bewilderment. *How?*

Images flashed before my eyes — memories of a man dying from the cold.

All right, so let's say I died. How did I end up in Ivan's body? Did I kill him? I'd started connecting to the cold in a way I couldn't understand.

"What's the last thing you remember?" asked Theophane, cutting into my thoughts and giving me a demanding look.

For a moment it seemed like that wrinkled face somehow grew considerably older after saying that.

I swallowed, gripping my seatbelt. I obviously couldn't tell him while he was distracted from the road that I'd frozen to death in another world and woken up in his student's body.

"I remember walking down stone stairs," I said, tracking down Ivan's last memory. "I was going to the ritual hall with my father." I went silent, trying to remember at least something else, but in vain — my memories cut off there. "And that's all. Then I woke up in Grandfather's room."

Theophane, thank the Savior, looked back at

the road and spoke resolutely with dry, clenched teeth.

"You died."

I was dumbstruck, to say the least.

Did he know I was an "intruder," and was he treating me the same as he always used to anyway? That couldn't be!

"The ritual revealed that you're an ordinary person, and your father killed you."

Oh. No, he didn't know, I thought, relieved. Then, realizing what he'd just said, I added:

"So why am I alive?"

Come on, I thought, prove that you're telling the truth, spill everything you know. I was really glad he'd already given away that Ivan's father killed him, and my soul accidentally filled the empty shell. I wasn't a murderer, I was just a replacement. Although I had to admit, if I had to choose between dying for real and taking Ivan's place, I wouldn't even consider it.

"The Master performed a forbidden ritual and spent the last of his life on bringing you back from the dead," said Theophane with a gentle sadness.

"Now YOU are the heir of the Morozov bloodline! You must be worthy!" That unknown, solemn voice overwhelmed my memory.

That was it! In some kind of forbidden ritual! Did that mean I hadn't taken Ivan's place by accident? Was I specially chosen to take his place? So that he could live? But why... me?

"You have understood with your very being

what piercing cold is!" that strange voice rang out in my head.

I sighed internally.

If someone had told me that dying from the cold could bring me new life, I would have just given him a cuckoo finger twirl.

An unexpected thought lifted my mood a bit.

It occurred to me that I was just one of many chronic drinkers, most of whom had also known the cold in some way, getting terrible chills after drinking too much, and any one of them could have been here in my place.

I figured that Ivan's grandfather here in this "other world" would have some choice words if he could see someone like that in the body of his family's heir. Or maybe he was already looking down on me and uttering those choice words.

"So my grandfather brought me back to life?" I asked. "And you're driving me out of here so I don't get killed again?"

"You could put it that way," said Theophane.

"And what are we planning to do after that? Where are we going?"

Theophane nodded approvingly.

"To start off, we're getting away from the Temnikov estate. We're going to disappear, get new documents, and settle down somewhere near the Wastelands." Theophane was silent for a moment, then continued: "I'll continue your instruction there. Now that we know you're a Normal, there's only one path left to you if you're going to revive the bloodline."

"And what's that?" I asked, knowing full well that I didn't want to revive any sort of bloodline, since it was surely a difficult and thankless task. All kinds of obstacles would be waiting for me on that path — plus, this bloodline was completely alien to me. I was just an "intruder."

Right now, all I wanted was to settle down somewhere peaceful, getting to know this new world. With the experience from my past life, I could earn money for a comfortable old age — enough not only for a little bread and water, but also for the things I really needed. But not every ancient bloodline revival was my kind of ancient bloodline revival. Or was it?

"You're going to be a warrior."

"Like you?" I asked.

"Like me," said Theophane. "Believe me, I've killed plenty of mages, and I'll be able to turn you into just as strong and skilled a warrior," he continued. "Even as a Normal, you'll be able to stand on equal footing with the heads of other families."

And what if I don't want to kill anyone? I thought angrily — killing made me sick. But I decided to keep asking questions. Information was more important than meaningless feelings.

"And why are we going to live near the Wastelands?" was my next question. "Isn't there a nicer place we could go? What's the reason for that?"

Ivan thought of the Wastelands as a dangerous place where arcane creatures lived. As a child, he'd been told stories of demons living there, but I knew that those didn't exist. It was most likely an allegory. Maybe there was high radiation in those areas? Uranium mines, for instance? Or the fallout from some kind of manmade disaster? All kinds of mutated animals could result from that. Or some mage was causing trouble out there, cross-breeding different species of animals. There could be two-headed wolves or six-legged boars with shark teeth running around there, for instance. Who wouldn't see those as demons?

"You're asking good questions," said Theophane. "Here's the reason. The destructive energy of those defiled lands prevent someone from being found with magic rituals, within about ten miles of the Wasteland borders. Rituals will just show that the person you're looking for is dead."

"If that's common knowledge, then they could just search for us physically near the Wastelands. There isn't an infinite number of them! They'll find us at some point!" I said, looking at Theophane. "They could even find us because of you, for instance. They'll be looking for a long-haired old man named Theophane and a ten-year-old boy."

"You're right, my appearance is plain but memorable. Thankfully, appearances can be disguised. What I'm wondering, though, is why you're so certain we're going to be searched for."

"You said it yourself!" I said indignantly, seeing that he was smiling. "We're going to hide out by the Wastelands so that I can't be searched for with rituals. That means someone's going to do it for some reason!"

Theophane laughed quietly. "I phrased that badly. Your father is the head of the family and an experienced mage. Do you think that he thinks you're dead or not?"

"Of course he thinks I'm dead," I answered without even thinking about it. "I'm pretty sure he can tell a dead person from a live one."

"So you insist that he's certain of your death?"

"I guess so."

"Well, look. At the very least, he knows that you died."

I nodded. Indeed, if my father had seen my dead body, he couldn't have doubted my death.

"We're hiding there," said Theophane, "so that if someone conducts a ritual of family, a living and healthy relative won't be detected."

"And what about my corpse? Won't it raise suspicion if it's missing?"

"Don't worry about that — before we left, I took a few measures to resolve that."

"All right," I said, then asked my next question: "And how long do I have to stay in hiding? My whole life?"

"No. But until you become a strong enough

warrior, at least at the Veteran rank, it's too early to talk about that."

I got lost in thought. The local system of warrior rankings was somewhat similar to the hierarchy of East Asian elemental martial arts, where after advanced mastery a warrior progressed to the final level — "dan." Here, the path of a warrior was called by special names: Novice, Junior, Soldier, Militant, Veteran, Knight, and Hero. Each rank, in turn, was divided into two levels: the first for the weaker representatives of the rank, and the second for the stronger. In principle, it was simple and easy to understand.

At the moment, Ivan was a second-level Novice, and he was preparing to move up a rank, which was both very unusual and very good for a boy of his age. As far as I knew, however, warriors of the Veteran rank were incredibly rare — even in the Temnikov family, there was only one! The rest were much weaker. So it seemed to me that I'd need something like thirty years to reach that rank, if not more. And warriors of the highest ranks (Knight and Hero) were almost a myth. I had no idea what Theophane expected — I might just not get good at it.

"Wait," I said, "to become a Veteran, I need to work at it for years!"

"Then so be it!" said Theophane sternly.

After that, I involuntarily shrank my head into my shoulders. Theophane very rarely used that tone of voice with Ivan.

"I understand," said Theophane with a grave sigh. "You want to become a great mage like your grandfather. You have an ambition that's hard to turn away from. But you must understand that life is a complicated thing. You're a Normal, and that means you won't become a great mage, but it's entirely possible for you to become a strong warrior... life is a very complicated thing, and at times it snatches away what we hold most dear. At times like that, the most important thing is not to break down. You have to simply grit your teeth and go forward step by step, despite the unbelievable pain and hardship of your circumstances bearing down on you, striving to reach your goal... over the course of this difficult path you'll suddenly realize that the pain has left you, the hardship is gone, and you can easily step over the obstacles on your path. Thus, the most important thing: go forward!

"For fate and fortune always smile on the persistent, the strong, and the determined. Go forward towards your goal, and everything will work itself out!"

Theophane spoke with such zeal, such heartfelt force, such passion, that I got a little uncomfortable. I sensed that I'd struck a nerve and reminded him of something he didn't want to be reminded of.

"How much time do you think we have until someone does a ritual to find us?" I asked after a bit, to break the drawn-out silence.

"A few days," he said after thinking about it.

"So soon?" It was my turn to be surprised. "Do they do them constantly, or what?"

"It's not that. After all the Morozovs are gone, your older brother George is going to help your father get access to the family's bank account."

I have a bank account? I thought with delight. Finally, some kind of upside to switching to this body. And who knew? The Morozovs were a very old family, so that meant they had a lot of money!

"I hope they don't manage it," I said, alarmed.

I'd have to find out just how they determined whose money it is — surely with the help of some kind of magic.

"They won't," said Theophane with a smirk. "The family's heir is alive! That means they'll have no access to the money."

"Aha, and when they have no access to the money, they'll decide to check for some Morozov heir nobody knows about!" I guessed.

"Very possible, and they won't find anyone."

"But then they'll do a ritual searching for the mystery relative! And looking for someone you don't know is a waste of time."

"Most likely, but if they look at the account statement, I think they'll decide not to do that."

"What's wrong with the account statement?" I asked, suspecting the worst. "And how would they even get their hands on it?"

"Your father has that right after your grandfather's death. However, I'm sure that he'll be very disappointed, since there's almost no money there."

"What?" I said indignantly. My illusory dream of a carefree future collapsed before my eyes. "How can that be? Our bloodline is ancient! There should be a lot of money!"

"It's almost completely drained. Many resources went to your mother's education and dowry. No one wants to talk to a woman without a dowry these days.

"A lot of money was spent on life support equipment, which isn't cheap, and very expensive potions for your grandfather. There is still some left, a small sum by noble families' standards, for your academic studies, but you won't be able to withdraw it for a few years."

"So we have no resources to live on?" I confirmed, upset.

"Oh, something will turn up," said Theophane with a casual cheerfulness.

Wow, you're a bad actor! I thought, looking at his wooden smile.

"Why do you think they won't start looking for the heir tomorrow? Why do you think we have a couple days?"

"I told you, I had to leave them some nasty surprises. Blew something up here, killed someone there, left a few pieces of false evidence pointing to the presence of rival families to keep them occupied with other things. Actually, though," Theophane added, "I hope they aren't quite the scoundrels that they seem, and they'll at least wait until the end of the mourning period announced after your death. That will give us a lot of extra time."

"So you prepared for us to flee in advance?" I said. "And why did you kill those people?"

"I killed them primarily because they saw you were alive. And yes, I did prepare this in advance. But that was just a standard precaution. I prefer always being prepared for the worst and using measures that I've already set up rather than improvising. I'm not as young as I used to be."

We drove in silence for a while.

"If we assume that my father didn't know the real situation and decided to seize the Morozov assets, then is it possible that he doesn't care at all if I'm a mage or a Normal? Could he have killed me so that the loss would be the death of my grandfather? Then the Temnikovs would get the Morozovs' assets without a fight. Isn't that right? And he'll say that I couldn't handle the ritual or died inexplicably from something. Isn't that right?

"You're a good thinker," said Theophane, confirming my guesses. After a bit, he said, "Get some sleep. We have a long way to go, and you need to rest."

I nodded in agreement and closed my eyes.

To an outside observer, it would certainly have been strange to hear an old man and a ten-year-old boy conversing like equals.

But, judging by Ivan's memories, Theophane's respectful relationship to him as a mentor was just the way of things. He was a seasoned warrior training the head of an ancient bloodline, not an everyday country boy. Although at times he liked to joke with and tease him, sometimes even getting too harsh with the latter.

At some point I fell asleep, and Theophane kept driving through the night.

* * *

"Demons choke you all!" Theophane cursed quietly, pulling over and stopping.

"What happened?" I asked, coming awake and looking sleepily out of the windshield.

"The road's closed," said Theophane. He squinted and turned to look behind us.

The Temnikovs can't have reacted so quickly, can they? I thought with some unease. I examined the road, which was blocked off by two big white vans. If they had, Theophane's skills were my only hope.

Theophane clucked his tongue and explained why he was so concerned:

"It's a hunter league! Demons choke them! They must be clearing this area, so we'll have to be held up a bit."

"What's a hunter league?" I asked, studying the vans with great interest.

I was fascinated by the beacons flashing blue, yellow, and purple on their roofs. They were flashing quite brightly and were easily visible from a distance.

Beacons were beacons — they were no different from the ones on Earth. I was definitely in some kind of parallel world, I thought amid everything that was going on.

As it happened, we weren't the only ones being held up by this situation. There were a few cars on the side of the road in front of us, which reassured me a bit.

"The hunter leagues are groups of mercenaries," Theophane replied. "They search for and destroy demons and their followers, prevent local infernal breaches, and defend the district."

I stiffened, trying to process that.

So that meant the "Wastelands," the "infernal" stuff, and the "demons..." they were real? Not generally accepted metaphors for something else? They actually existed? Here and now? I needed to ask him again! I must be completely misunderstanding something!

"What demons?" I asked.

"What do you mean 'What demons?'" said Theophane with surprise. "I told you! More than once!"

"Are you talking about real demons? Strange monsters? Who devour humans' souls?"

"Well, sure, maybe the most powerful ones can devour souls," said Theophane, looking at me incredulously. "What's gotten into you?"

He was serious as could be, and I realized he was telling the truth.

"I just thought those were fairytales, and they didn't really exist…" I babbled in confusion.

That got a big, sincere laugh out of Theophane.

That meant real demons did exist? I couldn't calm myself down. Real, terrifying demons? What was this world of nightmares? Where had I ended up? Forget my crazy dad who sent his own child to kingdom come over money that basically didn't exist — no, barely existed at all — now it turned out there were demons running around here!

And to make things even more dangerous, my own mentor Theophane was going to set me up not far from where those very demons lived — next to a Wasteland! Maybe I should just blow my brains out now so I didn't have to stew about it!

"If I wasn't taking the demons seriously, that's your mistake as a mentor!" I blurted out in the heat of the moment, irritated by Theophane's nonstop laughter.

At those words, he fell silent and seemed seriously offended.

"Are we going to be sitting here long?" I asked to break the uncomfortable silence that my words had caused. "Would it be better to take another road?"

"I don't think we'll be here long," Theophane deigned to answer after a bit.

"Why's that?"

"There aren't many vans," he explained. "Only two. That means the surge of infernal energy was fairly weak. There are a lot more hunters during serious energy surges."

"So we're going to wait until they kill the demons?"

"Yes," said Theophane. "But sometimes demons don't appear by chance — sometimes they're summoned, and in that case the hunters search for the ones who did it."

What kind of idiot would you have to be to summon a demon? I thought, perplexed, then reminded Theophane of my second question.

"Can we go a different way?"

"A different way..." he muttered. "A different way... no. First of all, because the league will also have the alternate route blocked. When infernal energy appears, they close off access to a fairly large area to prevent casualties. Second, even if we decide to go, an off-road vehicle turning around in front of a hunter league's barrier will definitely attract unwanted attention. We'll immediately be suspected of demon worship and thoroughly searched, which I really don't feel like dealing with."

"Oh, so they'll be able to remember us, and that information will get back to the Temnikovs, which will narrow down their search immediately."

"That's not the only reason," said Theophane, shutting off the car's engine. "There are a lot of special weapons and equipment in the trunk, and that'll absolutely get their attention."

The hunters might not remember a

grandfather and grandson traveling together, but they'd certainly pay attention to a peculiar old man with a pile of expensive, unique weapons.

I nodded, accepting the explanation.

If that was how it is, then we'd better not draw any unnecessary attention to ourselves.

I stopped asking questions, but my curiosity remained, so I took to examining the nearest van — or, rather, the hunter league's logo on the door — attentively.

The league's insignia was fairly simple — it was a black circle with a thin red border, and in the center of the circle was a horned demon's skull impaled by a flaming spear. Under the image was written in red Gothic script: *Venatores Foederis.*

Hunters of the unholy, I unexpectedly translated for myself. What was that, Latin?

"Remember our story," said Theophane, breaking into my thoughts. "You're my grandson, your name is Roma, we're going home to Kovgrad, we were visiting relatives. Got it?"

"Yes." I nodded. "If they start to ask too many unwelcome questions, I'll say that I want to sleep and act like a brat."

Theophane chuckled approvingly.

I followed his gaze and saw that not far from us, five soldiers in green camouflage with sewn-in elbow and knee protection, heavy thick-soled boots, and bulletproof vests were coming out of the woods. The hunters' faces were hidden by ski masks, and they had conspicuous helmets on their heads.

They were armed with pistols hanging from holsters on their belts. In their hands they were holding long black machine guns, of a design I didn't recognize, with spacious magazines for their ammo. The hilts of swords stuck out behind their backs.

I sized up the strong, powerful figures of the hunters and decided that they were exactly what people who fought demons should look like.

Each of them most likely had a couple of defense amulets too!

When the squad got to our car, a sixth hunter came out of the woods — he looked like he was a mage.

He was equipped like the rest of the soldiers, but instead of a sword he had a short magic staff with a blue stone at the top, and his machine gun was neglected on his back.

"Sit quietly and keep your head down." A suddenly gloomy Theophane left me behind for reasons I didn't understand, getting out of the car and approaching the mage.

As he walked up to the soldiers, similar groups came out of the woods near the other cars stopped by the curb.

What is this, a standard inspection? I thought in surprise. Were they looking for demon worshipers?

The passenger door on my side opened unexpectedly.

"Please don't frighten the child," said Theophane coolly, turning to the mage, who was holding a strange device.

"I'll try not to," the mage replied calmly, pressing some kind of button.

"Base to all units — sound off!" The radio on the mage's chest suddenly went off. "Over!"

"Twenty-one."

"Seven."

"Ten."

"Four." The mage inspecting us quickly confirmed his reception of the signal.

"The 'woodland' is compromised!" the voice from the radio rang out. "Repeat, the 'woodland' is compromised. Two intruders broke out of the ring and are quickly moving along the road in your direction."

"Move into position!" barked the mage to the soldiers once he'd heard about the approaching threat.

"Unit twenty-one to base!" I heard a man's confident voice. "What kind of intruders?"

"Nocers," replied the first voice. "Two approaching. Prepare for encounter."

Thundering hooves, the loud sounds of demons running toward us, reached us.

"Damn, they're fast!" spat the mage. "Grenade launchers!" he commanded.

I sat there, too scared to move. The noise from the radio had drowned out the squeaking of the mage's strange device near me.

What did that mean? Was I a demon? An invader in this body? And Ivan was what? Possessed? Or was it just leftover energy from Morozov's ritual? Who the hell knew? I hoped he hadn't noticed anything.

To my surprise, huge machine guns appeared on the roofs of the vans. They turned in the direction of the approaching demons and opened fire.

The firing hadn't gone on long before the vans were hurled aside with frightening force.

I froze, afraid to miss something important.

On the road stood two muscular, ten-foot monsters with dark gray skin.

The demons each stood on two powerful legs that ended in impressive-looking hooves. They had thickset bodies with well-developed muscles, broad necks, and frightful faces. Their eyes burned with red light, and they each had a monstrous horn just above a little snub nose.

In their long, three-fingered hands, they held axes with broad blades. Their weapons burned with ghostly crimson fire.

For some reason it brought the image of spilled vodka to my mind, when it was spilled on a table and lit on fire. The way the flames were burning was very similar.

The demons had flung the vans out of their path and stopped for a moment, and the hunters punished them for it — howling streams of gunfire engulfed them.

After the shots from the grenade launchers came machine gun fire, which left only one demon on the asphalt.

The second thrust out its axe, sent out the ghostly fire enveloping it in several directions, and formed a round spectral shield that it used to retreat behind an overturned van.

It probably would have managed to escape into the woods if one of the mages hadn't lifted the van off the ground.

Coming under a second round of fire, the Nocer rushed its approaching enemies with a wild screech. It did this nimbly enough for such a massive hulk of a creature that it had its first — and, as it turned out, last — stroke of good luck.

The blow of the axe caught a lingering hunter who'd managed to thrust out his machine gun in front of himself, and like a weightless baseball he was snatched a few yards off the ground and flung through the air down the road.

The demon raised its axe to strike again, but a powerful spell cut off its leg, and the hunters' machine guns finished the job.

Demons' sakes! I cursed internally, noticing at the last minute that I wasn't alone in the car. Theophane had gotten back in.

"Does this happen a lot?" I asked, gesturing to the side of the road, amazed at how quickly the hunters had taken out the demons.

"Breaches?" said Theophane. "No. According to statistics, they happen five or six times a year on average in our region."

"And is it a big region?" I asked, trying to understand the scale of the horrors hanging over this world.

"Fifty thousand square kilometers," replied Theophane. "Maybe a little smaller — I can't remember exactly."

That's only the size of the Astrakhan region! I thought with horror, knowing how big the world was. Then I flipped out: *They use the metric system in this world? How do you explain that?*

My thoughts were gloomy, so I didn't even notice how quickly the waiting time flew by.

"You can go!" said one of the hunters, and we got back on the road.

As we drove past the defeated monsters, I noticed people in protective suits neatly packing their body parts into black bags. I noticed a long, thick tail with a brush-like tip that I hadn't seen in the heat of the battle.

How can people live in a world where monsters like this exist? I asked myself a rhetorical question, then asked Theophane:

"Would you have been able to handle them?"

"The Nocers?" Theophane clarified for some reason. "Of course. They're not as strong of demons as they might have seemed to you. Believe me, after some training, you'll learn to take them out easily yourself, no question."

Somehow I don't believe that! I thought, hanging my head.

The clock showed four in the morning. The sky was starting to get lighter, which meant it was time for this worn-out child's body to get a little sleep.

Chapter 2

I WAS WOKEN BY SOMEONE gently shaking my shoulder.

"Huh? What? Are we there already?" I asked with a big yawn.

"Good afternoon!" Theophane greeted me with a smirk. "Not yet. We're making a stop — I have to rest and restore my strength a bit."

"Is it already afternoon?" I asked, puzzled, looking at the clock.

Hmm... one-thirty. I slept for quite a while! I thought in surprise.

"Well, it's certainly not morning," muttered Theophane, then hid his amusement and grew serious. "How do you feel? Did you rest well? Are you in pain at all?"

"I slept great!" I answered, yawning again. I took note of how I felt, and when I didn't find any traces of pain, I continued, "I'm definitely better in general, by a long shot. Nothing hurts or aches anymore."

"That's good," said Theophane, seeming happy and deep in thought simultaneously. "In that case, what would you think about doing a bit of meditation and exercise?"

I thought about it.

Yesterday's events had clearly shown me that this world, despite enormous similarities to Earth, was fundamentally different from it.

Before the encounter with the demons I'd entertained delusions of setting myself up nicely and living peacefully with the help of my knowledge from Earth, but now I was tormented by shadowy doubts about whether I'd hold out till eighteen or die young in shame.

It raised questions too, especially to myself. My thoughts about the future, my reactions to it, the conclusions I drew from it, my relationship to it had all been disturbed.

Why had I been categorically opposed to what Theophane said about training me? Why had I treated the warrior's path with disdain I barely understood myself? Why hadn't I thought it was a worthy endeavor?

Only a short list of complaints presented itself to me.

What was going to happen to me? What kind of normal boy in my childhood wouldn't dream of becoming a master of the art of battle? All boys dreamed of that! And we never forgot about it even after we grew up. I had dreamed about it too, incidentally. Why, in that case, had I even thought about turning down such a tempting offer despite all that?

I became lost in myself even further, frantically searching for the answers to my own questions. My head was roaring.

Maybe it was all about this transfer? The rebuilding of this body when it became the receptacle for a new soul? In the chaos of the memories that could never normally have stuffed themselves into my head? In the fact that what happened to me would cause stress in any normal person? In how much I had left from the dead boy in this body? His reflexes, his habits, his reactions?

If I carefully examined my memories of and reactions to yesterday's "stimuli," it was clear that I was thinking — so to speak — with my feelings. They had the first say in any decision I made. That was truly a trait more characteristic of children than adults.

Hmm. Maybe the problem really was that too much of Ivan was left in me.

If I thought about it, he would never have wanted to become a warrior, even though he had trained diligently. He'd done it to become a great mage. Like people said, healthy body, healthy mind. Or in our case, healthy magic.

That didn't mean all mages were in shape,

universally. Not at all. According to Ivan's memories, most of the mages he'd met had been weak, with rare exceptions, and the plebeian life of a warrior didn't interest them much — they had magic.

Ivan had learned about the benefits of physical exercise for mages from his grandfather. In those rare moments when they'd been alone together, he'd stopped hiding his ability to speak despite his age. He'd done this very rarely, spoken very little, but every word was worth its weight in gold. That was exactly what had pushed Ivan to give it his all.

My thoughts galloped about frantically, shifting at a frightening pace.

And what incredible luck that I had a consummate expert in the art of combat at my disposal, a man with an unbearably strong desire to teach me. It was truly my chance — to learn how to save my own life!

Although, now that I thought about it, how strong was Theophane really? Ivan knew that Theophane was his grandfather's personal servant and a master of single combat. That he practiced a style unknown to others called "Steel Autumn's Death." But what lay behind those words? I didn't understand them at all, personally. Maybe it was just a fancy name, and Theophane could barely do anything.

Although, on the other hand, hadn't he managed to kill those patrolmen back at the estate? That meant he could do that, at least, and was prepared to share that knowledge with me. I'd be a fool not to make the most of it.

My thoughts turned to something else.

How should I deal with these reactions Ivan had left me with? What should I do with them? How long would my mind and body stay in sync? When would the previous host's personality stop having this imperceptible influence on me? When would I finally be able to consider this body my own?

Ivan had wanted to become a great mage, and because of that, even now I felt lightly repulsed at the idea of becoming a warrior — despite understanding rationally what nonsense that was! Utter nonsense, at that! Because I, as it turned out, was a Normal. I had no say in it. I needed to grow as a warrior, but Ivan's emotions had a sharp bitterness to them.

But I could also understand him. What else would you dream of if every day since your early childhood it had been hammered into your head that your grandfather was an unsurpassed mage, a hero, a man who'd crushed hordes of his enemies? And you were the Morozov heir, duty-bound to be worthy of your line. That the Morozov family was great, and only by wielding magic could you be a worthy representative of your family!

"Ivan? Why aren't you saying anything?" asked Theophane, drawing me out of my train of thought with mild alarm in his voice. "You don't want to exercise? Then just sit in the car and wait. I'll be right back."

Was it just me or was he offended? Well, actually, it seemed like he was worried and thought I still hadn't recovered from dying. He didn't even know how right he was!

"Maybe instead of exercising you can just sleep?" I said. "It's better than trying to give yourself more energy. After a while you'll want to sleep again, and you'll be behind the wheel."

"There's no time to sleep now." Theophane shook his head. "So a short meditation will have to do. As you know, it's very good for replenishing strength. After that I'll exercise a bit and finally get myself back together. Then we'll go."

"In that case, I'll keep you company," I said thoughtfully, then went quiet.

My desire to learn from him had, of course, manifested itself — this was one hundred percent true. But now I had a new question: could I do it?

That is, would I be able to complete the full training like he wanted me to? Even at ten years old Ivan could confidently throw knives, juggle five objects, and complete up to ten sets of exercises armed and unarmed. He was a talented boy who'd worked under harsh discipline and still had great success.

But what would it be like for me in this situation? Would I be able to use this body's reflexes and skills? Or would I trip over my own feet ignominiously trying to do a simple set? How would Theophane react when he saw that his student had abruptly taken a turn for the worse and lost his carefully polished skills? Surely he would suspect something. My sudden death couldn't explain that kind of regression!

And if we added the significant changes in Ivan's demeanor and behavior to that, the whole thing became somehow sad and melancholy. Because Theophane couldn't fail to notice the huge difference between the former Ivan and me! Of course not! Theophane didn't seem like any sort of fool, if he'd lived to such an old age in this dangerous world.

To what lengths was he prepared to go to sort out this situation? I didn't know, I didn't have an answer, and somehow I didn't want one. The image of that dead man's lacerated body appeared in my mind's eye.

I had to get out of this workout I'd agreed to. In the beginning stages, I'd do it on my own. I'd investigate my skills and see what I could do and what I couldn't. Only after that would I work with Theophane.

These thoughts passed through my head in a moment, so I figured it seemed to Theophane that I'd simply hesitated.

"I could do some exercising," I said, "but I think it'll be better if I just meditate for now and postpone the exercise. Because who knows how my body will handle even a light workout, after being dead not long ago?"

"True," said Theophane approvingly. "I'm glad that you're learning to think with your head — that's a skill that will prove useful over and over again. Let's go meditate."

Phew! Looks like I'm off the hook! I thought with relief, not noticing the dangerous flash in his eyes.

"Sit down," said Theophane when we reached a place in the middle of a clearing, sitting right on the grass as an example.

I was used to assuming a lotus pose in imitation of Theophane, so I closed my eyes and went still — to my surprise, it came to me easily and naturally. It gave me some hope right away that I could get used to the skills Ivan had left me in a short period of time.

A ten-minute meditation was routine for Theophane before any workout, and this pose was likewise typical.

I closed my eyes and became absorbed in darkness.

My ears picked up on the sounds of cars driving by on the highway.

Aha, that means we're not far from the road, I thought, getting distracted, then tried to concentrate on the darkness.

Honestly, I didn't understand at all why meditation was necessary. Judging by Ivan's memories, he hadn't had much capacity to either. Despite his extensive studies, he'd never been good at meditating.

Theophane always said it was a very complex exercise that required years of training, and he always added that it was no good to get discouraged as long as Ivan had taken the first step — he'd learned to concentrate on the darkness. However, I disagreed that it required a multi-year training process — I figured Ivan was constantly getting distracted and thinking about unnecessary things. He was still an ordinary child.

From his memories I knew that after concentrating on the darkness came a second stage of "immersive" meditation — concentration on a concrete image.

This was when you took some kind of imagery, a landscape for example, that served to calm you. You relaxed, concentrated on it, and... that was all.

I didn't know what came after that. Ivan had never moved on to the next level, and Theophane had kept quiet about it to provoke his interest.

I decided to imagine myself first on a peaceful sea. For some reason I thought that image would calm me down, but as it turned out, I was gravely mistaken. I couldn't clear my mind. I tried to concentrate on the image for a few minutes, but in vain.

So I decided to go a different route and, submerging myself deeply, I started to search for the image I needed — the one that would help me, the one that I'd be able to concentrate on easily, the one that would calm me down.

After a short time, something began to form in my mind's eye.

Ice! That's what it is! I realized, cursing with annoyance. Come on, I was a Morozov — one who understood the cold with my very being! Why hadn't I thought of that right away?

I looked ahead to where an image of a bright slab of ice, shining with ghostly light, was beginning to form, cutting into my mind.

I gazed spellbound on the work of my subconscious and enjoyed the burning blaze of the illusory flames.

The slab was surprisingly realistic. The more I looked at it, the more natural it became. A crack appeared here, a sharp and perfectly straight edge there.

On some parts of it formed indescribably beautiful snowy patterns like the ones that could be seen out of windows in the winter.

I really liked what I saw...

* * *

During this time, a thoughtful Theophane suspiciously watched his pupil enter into a state of full meditation for the first time.

It was very strange. Before, Ivan hadn't been able to concentrate, constantly stopping at the first level — which, generally, was normal for a boy of his age. Just now he'd entered into full meditation fairly easily. And, from what

Theophane could tell, he was close to going a level deeper. What was this unbelievably quick progress? Such things simply didn't happen!

It can't have been his death that affected him like this, can it? he thought. *Or the ritual that the Master did? He said that Ivan would change, and that it would add years to his life.*

Theophane had no answers to these questions.

While Ivan meditated, Theophane pondered the changes in his character. He'd started to speak and think differently somehow.

Sometimes it seemed to Theophane like the Master was now living through Ivan — the head of the Morozov family had somehow managed to transfer his soul into the boy's body. But when he thought about that version of how these events had developed, he discarded it. If that were the case, Theophane would certainly have felt his master's terrible power. He was a great mage. Even Normals could sense it.

He glanced again at Ivan, who was sitting with a very solemn expression and — so it seemed — looking deep within himself.

Theophane was glad that Ivan was pursuing his meditation with diligence — now he just had to convince him to exercise in the same mood. He was no fool; he understood the young master's lack of desire to become a warrior.

Well, if Ivan doesn't want to learn, I'll make him want to learn! he thought to himself.

He froze. His astonishment knew no bounds — a stream of cold air had begun to emanate from Ivan. He sat there for a bit, and the sensation grew stronger.

Does that mean he's a mage after all? thought Theophane in shock and distinct relief. *I have a greater chance of fulfilling the promise I gave to my master... although...*

Theophane had a sudden thought. What was stronger: a mage, a warrior, or... a warrior mage?

What if he tried to make a warrior of Ivan all the same? Perhaps not a master, but a strong intermediate? Then the way of magic would be easier for him. He'd be able to fend for himself not only in duels of magic, but with his fists as well. Physical strength was always valuable in this world. Although today's mages had a disdainful view of warriors and their practices — this could provide additional hidden leverage for Ivan.

Theophane thought about all the arguments for and against it for another few minutes.

That's it! I won't tell him he's a mage. First, I'll instruct him in style and strengthen his mind, will, and confidence in himself. The disciplines of combat will cultivate the qualities he needs. When he gets older, he'll attend a magic academy, and once he's there, he'll go through the full initiation and continue his magical education. That's it.

"Ivan, can you hear me?" asked Theophane, touching Ivan's cold shoulder. *I need to draw him out of his meditation — it's too long for his first time.*

"Yes," said Ivan after a short time, not opening his eyes.

"Try to open your eyes without leaving the meditative state," said Theophane.

No harm in trying — perhaps Ivan would be able to go a step further.

Ivan, mustering his strength, opened his eyes.

"Excellent," said Theophane, looking in amazement at the burning blue glow of spectral flames in the boy's eyes.

* * *

I heard Theophane's words and slowly opened my eyes. It was as if my consciousness split in two. I was inside my head, in front of the slab of ice, and in the forest glade at the same time.

What in the world was this?

Without warning, harsh pain burned in my eyes. I yelled, shut them, and started rubbing them furiously. My state of meditation, of course, broke.

"Don't rub your eyes!" ordered Theophane, grabbing my hands.

"It itches!" I cried in some sort of pained, childish wail.

"It's nothing to worry about, it'll itch for a while and then it'll stop. But if you keep rubbing your eyes, you might hurt them and wear them down from overworking them. Do you want that?"

"Why do I feel so strained too?" I complained, knowing the reason for my discomfort was the division of my consciousness. "I made it two or three seconds in a meditative state with my eyes open, but then everything started... that's not enough time for horrible feelings like that."

"Hmph — well, what did you expect?" said Theophane. "To master a difficult tech without it having any impact on you? That never happens."

"What do you mean by 'tech'?" I noticed the unfamiliar word.

"Hmph," said Theophane again. "You succeeded completely by accident at performing the complicated tech known as 'Eyes of the Wolf.' And believe me, it's not known for being easy to perform."

"By accident?" I said indignantly. "You told me to open my eyes, and I did!"

"But I didn't expect that you'd be able to progress to such a deep level of meditation. It wasn't so long ago that you were unable to perform the tech."

There was a grain of truth in his words.

"So then why'd you tell me to open my eyes?"

"What do you mean why? I had to teach you the tech! Why not try then?"

All right, I got off easy there! I thought, then asked:

"So what's this 'Eyes of the Wolf' thing? And what does 'tech' mean? This is the first time I've heard it."

"You airhead!" said Theophane with amusement — he was clearly in a very good mood.

My two-second success with the "tech" hadn't cheered him up like this, had it?

"A warrior's techs are his special mystic abilities — that is, skills that a warrior uses in battle."

"And what are the 'Eyes of the Wolf' used for?" I asked skeptically. "Rubbing your eyes in pain right as your enemy attacks you? That's a great tech!"

"You're wrong there," said Theophane, a bit offended. "It's one of the techs any true warrior must have. Not everyone masters it, but it's unquestionably useful."

"What does it do?" I couldn't bear the taunting.

"It helps you to find invisible enemies and resist illusions."

"You should have said so right away!" I said, frowning. "And what was that about invisible enemies? Who can make themselves invisible? Mages or demons?"

"Both, but demons are much better at it. Some of them are born with the ability."

This world never stopped disappointing me. Not only were there demons wandering around, now they could make themselves invisible — twice as scary, in my opinion.

"Nasty enemies." Theophane confirmed my thoughts. "There's an entire class of small demons whose specialty is invisibility. They approach people unnoticed. And after they do that, they bite with small but very sharp teeth in their necks. They can tear away whole chunks of flesh!"

Augh! Disgusting! I shuddered.

"And what about illusions?" I asked Theophane.

I hoped this new information wouldn't be as shocking, and I'd stop being so scared of invisible mini-demons tearing out my Adam's apple.

"Oh!" said Theophane, reminiscing. "Illusions are a very interesting and crafty business. I became familiar with them a very long time ago when I ran into a group of unfortunate hunters in the Wastelands. Or rather, what was left of the group."

This is leading into something bad! I thought, and as it turned out, I wasn't wrong.

"A demon sorcerer had cast a complex spell of illusion on one of the hunters, who'd 'fought the demons' by killing his friends, then continued traveling with the demon and its mirages.

"When I came across this poor hunter, he'd lit a fire at the demon's behest and was roasting his friends' meatiest bits over it."

I wanted to vomit, but Theophane just kept going.

"With the help of the 'Eyes of the Wolf' tech, I discovered where the demon was and killed it. Thank the Savior it wasn't too strong a fighter."

"And the hunter? What happened to him?"

"The hunter was sick for a very long time. Later on, he nearly went out of his mind."

Was it just me or was I turning green?

I really didn't like this story anymore, and I would rather not have asked any other questions — what if I accidentally learned something else?

"But that's not the end of the story, you want a good laugh?"

There we go! You see what I mean?

"I think we have different senses of humor." I shook my head in response. "So I'd rather remain in blissful ignorance of this incredible epic's ending."

"Well, suit yourself," hemmed Theophane. "Maybe someday you'll want to know how it all ended."

I shook my head.

"Well, suit yourself," repeated Theophane, finally letting go of my hands. "You can open your eyes. How do they feel? Do they still itch?"

"No," I replied, paying attention to my feelings.

To my profound relief, the feeling of discomfort had gone away. However, a new problem had appeared. My stomach had started making shameless, unpleasant squelching noises. The unwanted reminders of food had played their role.

I felt a terrible hunger and remembered that I hadn't eaten all day!

I'd probably been in a constant state of shock

from everything that had happened since transferring to my new body — how else could I explain my lack of hunger?

"I want to eat!" I announced to Theophane, getting up from the ground.

"Hmm." He sheepishly scratched his head. "We don't have any food."

"What?" I cried. "Are you joking? I'm dying of hunger right now! You brought a child who-knows-where and you didn't even figure out the food situation? We're going to the nearest store or I can't be held responsible for what happens next!"

"All right, all right!" said Theophane, heading for the car.

I wasn't sure if the hunger had dulled my mind or if my self-preservation instincts had kicked in after the possibility of dying from hunger had occurred to me, but I'd completely stopped being afraid of Theophane. I even started to throw him bad-tempered glances every once in a while.

A few minutes later, we were tearing down the highway at high speed.

"Do we at least have anything to drink?" I asked, preparing myself in advance for another disappointment. However, to my great delight, Theophane wordlessly offered me a plastic water bottle.

Just like in my world. I read the label "Drinking Water" and took off the cap.

Terrific! I thought with satisfaction after drinking my fill.

It kept the hunger at bay a little, but I wasn't fooled — my body would figure out soon enough that it had been cheated, and the desire to eat would return with new force.

"There are clothes in the bag on the back seat there," said Theophane. "Change into something plainer."

Plainer? I looked over what I was wearing.

Only then did I pay attention to the unusual black fabric my suit was sewn from. Evidently, this was Ivan's usual attire, because I hadn't even noticed it.

If Theophane thought it was too conspicuous, I should believe him and change — I figured he knew what he was talking about.

There was indeed a small brown bag on the back seat with a bunch of different clothes in it. I picked out a pair of long black shorts that I liked, a simple dark blue t-shirt, and a bright red cap with some logo on it.

I decided to leave the comfortable gray sneakers I was already wearing on my feet. I didn't feel like changing them, and as it turned out, there were no replacements for them.

"That'll work," said Theophane, appraising my new look. "At least you look like a regular person."

"What did I look like before?" I asked, somewhat displeased.

"A noble heir," Theophane replied. "Anyone might've thought you were at least a rich kid."

"Is the suit that expensive?"

"And rare," Theophane added. "So it was better to take it off."

"A gas station!" I yelled, pointing to a road sign. Luckily, the little picture — a gas pump with a nozzle against a blue background — was easy to recognize. "I hope we can buy food there."

Theophane frowned. He'd clearly remembered something.

"As far as I remember, there should be a small village with a roadside cafe there."

"Let's hope so," I said optimistically. "I want to eat a proper meal."

My stomach growled in agreement.

Theophane turned out to be right — there was indeed a cafe in the village.

I examined the village with interest. It had the simple name Rudnia-Anton, according to the sign at the entrance.

What could I say? It was a typical backwater Russian village. It had old houses and simple wooden fences.

"After the encounter with the demons, I thought people's houses would be better defended."

"Why?" asked Theophane, surprised.

"What do you mean why? To protect themselves from demons!"

"You don't think fences will keep out Nocers, do you?"

"No, although that doesn't mean they won't

keep out other kinds. You said yourself there are really small demons."

"To defend yourself from demons, all you need to do is call the hunters on suspicion of a breach. Breaches don't happen in the space of a minute. Three to four hours, at the least. So hunters almost always get there on time, and they have all the necessary sensors."

"Wait, is it possible for them not to get there on time?" I asked.

"If the owner of the land or the lord of the region hasn't paid his protection fees or paid them late, sometimes they don't."

A typical business! I thought, annoyed. My image of the hunters as fighters for justice quickly faded.

A sign on a run-down single-story building read "Restaurant."

Questionable name, I thought, preparing for the worst. However, it turned out to be nothing. The inside of the cafe was far more pleasant than the outside.

There was a small bar counter where you could order and ten or so little tables packed tightly near each other, a few of which were occupied.

Made sense, there had been a few cars in the parking lot.

Going to the nearest free table, I threw my cap down on it and hurried up to the bar counter with Theophane.

We were greeted by a big, stout woman with ruddy cheeks and a wide, professional smile.

"Hello!" she said. "What'll you have? We have fresh chicken soup, fried potatoes, buckwheat, chops with cheese, and cutlets."

My mouth watered. I swallowed.

"We'll have two soups, two orders of potatoes and chops, two teas, and a couple of rolls. The portions should be adult- and child-sized respectively."

"Coming right up!"

"We'll need rolls for the road," said Theophane once we'd sat down at our table.

"Definitely," I replied.

At that moment, they brought us our soup, which I attacked resolutely.

Three boys, clearly locals, sat at one of the tables not far from us. They were about fourteen and wearing threadbare clothes, and they were giving me frankly hostile looks.

"From the brink of starvation... he's scared someone'll take it away... heheheh!" I heard the sounds of their voices.

Ugh, I thought, ignoring their insulting words. *I'm not really a child, it doesn't bother me!*

Theophane looked at the boys askance, which first got them to shut up and then got them to leave completely.

He also fell upon his food — he was clearly pretty hungry.

Despite his portion being at least twice as big

as mine, Theophane finished much faster than I did.

"You finish eating," he said, getting up. "I'm going to quickly go get gas."

I nodded.

The gas station was next to the cafe — he only had to drive about a hundred yards. I could finish eating and walk there. It wasn't far.

I ate a fresh and incredibly fragrant roll, washed it down with juice, and headed out onto the street with the leisurely gait of someone satisfied with life.

I was in a terrific mood, and a smile came out onto my face all by itself.

"Whatcha smiling at, freak?" I heard a boy's voice and didn't realize right away that it was directed at me.

A jerk on my t-shirt and a subsequent "imprint" onto the wall tipped me off that it was.

"You don't wash your ears or something? I'm talking to you! Whatcha smiling at?"

One of the local boys who'd been sitting in the cafe not long ago was holding my t-shirt. The other two were there, standing next to him and smiling impudently.

I looked to the sides. There was no one on the street — I couldn't even call for help. Or what if I screamed? A loud scream from a child should get the attention of the people inside the cafe.

I'd only opened my mouth when a harsh blow to my stomach knocked all the air out of me.

"What, you were gonna scream?" the guy holding me said gleefully, then added menacingly: "Give me your money, freak! Or I'll end you."

It hurt. Not only had he hit me unexpectedly, it had also been in my food-filled stomach. All the better that Theophane was constantly pushing Ivan — at least now I had muscular abs to soften the strong blow.

As I tried to recover my breath, my brain frantically tried to find a way out of the situation.

The three boys were older and much stronger in every way. Fighting back would be senseless — they weren't in my weight category, no question. So I decided to try and run away.

A second blow to the stomach put an end to my ideas of running and forced me to think more rationally.

I had to defend all my vital organs! I dropped to the ground right away and curled up in the fetal position with my back against the wall to cover my kidneys.

Let them hit me — I wouldn't give them the chance to hit in critically important places. Young rascals could start to overdo it a bit and accidentally, or maybe even purposely, make an invalid of me! As soon as I thought it, blows rained down hard and fast.

"Weirdo! Rich kid! You think your fancy threads make you better than us? Huh?" The boys yelled insults and got angrier and angrier with each blow.

They seemed drunk on their freedom from consequences and the weakness of their victim.

They snatched my cap off my head and hit me on the head a few times, and then two of my attackers tried to lift me up and stretch my arms out to the sides so that the third could kick my unprotected face.

The first kick landed not on my hands, but right on my head.

To my surprise, the older boys' strength wasn't enough to separate my weak hands. They couldn't lift me either — they only managed to sit me up.

The second kick to the head was really awful.

When the third kick landed, I instinctively loosened one hand and let one of the boys break through on his side. The guy pulling at me from the other side didn't expect this and got yanked towards me. A powerful kick landed right on his face.

"What the hell?" I heard a yell full of rage. "He loosened his grip."

I tore one hand free. Then I threw myself at the guy who'd lost his balance and stumbled backwards.

The fear of falling played a nasty joke on him — I sped up sharply and hooked him under his leg, and he fell to the ground with a thud that was music to my ears. My elbow in his "little sunshine" wasn't an accident at all.

I somersaulted forward away from him as he

tried to breathe, returned to my enemies' side, and stood in a fighting stance.

This reflex helped me avoid the kicks of the boy who was desperately trying to reach me with his leg high in the air.

I ducked under the flying leg and used every weak kid's classic move: the "nutcracker." Then I jumped away from him as he squealed and set to escaping my last opponent's punches. He was attacking ferociously, making wide swings with his long arms and clearly wanting to get even for the bruise his friend had given him.

Well, to be fair, it was sort of my fault!

I dodged a few punches, guessed the right moment, caught him as he stood up straight, grabbed his hand, and did a classic over-the-shoulder throw. You could say he fell on his own, and I just helped him a little.

It was no good to stand up straight and wave your arms around so recklessly! I elbowed the defeated teenager in the face a couple of times.

I sensed movement behind me and rolled to the side just as someone flew past me — the boy who'd "temporarily forgotten how to breathe" had come to his senses and was still trying to recover his breath but came to his friend's aid all the same.

I jumped towards him and dealt him a powerful "soccer kick" from above, right in the head.

After that I approached the one clutching his

groin and repeated my last move.

An eye for an eye!

Picking my cap back up from the ground, I set it on my head, walked past the groaning boys, and headed for the parking lot. I didn't even notice that Theophane had been watching the fight from afar.

* * *

"Hmm!" said Theophane with satisfaction. His pupil had done well for himself in the fight with the boys.

True, Ivan hadn't been prepared to fight at first and had wanted to call for help, but when he'd realized that he couldn't, he'd begun to act with great competence.

Theophane especially liked how Ivan had finished off his opponents. Vindictiveness was a good trait for the head of a family — he would become dangerous and unpredictable, and he'd always remember his enemies!

Theophane inspected the site of the recent fight again.

"The boys earned their money," he said. "I hope, Ivan, that this lesson forces you to take your training seriously, otherwise I'll have to think of something else."

Chapter 3

GALINA TEMNIKOV, maiden name Belov, was bearing down on the family target range with every malicious bone in her body.

Scoundrels! Wretches! Mongrels! I hate them! the young woman screamed internally, methodically shattering textured stone targets with powerful spells.

She wanted to destroy them, cut them open, hurl them across the room, tear them to pieces, and gut them. She wanted blood, all the blood of whatever remained of those sly, nameless enemies who'd brought this sudden and treacherous attack on the estate.

Although, why am I assuming they're nameless? she thought, messing up her rhythm. What about the Vorontsovs, the Paskulins, the Simonovs? Those scoundrels wouldn't hesitate to put a knife in her defenseless back. You turned your back for a moment and you got a shard of magically sharpened steel between your ribs. They wouldn't turn down a chance to stick it to her.

But when it came to them, there were questions of their qualifications. Were those marquis families strong enough to pull off an operation like this?

At the idea that her enemies were all nothing but mediocre "silver" families, Galina smiled contemptuously.

Despite the intrigue and competition from those families, she was the one who'd succeeded in snatching the "gold" — the widower prince Yegor Temnikov — from their hands, wrapping him around her little finger, and becoming his lawfully wedded wife in the end.

Galina stopped, shook her head, sat on the ground, and closed her eyes.

The heat from the targets she'd burned up after she'd hit them with the spells and the rock bits of various shapes and sizes didn't cause her any discomfort.

On the contrary, contemplation of her own far from meager strength, and thoughts of how she was capable of defending herself if necessary, reassured her and gave her some feeling of safety.

Yes, but who could pull off something like this? thought Galina. Who could simply — and completely imperceptibly — fight their way onto the grounds of the Temnikov estate, which was protected by old magic?

Who could silently make short work of two soldiers who'd spent ten years in training and a mage, all without disturbing one signal line or catching the eye of a single servant? And all when the head of the family was at the estate.

It was just beyond all reason! If she told anyone, they wouldn't believe her. Apparently, the family magic had temporarily abandoned Yegor — after all, he had killed "one of his own blood."

Galina clenched her fists furiously. Associations with the word "blood" would be bringing those images back to her mind for a long time to come. Images of her personal servants, guards, and mages slaughtered by her treacherous enemies.

Who hated Galina viciously enough to butcher her subordinates, without touching any of the Temnikovs'?

"They didn't even spare the servants," she whispered quietly.

POW! One of the targets couldn't hold out against a fire spear filled with her primitive rage and shattered into a hundred pieces.

"Even the servants!"

In her mind's eye rose the image of two young girls, her personal maids, whom she'd found murdered in her own bed.

Could they have been coming for her?

And how those two little girls had been killed! They'd been literally gutted on her bed! Like they'd been tortured by some great maniac, or — so to speak — demon. Certainly not a soldier.

Scoundrels! Why the girls?

Galina destroyed a few more targets.

What was this? A threat? A warning? Why focus on those victims?

There's no answer, thought Galina after several minutes of racking her brains. And the essential question was still who could do something like this — that remained unsolved.

This whole situation reeked of inaccuracies and impossibilities!

For starters, how much intelligence data would be needed to carry out an operation like this. From a detailed floor plan of the house to a schedule of which servants could potentially stumble upon the attackers and raise the alarm.

Operational information about the protection of assets and resources would have been essential to the success of the mission. For instance, information about the numbers of their soldiers, mages, and patrol squads, charts of the patrol routes and the locations of the alarms, and also their offensive spells. In short, it would require all kinds of strictly limited-access information.

Besides, security wasn't standing around twiddling their thumbs — just days ago they'd unmasked a servant who'd been reporting the house's goings-on to the Department of Imperial Security. Maybe what had happened was the DIS's doing?

But what would the DIS want with her? They were more interested in the Morozov fortune than the Temnikovs' doings.

Or had there been another mole who'd been taken out after the events? No one needed witnesses who could give them away, after all!

Stop! Galina thought to herself. Her thoughts were getting out of hand. She had to try to look at this from a different angle.

"No matter what Yegor says, one thing is clear," Galina said slowly, convincing herself of her own words. "This was directed at me personally, and not at the Temnikov family."

It was only logical, since her security and all her subordinates had been killed. The unknown saboteurs had even managed to find the security camera operators and scrub all traces of their presence.

"That's decided," she said. "Next question. Does the DIS have a connection to this?"

On the one hand, they aimed first and foremost to combat reconnaissance from neighboring governments, to counteract demon worshipers, and to search out and destroy forbidden covens — never to do surveillance on the nobility. There was a department of gendarmes for that.

On the other hand, it seemed very suspicious that the attack had come on exactly the same night that the Morozov heir and prince had died. Just what the DIS was following so closely! Such simple coincidences didn't happen in a world devoid of simplicity... wasn't that right?

What was this? Revenge for the extinction of a once-powerful family? But why kill so many Belov servants, if not to get at her specifically? And why hadn't the murderers, despite their professionalism, finished off Yegor?

No. This wasn't the DIS, and this wasn't a vendetta against the Morozovs. No one had known Galina's plans, not even her husband.

She saw that image of her eviscerated maids in her mind's eye.

POW! She smashed another target to bits.

It was a clue! That's what it was, a clue! Could it be that the murderers had been after her, but they hadn't expected that she wouldn't be home? Entirely possible. She wasn't in the habit of going anywhere at such an hour. But she'd had to be on urgent guard — there had been no telling what the old, very powerful mage living in one of the cellar rooms would do when he found out that the heir of his bloodline was dead. He could have turned the whole house into an icy grave.

Galina smacked her full, beautiful lips with satisfaction.

All the better that the plan worked as expected.

God only knew what she'd had to go through over the course of this month to consistently, and without being detected in any way, give her husband a very rare type of mild drug that provoked uncontrollable emotional outbursts.

Galina had found an ancient recipe for it long ago in her childhood, in the Belov library. In a special and secret section, only for the viscount and his heirs.

As the youngest daughter of a small, third-rate family, she'd understood even in her childhood that her fate was in her own hands. No young, wealthy nobleman from a first- or second-rate family would marry her. Her lot was either a poorer husband from a viscount's family or a very rich commoner.

She'd turned that on its head.

From an early age, she'd practically lived in the library and the family target range, wanting to become strong and self-sufficient.

Such an approach was highly approved of in her family circle.

Galina had gone to the Ikorilin Academy of Higher Magic for her education, already holding a second-level master's degree and very close to a low-level doctorate. Thanks to her competence and talent, she'd become a tempting match for several wealthy suitors from marquis families.

She'd even planned to marry one of them. But then the news of Olga Temnikov's death and the widowing of her "gold-ranked" husband became public knowledge. Galina couldn't pass up a chance like that — she broke off her engagement and left everything behind, that she might only take her rightful place. As the years had shown, she had not miscalculated...

The Temnikovs had great prospects and not many relatives on the husband's side, which had allowed her to take a high place in the hierarchy of her new family.

But only a naive fool would believe that just by becoming the head of the family's wife, she'd wield unquestioned authority, give orders, and be obeyed. Yes, when it came to servants, it was true, but only in part. One also had to know how to manage servants the right way. Let alone the rest — mages, soldiers, and stewards of all levels...

Over ten and a half years of marriage, with hard work, responsibility, cunning, rancor, and vindictiveness — and a sharp mind — Galina had forced everyone involved with the Temnikov family to respect her, from the stable boys to the professors of magic.

BANG! She hit the next target.

Who knew — if Professor Petius had been in place, perhaps everything would have turned out entirely differently? Perhaps he would have been able to ward off the attack? Perhaps she'd snuck him out of the house for nothing?

Galina knitted her brows again.

On the other hand, the professor probably would have prevented Yegor from killing his son. And that would have threatened the plan to eliminate Morozov. But then again, despite all the unpleasantness, they'd gotten access to the Morozovs' money, which would really help in the development of her new ambitious projects.

Unfortunately, Yegor hadn't proven himself especially capable of earning money. He was content to receive his inheritance, and he led an idle life. The Temnikovs' money and assets were enough, but that road would lead to failure sooner or later!

It wasn't for her — she would do everything to bring her family into strength and wealth, to pass all that wealth on to her children in the future.

Galina gently stroked her thin stomach.

Everything was going to be all right! It would all go to a son of hers! And not to some Morozov mongrel!

Their elimination was well underway — Yegor's third son had already been killed. She still had to get rid of the fourth, and she could leave the daughters alive.

Galina smiled greedily. Sooner or later they'd all die — she would be thorough and unobtrusive. They'd never suspect her. No matter what, she'd get what was hers. That was the way it had always been.

* * *

"Hey there, handsome!" said Theophane, looking at me with some kind of nasty smirk. "What happened to your face?"

"I fell over!" I snapped at his unexpectedly malicious tone.

So his student walks over with his face all beat

up, and he just wants to make fun of me! I thought angrily. *Forget this! Not even a hint of concern!*

Theophane chuckled and examined my face again.

"What are you looking at?" I asked, feeling that my split lips and the kicks to the cheek I'd taken were starting to swell a little and thus tingling unpleasantly. "Did you get gas?"

"Yes, a while ago," he replied. "I've just been waiting for you here."

"Well then let's go, why are we sitting around chatting?" I said, opening the door and jumping into the car.

We had to get far away from here — I really didn't want the cafe customers or any local residents to stumble upon the beaten-up boys and start looking for the guilty parties. That threatened not only to lose us time — which we already had little enough of — but also to rattle my nerves, which despite my youth were very precious to me.

Theophane silently got into the driver's seat, and the car jerked forward rapidly.

A tense silence hung over us. I started to register little by little who I'd just been taking that tone with. I only had one excuse: I was worked up and very, very grumpy.

The first thing was the absurd reason for the fight. The second was the fact that a child had had to defend himself against a couple of burly mugs, and he (me, that is) hadn't had anyone come to help him. And the third was that Theophane didn't give two cents about the state I was in! It was like it didn't matter to him that they'd beaten me up, and like he wasn't the only adult responsible for me! Maybe his harsh warrior's soul didn't see a skirmish between little boys as a very important matter, but couldn't he at least have shown a little interest for the sake of propriety — who I'd been fighting, why, whether I'd won or lost? He was my mentor, after all! Instead he'd just made fun of me! He'd been satisfied with my answer and was just driving in silence.

I was bursting with childish resentment. Rationally I understood that I was a grown man, and it was no good being angry at Theophane. But, clearly, there was a lot of Ivan's childishness left in me.

I think Theophane had decided I was upset about my black eye and bleeding lips — that I was really embarrassed, and that was why I was being quiet.

That wasn't it, though.

True, if I were really a ten-year-old boy who'd been beaten up, I would be embarrassed. But I was a grown man, so instead of shutting down I started analyzing what had happened and what had led up to it.

And the longer I spent doing that, the more I felt that something about what had happened was wrong. Something didn't add up, something wasn't as it should be.

I got this from not only my analysis of the

situation but also from my intuition screaming at me.

First of all, I was bothered by Theophane's reaction to my getting into a fight and his relationship to my fighting-related — I wasn't afraid of this word — trauma.

Here was the thing.

Not long ago, when we'd been meditating in the forest glade, Theophane had fussed over me like I was a baby. He'd asked me about how I felt with clearly noticeable anxiety in his voice, and he'd been interested in my health and so on. But now I showed up with my face bashed in and he didn't react at all, not even a little! Well, more accurately, he'd of course reacted, but not at all how he should have.

Surely he couldn't have changed his outlook on my health so fundamentally in such a short period of time? Or could he?

If so, why? Because of my success with the meditation and mastery of a new tech? Did he think that since I had the strength for that, I wouldn't die anytime in the near future?

It was very possible, but it was a little far-fetched, so I ditched that idea.

In any case, he should have tried to figure out who I'd fought and why, rather than being satisfied with the childish excuse I'd shouted at him angrily.

After all, in his mind, I was getting out into the big world for the first time. It was the first time in my life that I'd fought with strangers or someone had hit me.

But no, he wasn't saying anything — as if he knew all that. What happened, how it happened, who was there.

Hmm. A suspicion of exactly that formed in my mind — that he knew it all.

To corroborate that suspicion, there was also the fact that he'd left the cafe so quickly for no reason. What had he been thinking, leaving the hope of the Morozov bloodline alone in an unfamiliar place? What had he been hoping to do?

Teach me to be independent? Get me used to being left alone? Stop me from getting lost in case something similar happened again? Or was it actually because of this?

These ideas were far-fetched too.

The guy was just such an expert mentor that he'd thought of everything down to the last details.

Somehow I doubted it.

So let's say the reason he left the cafe was something entirely different. He could just have waited a few minutes, and we could have left the place together. A measly few minutes that wouldn't have caused any trouble. But he'd done what he'd done, and there was some reason for it. But what?

Maybe the reason had been to cross paths with the boys who'd left the cafe and somehow provoke the fight?

How? Hell if I knew.

He could've heckled them, for instance, called them bums, and told them that Ivan had money and didn't "look like a regular person" and so on. In short, he could have provoked their desire to beat me up.

If I really wanted to be paranoid about it, I could assume he'd left early so he could pay the boys to fight me. To make me understand that my training was important, that without it I'd be a piece of garbage who'd constantly get clobbered. To motivate his student, you could say. No wonder I'd heard such offense in his voice when I hadn't wanted to exercise.

I giggled nervously internally.

No way! That was stupid! Theophane could never behave so despicably! Or could he?

Because... how had the fight started? What was it they'd accused me of?

First they'd said, "Whatcha smiling at?". Then they'd said, "Give me your money!". And finally, they'd said I was wearing expensive clothes. I think that was everything.

Somehow it seemed like too many reasons to bash my little face in — a strong desire to do it, but no clear understanding of why.

True, boys their age rarely thought with their heads, and they didn't need a serious reason to swing their fists. But when I analyzed the situation and searched for evidence of Theophane being to blame, I could throw that likely possibility on the heap of oddities too.

I put the boys aside for now and tried to understand the illogical behavior of my so-called mentor.

Why hadn't Theophane come back for me at the cafe when he'd finished filling up the car?

I may have been a grown man in a child's body, but he didn't know that! The real Ivan most likely wouldn't have gone to find the gas station himself — he would've waited for Theophane to come back. I'd noticed the sign with the prices, so I'd understood where I needed to go.

What was this? Another test of wits? Another weird lesson?

No, enough making excuses for this jerk.

It all made sense — Theophane had deliberately set me up!

Incidentally, he couldn't possibly not have noticed the hostility that the three boys in the cafe had taken out on me! They'd left the cafe right after he'd given them a few sour looks...

Once I'd determined that the fight was Theophane's work, how was I supposed to get on with him now? What should I expect from him?

What would he do the next time? Set a couple of grown men on me? Then bandits? And then actual demons? Just to get results?

Rotten sadist.

But how should I know if my reasoning was really correct, or if these were the ravings of a runaway imagination?

"How's your face?" Theophane drew me out of

my unpleasant thoughts.

I ran my fingers over my swollen lips and my burning cheek, where a little bump was starting to grow, and responded:

“Not great, but I’ll live.”

Theophane chuckled.

“So who were you fighting with? And why?”

I looked at him with suspicion.

How I wanted to shout accusations in his face. Say that he knew it all, he’d planned it all, and then he’d listened to my excuses. But to be honest, I was scared to, so I decided to go about it differently. I hoped that my “earthly” knowledge would come in handy.

“Where’d you get the idea that I was fighting with someone?” I asked him.

“Ivan,” said Theophane condescendingly, looking at me. “I’m an old warrior. Do you really think I can’t see the signs of a fight, or at least that you were rolling around on the ground with someone?”

I shook a blade of grass off my shoulder and, mustering a tone of importance, responded:

“Actually, I think that you’re not only an OLD warrior, but a very skillful PLANNER too.”

I was paying careful attention to him, so I was able to notice his eyes shooting up and to the side for a second.

I have you now, my friend!

How well I remembered it from books about nonverbal communication — that eye movement meant someone was lying or thinking about lying.

"What are you talking about?" Theophane frowned, acting like he didn't understand, but he couldn't fool me.

"About what you've always taught me," I answered evasively, seeing that the outwardly calm Theophane was starting to become a bit tense.

"What do you mean?" he clarified anyway.

"I just mean," I said, "I'm always getting these stupid thoughts into my head. Probably because I'm looking for excuses for my own weakness and wounded pride."

I didn't know why, but openly chewing Theophane out was scary, so I decided to tell him what he wanted to hear. That is, that I was weak and had a newfound desire to train with him. But, of course, I'd come to the conclusions I needed for myself, and I'd keep a sharp eye out around him. Who knew what he'd think of next?

"Because you need to train more!" He raised his finger instructively, starting to calm down a bit.

"I already know that." I nodded, looking down. "Although, is there maybe some kind of healing tech for warriors? Like the Eyes of the Wolf," I explained quickly. "If I managed to master one tech quickly, is it possible that I could master a second one too? I could try to learn it while we're on the road."

"Why not?" said Theophane with a somewhat

tense smile. "You could try. But I think it's better to start with securing confidence in your ability to enter and remain in a meditative state. At a certain level that tech increases cell regeneration several times over, as you already know, which allows for quick restoration of strength. As you've understood: I can make up for about five hours of sleep with one hour of meditation. In your case, though, you'd have to meditate for four whole hours."

Wow, he was talkative. I smirked internally as I watched Theophane from the side. He was dumping buckets of information on me just so I wouldn't start suspecting his involvement in the fight again. He'd even forgotten to ask again who I was fighting with. Was it because I'd made him nervous? He could lose the Morozov heir's trust just like that, and how was he supposed to keep working with him then? I hoped ideas like that would make him think twice next time before planning "practical" lessons like this for me.

"All right, let's practice my meditation," I said obediently.

"In that case, go sit in the back," said Theophane, "otherwise it'll be hard to concentrate and you'll be constantly distracted."

I agreed that that made sense, so I crawled into the back seat, settled down comfortably, and closed my eyes.

It seemed like it wasn't necessary to sit in the lotus pose to enter the meditative state. It was likely a kind of anchor to help new learners master the tech in the beginning stages of their education.

That is, when you're constantly using that pose to immerse yourself in meditation, you just have to assume it and your body starts to enter into the right framework without your help. Something like developing a habit for yourself. You basically program yourself. You sit in the lotus pose, you're meditating.

Like Pavlov's dog! I smirked.

I entered the meditative state very quickly. One moment, and before my eyes was the familiar and incredibly beautiful slab of ice, radiating some kind of pleasant energy.

I knew how to get in, now I should try to get out.

I tried to make myself aware of my body sitting on the soft seat and my hands touching the leather covering, and I came out of the meditation right away.

I did it!

"Problem?" asked Theophane. He had some way of sensing whether I'd done the exercise or not.

"On the contrary," I answered. "Everything is coming to me really easily. I just tried leaving the meditative state on my own."

"Then go in and out five times. You need to be secure in that ability."

"All right," I said, and went about completing the exercise.

"Very good!" said Theophane, clearly pleased with my success, once I'd finished.

"Thanks," I said.

I hadn't expected myself that it would come to me so easily. Evidently, meditation was like riding a bicycle. Learn once, you'll be able to ride one for the rest of your life.

"Now just meditate."

I nodded and sank deep within myself again.

Admiring the icy beauty for a few minutes, I asked:

"And do I have to be in this state long before I see at least some kind of clear results?"

After repeating the question a few times and not hearing an answer, I realized that Theophane simply couldn't hear me. It was like I was talking inside my mind.

I tried to feel my body in the car without falling out of my meditation when I did that. It was difficult, but I managed it all the same.

Not opening my eyes so I wouldn't accidentally activate the tech I already knew about (because I remembered the feelings that had come with it the last time I'd used it), I asked:

"And do I have to be in the meditative state long before I get results?"

It was actually really hard to talk like this — I didn't understand how Theophane had managed to get through to me last time and how I'd responded to him.

Now I understood clearly that it was

incredibly difficult. Small beads of sweat were already rolling down my forehead.

"I'm not going to tell you just yet how the restoration will happen to you — you need to experiment." Theophane's hoarse voice reached me. "Start by meditating for at least an hour, and then we'll see if there's any change. After that I'll be able to answer your question."

"In that case, mark the time," I said, and went back "into myself."

Everything there was as it had been before. The beautiful ice slab was peacefully, serenely cheerful in the air. I went in a little closer.

If I could go closer to it, that meant I was walking somehow, didn't it? I looked down.

It turned out that I was standing on an ordinary concrete floor.

Hmm. Why concrete? Why not something else?

I had no answer.

The floor was dark gray, unvaried, and — upon observation — located where I could see muted light coming from the ice slab.

Outside the borders of this unusual light, it was pitch black. Which, I admit, was somehow frightening for me to approach.

Interesting — if the ice weren't creating the light, would I be able to see anything in this place? Or would I just be in pitch blackness with no idea where I'd wound up? I was glad that I had this light, at least, to brighten up the existence of my internal world.

It was an internal world, right? Wasn't that what it was? It was just a bit empty in here. Could I try to create something? It was my internal world, after all — I was the king here, the god. Why not?

The first thing I wanted to create was a soft, comfortable armchair — I didn't want to stand here for a whole hour. Right?

Unfortunately, my wish was very difficult to carry out. I couldn't do it the first time, the tenth time, or even the twentieth time. Although a featureless heap of who-knows-what appeared every so often.

I gave up on the soft, comfortable armchair after a while and tried to imagine at least a simple wooden stool for myself, as ordinary as could be.

Again and again, however, some featureless wooden construction vaguely resembling a chair appeared in front of me.

Finally, I managed to create a simple wooden cube with edges that weren't completely straight. I sat on it right away, only to feel the hard floor on my tailbone a second later.

Argh! Do I really have such a terrible imagination that I can't dream up a piece of wood? I thought, irritated. Although there was one small benefit to knowing this. Despite my lack of success, I'd discovered the most important thing: I was able to create things in my own internal world, but it was very difficult.

Frankly, I didn't want to continue my difficult

task, so I decided to do a workout.

I had a body here — why not try to practice some moves?

I decided to start with testing my unarmed exercise sets.

It was better not to do a warm-up — this body wasn't real, so I wouldn't suffer any damage or injury anyway.

Kick, kick, kick, jump, roll.

I was easily able to do everything Ivan knew how to do. I did each set a few times, then moved on to doing them at random. I imagined hundreds of enemies surrounding me and set to destroying them.

At a certain point I started to feel a kind of force that went towards the enemies with my blows. I'd bet anything that Ivan hadn't felt anything like it before he'd died.

I repeated the sets in random order and felt the energy accompanying my blows again.

Theophane had constantly talked about this during my studies. Spiritual energy, or — as he'd called it — "Shiki-Cho."

If I understood right, the ability to sense Shiki-Cho was a completely new level of power in the art of combat.

With each blow I honed, I felt destructive energy leaving my body. It was so unusual that I couldn't possibly stop, and I kept experimenting. I wanted to figure out more and more new moves.

I'd have to test this kind of workout in some

real capacity. I couldn't wait to find out if I could really use Shiki-Cho now or if it was only a game my sick imagination was playing, locked within my subconscious.

"Incidentally, how long have I been in here now?" I muttered in amazement. "Definitely longer than an hour."

Leaving my meditative state, I opened my eyes decisively and saw that we were still on the road, but the sun had almost set.

"You back?" Theophane asked right away, once again somehow having a bead on my return to the real world.

"Yes," I replied hoarsely. My throat was dry. "Why didn't you shake me after an hour, like we agreed?"

I reached for a water bottle, twisted the cap off, and took a couple of big gulps.

"No reason," he replied. "I barely saw any changes in your face. So I decided to give you the chance to train more. It's your new tech, after all. Besides, I'm surprised you managed to hold out for so long. Not all novices can meditate for a whole hour, and you held out for more than six. How did you do that?"

Believing there was no reason to hide this type of information from him, I answered honestly:

"I was working out. I did some unarmed sets, and it seemed like I started to feel some spiritual energy."

Theophane tore his eyes off the road for a bit

and stared at me attentively. After that, he kept moving with a very satisfied look.

After a few minutes of silence, he finally asked me:

“And how exactly do you meditate?”

I was surprised by this question, but I answered anyway.

“I close my eyes and imagine a fixed image in front of myself, and it’s as if I pass into an internal world. I can walk there and do whatever I want. I tried to make a chair,” I admitted, “but for some reason I couldn’t do it, so I decided it was pointless to waste my time and I should work out.”

Theophane went into a coughing fit.

“You’ve already accessed the internal world?” he said, dumbstruck. “And you’ve already tried to create things?”

“Well, I think it’s an internal world,” I answered after thinking about it. “There wasn’t really anything there besides a floor and a slab of ice in the center.”

“A slab of ice...” Theophane muttered audibly again. “So that means... strong bloodline.”

“Why do you ask?” I asked out of curiosity. “I’m not meditating wrong, am I?”

“You’re meditating right,” he replied. “But in order to reach that level, a warrior needs to train intensively for several years. And you somehow managed it all on your own.”

“You don’t say!” I said, dumbstruck too.

“And how do you feel?” asked Theophane. “Do

you feel anything unusual? No unpleasant sensations?"

After he said it, I realized I was spilled across my seat like an amoeba, and I had almost no strength left even to move.

"I feel weak," I answered, stretching, trying to lie more comfortably.

My legs and arms were starting to burn a little in the places where the spiritual energy had come from them with each blow.

"And I feel some mild burning."

Theophane nodded.

"That's how it should be after a long training session with Shiki-Cho in the internal world."

"But why does it burn?" I demanded with the last of my strength. "I did the workout in the internal world. That means nothing should hurt! I wasn't even doing a workout, really!"

"You were doing a workout," Theophane disagreed. "It's just that you weren't training your body, but your spirit. And, judging by your condition, you did so very energetically. Now your physical body is adapting to your spirit's new strength, and because of this process you're feeling slight discomfort."

Theophane said something else, but I — much to my regret — was already too far gone to hear him.

Chapter 4

I HAD A DREAM ABOUT MY HOME, my home on Earth, where I was loved, and valued, and respected, and eagerly awaited...

Comfort, peace, and warm-heartedness reigned there.

But this time it was somehow different. It was too gray, gloomy, quiet, and melancholy.

I shuddered.

Neither the computer, the TV, nor the radio was on. I couldn't hear my beloved wife's dear voice, and my kids weren't making any sound in the other rooms.

I felt empty and really lonely inside — I sensed a painful loss and a feeling of unhappiness hanging over the place.

With a heavy heart, I started walking through the rooms in the hope of finding at least someone.

And I did…

My chest tightened painfully at what I saw.

A beautiful woman, her face exhausted by grief and her dark hair covered with a shawl, was sitting at the table with her head resting on her arm.

She stared ahead miserably with her eyes full of tears and sadness.

"Why… why did you leave us?" she asked in an incredibly mournful voice, and sobbed bitterly. "Why did I let you go this time? Why?"

My heart ached.

"Forgive me, dearest Masha, forgive me!" I whispered in a lifeless voice, taking a few steps forward.

On the table I saw a photo of myself with a funeral ribbon in the corner.

Angry tears started to flow from my eyes.

What was this for? What was this all for? Why had this happened specifically to me? Why? Why had I wound up in the body of a little boy from another world? To what end? I wanted to go back to my world! To my family! How were they going to live without me now? How?

"Take me back home!" I cried fiercely, not expecting it myself. "Take me back home! Take me back home! Take me back!"

I sat on the floor near my wife and sobbed bitterly.

I wanted to hold her, to feel her warmth, so dear and so far away, but my hand met with no resistance and passed through her.

"NO! NO!" I screamed furiously. "I want to be warm again! I want to be warm again!"

Somehow I sensed that this would be our last meeting, our last chance to say goodbye, our last moment together.

Knowing that made me endlessly sad.

"Take me back… take me back… back…" All I could do was mumble, hiding my face in my palms and wiping away the tears endlessly pouring down my face. "Back…"

"Ivan! Ivan! Wake up! Ivan!" I heard Theophane's voice as he shook me. "Wake up!"

Needless to say, waking up was horrible.

I opened my eyes and looked at Theophane, and for a moment even he recoiled.

I think it was because a man who'd lost everything most dear to him in life was looking at him through a little boy's eyes.

As soon as I woke up, it was as if a mountain of grief collapsed on me. I couldn't even move my arms or breathe. A feeling of guilt crushed my furiously pounding heart painfully, and I started to suffocate.

A few slaps to the face and a couple of light thumps to the chest brought me out of this horrible state, and I finally drew in a deep breath.

"Breathe, breathe, Ivan! Breathe!" said Theophane, his face red from the fright. "Breathe!"

Realizing that I wasn't getting enough air, he quickly dragged me out of the car.

"Breathe, Ivan, just breathe. It was just a nightmare."

Hardly just a nightmare, I thought wearily.

"Put me down on the ground, I'm already feeling better," I said to Theophane after a bit.

"Really?" he asked with audible doubt in his voice, but he did as I asked all the same. "How do you feel?"

"Much better already," I answered, wiping my face dry from the tears.

Forgive me, my love! I begged in my mind, clenching my teeth till it hurt. *Forgive me...*

"Is it happening again?" Theophane asked, tensing up.

"No."

Interesting — what did he think about what had happened? What had he seen? Had I started to cry in my sleep and mutter something? Had I started screaming? Did he perhaps think I was going crazy? Or that my death had had a negative impact on me? Surely now he'd start being afraid to leave me alone for long, so that this kind of thing wouldn't happen again.

Thoughts about my loved ones I'd left in the other world were weighing heavily on me and constantly surfacing in my mind.

If this went on, I would just go mad. The sadness and grief were starting to pursue me constantly. Yes, humans were of course creatures that could get used to anything, and I was no exception. The feeling of loss would subside little by little over the course of time until it was almost gone. But I still had to live through everything until I reached that point. I wasn't fit for anything saddled with these feelings — I needed some way to take the edge off of them, because no matter how much I wanted to, I couldn't change anything. Thankfully, I'd left my family an apartment and a decent sum in the bank. They weren't goners.

I remembered waking up in Ivan's body right after I'd transferred into it, how my emotions had been seemingly locked behind slabs of ice, which had allowed me to behave properly and not make a fool of myself.

Maybe I needed to try to return to that state, just consciously.

Concentrating, I imagined that I was collecting my thoughts and memories of my loved ones and embedding them in a block of ice. That they could rage within the ice, but they couldn't break out.

I felt better.

The sadness and pain of loss weren't gone. They were somewhere deep inside of me, but they weren't constantly consuming my thoughts anymore.

"Where are we?" I asked, looking around at the forested road that we'd stopped on after leaving the highway.

"What, you can't see for yourself?" Theophane sneered. "In the woods."

That tone seems uncalled for, I thought, but I

didn't even make a face at him. Was he somehow trying to distract me from having another nightmare? To some degree, it was working. Except, unfortunately, that had been no ordinary nightmare. It was something much worse...

It felt like there were needles jabbing into my head again.

I don't even want to think about this! I decided.

I held the emotions back, but an invisible vise crushed my heart again.

"I need something to distract myself," I said to Theophane. "So that nasty thoughts won't creep into my head. Can we do a workout?"

"A workout?" He stared at me questioningly and added with doubt, "Are you sure? Maybe it's better not to risk that yet."

"No! I want to work out!" I said a little too sharply.

"For crying out loud..." Theophane heard my choked voice. "If you want to. A workout is a healthy thing — drives away all the nasty thoughts! Actually," he added, "while we have the chance, we need to check if you can use Shiki-Cho now."

After a short warmup (Theophane said there wasn't much time before sunset, so we had to hurry), I moved on to practicing some combat sets.

"Let's start with number eight," said Theophane, who was constantly keeping an eye on my condition during the physical exercises. "Number three..." He suggested an order for me to do the sets. "Number five..."

To my great regret, it didn't work at all for the first twenty minutes — I couldn't pick up on an ounce of spiritual energy. Even if I diligently tried to reproduce the feeling I already knew from my internal world.

Stupid Shiki-Cho! I thought angrily after yet another failure, punching straight ahead with my fist. And at that moment spiritual energy accumulated in my hand, broke out, and smashed the trunk of a birch tree a few feet away.

Lightning-fast, I jumped to the side away from the falling tree.

"Whoa!" I exclaimed, surprised and happy at the same time. "Is that how powerful Shiki-Cho is? That's incredible! I didn't think it was such a destructive art! I thought spiritual energy would just strengthen my attacks, but look at that!"

Theophane scratched his head, puzzled.

"Actually, you did it," he said, "but you put more energy into your blow than was remotely warranted. It's like if instead of just splitting your enemy's skull, you smashed its head to bits, and wasted a great deal of energy doing so. And by doing that, if you do that, you'll of course see results and win fights, but at what cost? If you expend your Shiki-Cho so disproportionately, you'll lose your strength quickly and be unable to withstand large numbers of enemies."

"That was my first time doing it!" I said, a bit indignant. "Of course I don't know how to evenly distribute the amount of spiritual energy I put into my punch. It would be stupid to expect anything else!"

"I certainly didn't want to offend you," said Theophane sincerely, raising his hands. "On the contrary, I'm amazed by your progress. And the fact that you've managed to master very difficult techs at your age, I confess, is a little shocking to me. Now, can you tell me how you did that?"

"I was angry," I admitted to him. "Everything came to me fairly easily in the internal world, but out here it's like it's gone numb — I can't get it at all. I didn't feel an ounce of spiritual energy inside me, so I got upset."

"I'll try not to annoy you from now on," said Theophane with a smile, then continued more seriously. "You are truly a surprising child." He explained: "Warriors only start to get a grasp on Shiki-Cho at medium rank, and even then not all of them do. Many of them simply aren't able to feel the energy. And here we have you, only a second-level Novice, and you're already succeeding. So what you were able to do just now — " He gestured to the birch tree. " — was already an incredible result. Which I can explain, though not fully."

"How's that?" I asked, intrigued.

"The most important thing is strong ancestry." Theophane crooked his finger. "That has allowed you to reach deep levels of meditation and master difficult techs. The second thing is the combat exercises we started doing in your early childhood. Those sets have the basic movements used for the techs that control spiritual energy."

"You could say it's an inborn talent," I said, "which would sound more motivating than it really is — all my achievements are just good blood."

"But that's true." Theophane squeezed my shoulder. "It's just that — your blood — that makes you what you are. I want you to always remember that you're a Morozov!"

I nodded in agreement.

"But," Theophane added, "you can't ever forget that, in the end, what you make of yourself depends only on you. Whether you'll stay at the Novice rank or whether you'll make it to, for example, Knight."

Theophane took a deep breath.

"More than once I've encountered people who squander their great talent in mediocrity because of plain old laziness — they don't even try to develop it. But I've also encountered people who have blown blood vessels trying to eke a decent substitute for talent out of their paltry skill, and they've reached incredible heights. So, as I said, it all depends on you."

I nodded again.

What was this, an unscheduled pedagogical brainwashing?

"We have very little time left before the sun sets," said Theophane, looking at his watch. "So let's continue your training, and you try to sense Shiki-Cho again while it's still fresh in your memory."

To my great disappointment, I wasn't able to sense any energy within myself for the rest of the training session.

"Don't worry," Theophane reassured me. "You've done it once — that means you'll be able to do it again. You just need to train more, both in the real world and in the internal world."

"But why could I do everything there, while here I can do almost nothing?"

"Because your physical body isn't yet synchronized with your spirit, which became noticeably stronger after your death. Hmm." Theophane paused. "In fact, after you died, your spirit became so much stronger that now you can use Shiki-Cho. That's very interesting..."

I froze internally.

If this bloodsucker believed there was a direct relationship between death and a growth in spiritual energy, then things were about to get really bad for me. He'd start every day by stopping my heart, inducing clinical death, and then "resurrecting" me.

"So what will happen after they synchronize?" I asked, hoping to distract him from that idea.

"Well... that... see... it allows you to freely use your spiritual energy in the real world just like you do in the internal world," Theophane replied, confused for some reason and still lost in his thoughts.

"I'd like that. Is there any way to speed up the

process?"

I admit I really liked this power that could give me combat skills. And if I'd been skeptical earlier when Theophane had said he could easily take out two Nocers, now I saw clearly that he could wipe out twice that many demons easily.

I just wanted to be able to defend myself if I needed to, and I hoped that as soon as I was able to use Shiki-Cho confidently, I'd reach that goal.

Say what you will, but being able to support your opinions with your fists always has a positive effect on any normal man's psychological state. And I was still just a child who could get my feelings hurt by everybody.

"Of course there's a way to speed it up," said Theophane. "Constantly being in your internal world and working through the sets you know there. The more you do that, the faster the synchronization process will go. But it's very hard to do that. Few can spend long in self-development and then lie around with no energy for several hours."

"Hold on," I said, not completely understanding. "But if I train in my internal world, then my spiritual body will become stronger and stronger, and my physical body will stay the same. And they'll be out of sync again. Surely in that case I wouldn't be able to use Shiki-Cho, right?"

"You would. The greater the disparity between one body and the other, the quicker they synchronize," said Theophane. "Let's stop talking and go. There should be a roadside hotel somewhere nearby — we'll stop there. I'm a bit tired," he said after I sat down in the car.

"Not surprising." I shook my head as I looked at him.

He was cheerful, but he seemed rather unwell. He had swollen bags under his eyes, which had grown dark from not having slept in ages, his wrinkles had gotten even deeper, and his skin was sallow.

Geez. I'd seen prettier corpses. I shook my head and knit my brows. Although I'd looked much worse at my own funeral.

I looked again at Theophane, who was holding the wheel firmly and carefully watching the road.

The old man was weakened — he was so tense. He was clearly afraid of falling asleep. I noticed that even his noble-looking head of gray hair somehow looked off. Why make such sacrifices? Did each day really count for so much? I hoped the hotel really was nearby. With such a "raw" driver, it was fully possible to get into an accident.

An amazing transformation had happened before my eyes! In the place of the deadly and dangerous butcher-warrior, I saw beside me a very tired old grandpa.

Maybe he'd been making stupid jokes not because he was a maniac, but because he was really tired? The criticality of his perception had decreased — he'd gotten worse at analyzing situations. He was hardly young anymore, and he hadn't slept in a few days — two at the least, possibly more.

While I was thinking about the reasons for Theophane's fatigue and calculating how much strength he had stored up, we passed a road sign that showed a hotel in the woods coming up.

"We'll be there soon." Theophane confirmed what I was thinking.

Somewhere half a mile later, we came across a nice little hotel and headed towards it.

"Are you hungry?" Theophane asked gloomily, parking in the empty lot.

My stomach growled treacherously.

"Understood," he said. He opened the door, went to the trunk, and like a magician produced a paper bag stuffed full of food.

"Where did that extravagance come from?" I asked immediately, mentally composing a fantasy entitled *What We're Going to Have for Dinner.*

"While you were meditating," said Theophane, setting the alarm on the car, "we went past a large shopping center, and I decided it would be a sin not to stop in."

"A large shopping center?" I repeated skeptically, picturing the situation, then decided to get clarification: "On the highway?"

Theophane sighed heavily.

"Not in the middle of the highway, of course. There was a fairly big city nearby."

"Now I understand."

A smiling, rosy-cheeked young man of about twenty-five with an easygoing, good-natured face met us at the entrance to the hotel. He stared in fascination at our Jeep.

"What is that? A Mountain Commander?" he asked, looking at the car with shining eyes.

Mountain? Was that the make of the car? I looked back. Hmm. There was indeed something depicted on the logo that looked like a mountain. So that was most likely it.

"Yes, that's right," said Theophane in an incredibly tired voice.

"That's a very expensive car," said the guy, looking us over attentively. He added weightily: "In that case, I'll prepare our best room for you!"

"And make it quick," Theophane begged quietly, and explained: "I just really want to sleep."

"Decided to treat your grandson to a road trip?" the young man asked us amiably as we walked to the room. "Then I suggest you visit St. Kelemet's church — it's very beautiful, and it's only about ten kilometers from here."

"Yes, we're on a road trip," said Theophane. "I think we'll stop by the church to check it out."

I liked the room.

It was simple but tidy, with big beds made up with clean linens and a separate shower.

Everything that tired travelers needed after a long journey.

"Will you be paying now or at checkout?" the young man asked Theophane.

"Now."

"In that case, it'll be twenty thalers."

Theophane wordlessly reached into his pocket and handed him money.

"The key is in the door. Call me if you need anything," he said, leaving.

* * *

After he shut the door to the room, Artem went at an unhurried pace to his workstation, picked up a simple black telephone from the table, and dialed a number.

"Hello?" came a man's husky voice through the receiver.

"Boss, it's Canute," said Artem. "I have good news."

"Go on," said the man on the other end, immediately interested.

"There's a Mountain Commander in our parking lot. The driver was a tired old man of about seventy — could barely stay on his feet — traveling with his young grandson. Is that of interest to us?"

"What was the old man?" asked the voice. "A mage? A warrior? Or a civilian?"

"Hmm..." Artem thought about it. "He didn't look like a mage — he looked like a civilian. Most likely a former warrior. Tall and muscular. But clearly not a fighter anymore — he was green in the face from exhaustion."

"Send me the security footage," the boss ordered. "I'm curious."

"Right away," Artem replied, predicting how this would go.

The boss, of all people, was rarely a man of logic and foresight. He only made decisions about his work after he saw the visitor in question for himself.

"Our client!" said the voice in the receiver smugly. "I'll call you back. Won't be long."

Artem hung up the phone and, looking at the very expensive car, smiled with anticipation and dreamed of what he'd spend the dividends from this job on.

He was so lost in thought that he didn't even notice the old man watching him from the darkness of the hallway with the grin of a predatory beast.

* * *

"Go take a shower and change," said Theophane, handing me a package with clean underwear and needed supplies after our escort had closed the door behind us. "I'll fix us something to eat in the meantime."

Inspired by the thought of eating dinner soon, I gladly cleaned myself off in the shower and even carefully brushed my teeth with the toothbrush he'd put in the package, then returned to the main room freshly steamed and rosy.

I found Theophane there with some skilfully cut smoked meat.

My mouth watered immediately.

“Eat,” he said, pushing a plate of sandwiches towards me.

“Thanks!” I said, attacking the food greedily and not forgetting to take a swig from the glass of apple juice.

“There’s more juice when you finish that,” said Theophane, placing the juice bottle near me and heading for the bathroom. “Finally, a chance to wash up properly!” I heard his quiet voice, and the door closed.

I ate my fill surprisingly fast (only three big sandwiches!), drank some more juice, and resolutely reached into the bag. I was curious to see what else Theophane had gotten at the shopping center.

The first thing that caught my eye was a couple of small chocolate candies with thick wrappers, which I set aside right away — I’d eat those a bit later.

Ivan would have just loved those. And I also loved them now, clearly, even though I’d been entirely indifferent to sweets in my own world.

The second thing I found, which made me very happy, was a new cell phone still in the box. There were also a few other phones and one fairly large tablet.

That meant this world wasn’t behind mine on a technological level, I thought happily. I resolved again not to be surprised by such amazing similarities between my new home and Earth.

I put the phones back in the bag and started unpacking the tablet.

ИК. Прогресс, read the inscription on the case — "IK. Progress," in the Cyrillic alphabet.

Hmm. Nothing out of the ordinary, aside from the name of the manufacturing company, I thought. I'd gotten used to the Roman alphabet taking over in my world.

"A tablet is a tablet," I muttered quietly, carefully examining the gadget from every side and pressing the small "ON/OFF" button.

After a fairly short loading time, a prompt appeared:

Choose your language.

For the sake of curiosity, I scrolled through the list of languages underneath and discovered that most of their names were written in the Cyrillic alphabet. That was a bit unusual to me, because again, in my world I was used to the Roman alphabet dominating.

The rest of the languages on the list were divided into four almost equal sections. The first group was in the Roman alphabet. The second was in something that looked like Arabic script. The third I identified as characters like in Chinese or Japanese (where would we be without them?). The fourth — completely out of the ordinary — looked like Egyptian hieroglyphs.

It would be really interesting to learn about

the latest developments, I thought, but I selected "Nosirian," which was highlighted in red by default.

Enter date and time or connect to wireless service, read the next window.

This place has its own internet? I thought gleefully. *Awesome!*

With the help of the pop-up prompts, I quickly opened a network search.

I chose the only option that turned up: "Harmony Hotel."

A new window immediately appeared. *Enter password.*

Sheesh, what does this hotel need an internet password for? I thought, annoyed. The place was in the middle of nowhere — there was no one but the staff and the guests here. Why set a password? What were they protecting their data from? The squirrels? Or what if it had been done for a special reason? Say, what if the network wasn't free? Pay for the service and you could only use it after that?

Looking around the room attentively, I noticed a landline phone on one of the bedside tables.

There was no pad to dial numbers on the phone, so I just picked up the receiver, hoping it would connect automatically to the administrative desk, and I wasn't wrong.

"Good evening, how may I help you?" I heard the voice of the guy who'd greeted us.

"I'm calling from room number five," I said to

him. “I need the password to the wireless service.”

“To the what?” said the guy in surprise, then exclaimed, “Did you mean the wi-serve?”

“Yes,” I replied. “I meant the wi-serve.”

“I was thinking, ‘What does he mean, ‘the wireless service?’” the guy laughed. “You talk like my grandma.” He added, “Here’s the four-digit code.”

“Thanks,” I said. I was about to put the phone down when I heard his voice abruptly become suspicious:

“And does your grandfather know that you’re planning to spend all night playing games? What, is he already asleep?”

“No, he’s still in the shower,” I answered glumly. “Once he gets out I’ll have to go to bed.”

“Well, be careful,” he said in a stern voice and hung up.

Something seemed off to me about those words, but I cast those unwanted thoughts aside and focused on more interesting things. I was absorbed by the tablet, or more precisely, by the new knowledge of this world that I could get with its help.

People these days had the ability to very quickly (practically on an intuitive level) understand new gadgets. So that didn’t take me much time. To be honest, I didn’t see any particular differences between the operating systems I was used to and this one. It was just a slightly weird Android device, that was all.

All right, it's finally time to learn about the world I've arrived in, I thought, eagerly tapping the icon of an application called "Pathfinder."

As Google and Yandex's local counterpart informed me, today was June fourteenth, 7752.

Whoa! What on earth was that? Why was the year so high? I was astounded, subconsciously expecting to see numbers closer to the two thousands. Give or take two hundred years. But this differed from my expectations by more than five and a half thousand years. It was a bit too much... was this really a parallel world?

Although, of course, on an intellectual level I understood that this world was very different, and the chronology here could start from any year. Even on Earth, every civilization used to have its own calendar, and time had been counted starting from different dates. Nonetheless, it was unexpected.

Unable to overcome my present curiosity, I discovered that the local chronology started with the Great Hero's death day.

I rummaged through the search engine and understood why it had such a strange name. It turned out that this date was related to a time in history when humans could have lost to the first onslaught of demons.

It was then that the Savior appeared in the world, using his Avatar. After a grand battle with the demons, he succeeded in sealing off two of the smaller and one of larger Wastelands, which at that time were located in the territory of the present-day Nosiriansky Empire.

Of course, the Savior's Avatar — as one can count on from a true hero — was killed. His heroic deed, however, allowed humans to muster their strength and stand their ground.

I wasn't happy with the first conclusions I came to after studying this information on the local equivalent of the internet.

First of all, it turned out that gods did indeed exist in this world. It was unpleasant knowing that there was such a powerful being somewhere in your vicinity when you hadn't prayed for a couple of days. And second, it turned out there might be quite a few Wastelands.

"Twenty-two..." I was dumbstruck as I read the answer to my question. "Stars above! Isn't that too many Wastelands for one world?"

As it turned out, certainly not.

Twelve of them were considered small.

These Wastelands spanned about three thousand square miles. Which, in my opinion, wasn't small at all.

Six were considered mid-sized. These were about four times as big as the small ones.

And then there were two large Wastelands: the Samerkan Wasteland and the Gorbovich Wasteland. They spanned about forty thousand square miles. What I liked least of all was finding both of them right on my own continent. And the Gorbovich Wasteland, the biggest one, had made itself at home right in the Nosiriansky Empire.

Now I understood what Theophane had said about how I'd be very difficult to find. With that kind of square footage in the Wastelands, it would be stupid to suggest otherwise.

I cursed internally. Something told me that Theophane and I would be moving to that exact Wasteland, the biggest one. In the place with the highest chance of the next infernal army attack spawning! That was great, that was just perfect!

I was frustrated, but as it turned out, that wasn't all the bad news there was for today.

I was still missing two Wastelands by my count, so I opened the world map and got a shock.

Out of eight continents, two were under the full control of demons.

Two continents and the nearby islands, I realized!

I mulled over the situation and examined the world map.

I needed to study the Wastelands in greater detail — how they'd gotten there, when, and why the demons hadn't taken over the rest of the world yet.

I had so many questions now.

"You already managed to find the tablet?" Theophane's tired voice caught me by surprise. I'd been too lost in thought.

"I was bored," I sighed, burying myself in the screen. "I decided to entertain myself a little."

"Go ahead, but don't stay up too late," he

replied, walking past me. He didn't even make it to the bed and collapsed unconscious on the floor.

"Oh no!" I jumped up and ran to him.

I turned him on his back, noticing that there was blood coming from his nose.

There's a pulse! I thought with relief when I found a blood vessel.

The prospect of being deprived of my only protector in this world was frankly terrifying. Although not long ago I'd been thinking about how I could survive just fine on my own.

"Theophane," I said, and started slapping him on the cheeks. He didn't react.

Pouring water on his face didn't have any effect either. And my attempts to lift him were shamefully unsuccessful.

"You weigh so much!" I growled after yet another failure.

What a dilemma.

I couldn't drag him onto the bed, and I couldn't leave him on the floor.

I resolved this problem simply. I knocked the orthopedic mattress off the bed, put it down next to Theophane, and tried to roll his bulky body onto it. It didn't work on the first try — more like the tenth — but I managed it all the same.

"Phew!" I breathed, collapsing next to him. I wiped away the beads of sweat that had appeared on my forehead with my hand and tried to catch my breath. "You need to take better care of yourself, you're not so young anymore," I said angrily to Theophane — who, of course, didn't answer. I begged internally:

Please let him get through this without consequence! Traveling with a feeble, disabled man would be very bad.

To the bathroom first, I decided! Then I could return to my goldmine of valuable information. Besides, I still hadn't opened the package of my favorite chocolates.

I washed up quickly, dried myself off, and left the bathroom. Outside, I heard the sound of a car approaching, and the beams from its headlights flashed into the room.

Going into the bathroom, I completely automatically turned off the lights in the room — this way I'd be able to fearlessly get a peek at the car that had pulled into the parking lot.

I really didn't like what I saw. By the light of the streetlamps I could see four men who clearly looked like bandits.

They immediately went up to our Mountain and started looking it over like they owned it.

I got a terrible feeling in the pit of my stomach.

I saw the hotel administrator quickly approaching the men.

Greeting them with a handshake, that smiling and cheerful young man with such an honest appearance pointed out our windows to the bandits.

We were done for!

Chapter 5

ONE OF THE BANDITS — the one who'd talked the longest with the hotel employee — somehow noticed my head sticking up through the window and instantly gave me a friendly wave.

Oh, nether-demons! I cursed. And screw this new world and its incomprehensible magic! Did this bald brute know the Eyes of the Wolf tech too? Or something else like that? How else could he have noticed me? And when would I finally remember that I wasn't on Earth anymore? That this world had its own rules?

Panic overwhelmed me in moments — I just froze up and watched the men in the parking lot like a rabbit hypnotized by a snake. In that time I tried to come up with a way to resolve the situation happily.

The man who'd noticed me barked an order

at his people, and they went to the hotel entrance with nasty smiles. Once there, one of them separated from the group and moved towards our window so he could control the perimeter and prevent me from escaping.

There's nowhere I can run! I realized then and there. The escape route through the window was blocked, and the bandits were already in the hotel. I needed to do something quickly! If I didn't, I was a goner!

"Theophane! Theophane!" I cried, leaping to his side and slapping him in the face a couple of times fervently, hoping it would make him come to. "Wake up! They're coming to kill us!"

But my efforts didn't have the effect I intended — he kept lying motionless on the mattress.

Demons' sakes! I cursed, not knowing what else to do. Panic flooded my mind.

I understood clearly that there was no way I could go up against four adult trained thugs. Besides, I really just didn't feel like dying twice in a row in such a short time. Fate had given me a truly incredible chance — it had given me a second life in a new, incredible and unusual world. I didn't want to waste it so foolishly.

If I got killed, the chances that some old mage from another strange world needed the soul of a boy who'd been killed by bandits were slim to none.

I closed my eyes, imagined the slab of ice in

front of me, and transferred all my doubts, fears, and emotions into it. I immediately sensed the cold enshrouding my mind. I calmed down and opened my eyes.

Cleansed of unnecessary thoughts, my mind could concentrate fully on surviving. I started to think up a plan for the fighting I'd have to do.

I'd need a swift and merciless victory so that I wouldn't have to withstand confrontation for long. So, first of all, I was counting on the element of surprise.

I grabbed the fighter's knife that Theophane had used to cut the sandwiches from where it lay on the table and checked how sharp it was.

It was very sharp.

Excellent!

A knock sounded at the door.

"If you touch a hair on my head, I swear," I said loudly, while noiselessly putting a chair in front of the door. I had to keep the bandits from bursting into the room for at least a little bit — those few moments would decide everything. "The house of Temnikov will find you and your whole family, and they'll slaughter you and your third and fifth cousins!"

The bandits went quiet, probably because of the coldness and the confidence they could hear in my voice — they lost their nerve a little.

"The boy's lying," said the hotel administrator's somewhat nervous voice. "The car is registered to his grandfather. And he's an ordinary commoner, even if he's rich. He's got nothing to do with the nobility. Look, I ran it through the system."

It sounded like the hotel employee was giving the bandit a tablet or a phone so he could look at that information.

"The old man passed out something like half an hour ago and didn't get up after that," he continued, as if to reassure the bandits and thereby resolve their subsequent doubts. Besides, they were probably angry that they were scared of a child.

Oh no! How did he know that Theophane passed out? Were there cameras in here or something? Instinctively, I spun my head from side to side, but I didn't find anything by doing that.

"Lying is naughty," said the bandit leader in a rather nasty tone, then spoke to the hotel employee. "You got a key to the room?"

"Yes, here, I brought it for you."

"Then open it up," ordered the bandit leader.

The hotel employee dawdled a bit, but after a moment I heard him inserting the key into the keyhole and turning it.

The key that had been left in the door on our side didn't interfere with it at all.

I silently slipped closer to the door, squatted a bit, and went still. I counted the seconds as they passed.

I was counting on three things: that the door

opened in the direction of the hallway, that the bandits were off their guard because they were trying to kill a child and an old man, and that I had the element of surprise — none of them would guess that their harmless little victim would be prepared to defend himself.

Clenching the knife confidently, I concentrated even harder.

As soon as the door started to open, I came forward out of the opening at half-pace and — with a sharp movement up from below — dealt a blow to the closest bandit, who wasn't expecting it at all, straight to the groin.

A sharp jerk of the knife downwards, a precise rebound, and I was back in the room.

Despite the speed and unexpectedness of my daring attack, I'd provoked a reflexive response from one of the men, but thankfully it was a blow that barely hit my shoulder.

Sharp pain shot through my arm. But I got a hold of myself handily. No big deal.

Everything's fine, let's keep dancing! I thought, preparing myself. Now began the second act.

The second bandit came after me, his face warped with rage, fear, and disgust, and ran into the chair I'd put in front of the door.

He was very confused, and that kept him from thinking straight. Imagine what you'd think if your friend got such a cheap shot right in front of you! Any man would understand that even the idea of such a thing would provoke illogical terror and panic.

The chair that he'd stumbled over wasn't an insurmountable barrier for the attackers. Its role was just to distract the second attacker — to make him look down. And my barrier played its role. When the bandit, completely by reflex, looked down towards the object that had caused him the sharp pain and realized that it was just a chair, he looked back up to find me and immediately got a knife in the eye. He didn't even know what killed him.

A brief thought flashed through the depths of my mind — all of Ivan's reflexes were good, but these frozen emotions were freeing me from doubting this body's capabilities!

But I didn't stop to dwell on it — two bandits and the hotel administrator were still left alive, and I didn't know what to do with them.

I no longer had the element of surprise, and the bandit I'd gotten with the knife to the eye had collapsed face-down on the floor, driving the knife deep into his head — I couldn't just pull it out easily now. Basically, I now had no weapons left. My only choice was to put my trust in the ability I'd recently learned and absolutely not practiced — punching with Shiki-Cho.

The third bandit, the most dangerous-looking one — the leader — came into the room. Instead of going up against me hand-to-hand, he drew his pistol. I immediately realized the situation had gotten really bad.

This man was the leader for a reason. He was so good that he'd quickly evaluated the situation and decided not to mess around with an empty-handed kid. That certainly deserved some praise and spoke to a good mind. Not everyone can admit honestly that they're in no condition to deal with an enemy known to be weaker than them, let alone a ten-year-old boy, without resources at hand or outside help. But he could move this forward if he didn't swear off his weapons.

I'd rightly praised the reflexes hammered into the innermost parts of this body's brain. As soon as I laid eyes on the bald bandit's pistol, my body started to move...

Do you know what the "Pendulum" is? I admit I didn't know either — until that moment, that is. I'd read about it, of course. With this tech, you could avoid bullets, but to be honest I'd found it impossible to believe.

But when I did it, it turned out that when someone points a loaded firearm at you, absolutely anything becomes possible.

Even speeding up my mastery of Shiki-Cho, as it happened.

I made three quick jumps from one side to the other, found myself in front of the bandit leader, and punched him in the stomach.

Blood, flesh, guts, and turds — that was what I'd associate that energetic punch's tech with now. Believe me, just that!

Despite my frozen emotions, I was in shock at what I'd done with nothing but my own hands.

The last bandit left alive brought me out of that. He heard the sounds of the fight and hurried to his companions' aid.

The wild cry that he let loose at what he saw, and the chaotic gunshots that followed, brought me back to my senses.

I didn't know how, but I was able to get out of the line of fire and avoid getting injured. It was probably thanks to the fact that he was in shock from seeing the bloody bits that used to be his boss not long ago. Believe me, it wasn't a pretty sight. I was saved from having the same reaction as the bandit by those frozen emotions and my sense of self-preservation.

When the bandit's pistol ran out of bullets, he kept uselessly pulling the trigger and yelling wildly. A dash forward and to the side, and I snatched up the gun from the bandit leader who'd met his untimely demise.

My small hands firmly and confidently gripped the handle. A shot rang out, the pistol recoiled hard in my hands, and it slipped from my fingers.

But the gun had done its job. The young bandit clutched his stomach and fell to the floor.

Good thing the leader's pistol had still had bullets in it. I'd had no strength or desire to use Shiki-Cho again. I couldn't recover from the first punch.

Remembering the golden rule of American war movies, I removed the knife with difficulty from the first dead guy's eye socket and mercilessly finished off the wounded ones. Leaving enemies behind your back always causes no end of problems.

I found the guy from the hotel administration in the hallway. He was sitting in the corner, shaking from fear and staring at me — a little boy covered in pieces of bloody flesh — with wide eyes.

I probably looked like the very Devil incarnate to him.

He didn't wait for me to approach him before he fainted.

I stood motionless for some time until my mind registered that it was all over. Then I doubled over — I was sick to my stomach.

After freeing its contents, I got a hold of myself and hurried back into the shower. I had to clean up our room and the hallway and hide the bodies, but I couldn't do that looking like this.

First of all, someone could show up at the hotel — new guests or employees. Second, it was pretty damn unpleasant walking around looking like a bloody little demon. Besides, the smell of this atrocity was just horrific, and dried blood was starting to pinch my skin.

Pulling myself together quickly, I mentally thanked Theophane for buying a few pairs of underwear, got changed, picked up the knife, and went out into the hallway.

The hotel employee was already awake. He was looking around in horror at the blood-covered floor, afraid to move.

"I'm glad you only fainted," I said in a cold voice. "Now I have a helper. You will help me clean up, won't you?"

He didn't answer.

I set his head straight with a good punch, and his eyes focused on me.

"Do you want to live?" I asked with conviction.

"Y-y-yes," he said, nodding.

"And do you have a family?" was my next question.

He didn't answer.

"Do you have a family?" I asked, putting even more coldness into my voice and dealing him another sobering blow.

"Y-yes," he said. "I h-have a mother and a sister."

"That's good." I nodded. "Family is important. I have a family too," I said, and explained, "a noble bloodline. So I'll warn you in advance right now: if you try to run or if you don't make an effort to do as I ask, my family will kill you and your family. Understood?"

"Y-yes!" He nodded. "Y-yes! Understood, I'll do everything you say."

"Then drive your friends' car closer to the hotel, open the trunk, and start carrying the bodies out to it."

I got into the bandits' car with the hotel

employee — what if he'd lied about his family, or what if he didn't care about my threats and tried to run?

Carrying the bodies and the various remains didn't take much time. Although a few times the guy did the same thing I'd done — dropped to his knees and heaved.

When we finished with the bodies, we returned the car to the parking lot. We got busy cleaning up more. Of course we had to drive the bodies out of here, but we didn't have time for that. Cleaning up was more important.

The hallway didn't take us much time, since it turned out that this world also had vacuum cleaners for wet cleaning jobs.

The room was worse. The walls, floor, and ceiling were splattered with highly unpleasant substances.

"Wash it for now," I said to the guy. "You can paint it later, and the room will be as good as new. You still work here, after all."

What I said had a positive impact on his work ethic. He thought I intended to spare him. Naive — he didn't know yet how wrong he was. It was like I'd forgotten who'd insisted that Theophane and I were ordinary people...

* * *

Theophane was in deep amazement. It had all started when he'd overheard the doorman's conversation on the phone — he'd decided once again to demonstrate to Ivan that he couldn't defend himself on his own, and that meant he needed constant, purposeful training.

After "losing consciousness" in the hotel room, Theophane had gotten Ivan to learn what he wanted him to: he was alone, and he had no one to rely on in that moment but himself.

Theophane had been glad to see Ivan's persistence in trying to get him onto the mattress. It meant he wasn't indifferent to his old teacher, at least.

But here was the most interesting thing.

When he'd looked out the window, Ivan had somehow determined that there were bandits in the parking lot, and he'd started to prepare for the fight in advance, knowing honestly that he didn't have the strength to deal with them.

All right, Theophane had thought as he'd pretended to lose consciousness. *You'll take a couple of serious hits, you'll realize you don't have a chance, maybe you'll hit someone with Shiki-Cho, and then I'll come to your rescue. Just to show you once again who your only protector is and whose skills you need to match. Then you'll understand that your training is vitally important to you, because I won't be around forever.*

But Ivan's actions had simply stunned him. The audible coldness in his voice, his threats. He had tried to find some way to resolve the matter without bloodshed! And he might even have succeeded if not for the doorman.

To take things further, instead of quietly waiting to die, he'd decided to attack. And he'd done well! No, he'd done spectacularly.

A few seconds of fighting and two of his enemies had been dead.

Could Theophane have imagined such a thing? No! He was thoroughly confused. That hadn't stopped him from guarding Ivan while he'd been dancing between bullets. It was precisely for that reason that the last bandit hadn't hit him, even though two bullets had headed straight for his chest.

Once he'd dealt with the bandits, Ivan had taken to restoring order. He'd assumed that Theophane could remain unconscious for a bit longer and decided to make the hotel into a temporary base.

After meditating a bit and having a good rest, Theophane decided to get up. Ivan needed to sleep, and Theophane needed to get rid of all the evidence and ponder what had just happened.

* * *

When Theophane woke up a while later, he was extremely surprised by the changes to the interior of the room, his appearance, and my nighttime adventures.

He offered to let me rest a bit in the room next door, then took the hotel employee in his arms, brought him out of the room, and hastened to familiarize himself with his version of events.

I knew Theophane's methods. They were, needless to say, very bloody and cruel. Although, this guy had done whatever I wanted at the slightest threat of force. He was a thing of value, not a prisoner.

I took the key to the room next door, let Theophane know where I was going, and lay down to sleep. I was shaken up from the stress I'd just gone through. So when my head touched my pillow, I passed right out in a very clichéd manner. It was good that I was able to entrust my problems to an adult who knew how to solve them.

I woke up at around eleven o'clock in the morning, and we were already on the road. The night's adventures had been so exhausting that I hadn't even felt it when I'd been carried out to the car.

"Have we been driving for long?" I asked with a big yawn, having a nice stretch in the passenger seat, all the way to the fully reclined headrest.

"Yes, we have," said Theophane, looking at his watch, then asked, "How do you feel?"

"Fine," I answered, realizing what he meant, then adjusted the seat so I could sit comfortably.

"I'm saying I hope your conscience isn't bothering you," Theophane clarified all the same, once I'd seated myself normally.

"They were bandits, they were there to kill us," I declared with unshakeable confidence. "So I don't regret anything. It was either us or them."

"You're right," Theophane agreed. "Either us or them. I'm glad you understand that. They crossed swords with us, and it got them killed." Theophane paused for a bit before continuing. "The young man from the hotel had a police database on vehicles. He was using it to monitor non-aristocratic Normals staying in the hotel and send for the bandits. You know the rest. They've already killed around twenty people this way."

"Monsters," was all I could reply. Then I said, "I think that guy paid for what he did."

"Of course," said Theophane. "Worms like that don't deserve to live. Because as it turns out, he approached that gang of bandits himself and suggested that they work together. If I'd left him alive, he would've returned to his trade soon enough. Besides, he heard the name Temnikov and couldn't be allowed to live."

"I wanted to try to resolve the situation without violence. What if it had worked?" I shrugged, and decided to ask just in case: "Oh, and what about the footage from the surveillance cameras? You know there were some in the hotel rooms, right?"

"I know," said Theophane. "I found them all and erased them. Anything I couldn't erase I burned."

So that was why I thought he smelled like a campfire. He'd made a fire in the hotel to hide the traces of our activities. All right.

"And can I now congratulate you on your mastery of Shiki-Cho?" Theophane asked.

I shrugged.

"I don't know, I need to do some more good practice so that it works every time and not just every once in a while. But I think being able to use it once when I really need it is good enough. As for any punches that follow, I don't know yet — I'll find out in training."

"After you recover, we'll definitely check," said Theophane. Then, very slowly and carefully choosing his words, he said, "And, Ivan... thank you... for saving my life.."

"Oh, it was nothing," I said, suddenly embarrassed for some reason. My first idea had been running away, my second had been surviving, and only after that had I thought about Theophane as someone I didn't want to lose. "I only did what I had to."

"That may be so, but I can't let that go without rewarding you for it. You're only ten years old, but you've already managed to take on four grown men, even if they were only Normals. So, as your teacher, I'm promoting you to a second-level Junior."

"A second-level Junior?" I was a bit astonished as I recalled the warrior hierarchy. "So that means just a little more and I can become a Soldier? A full-fledged Soldier? Why so far in advance? Because I saved your life?"

I remembered that talented children usually

made it to the Junior rank at around twelve or fourteen. Like my older brothers Simon and Ignatius, for example. But never at ten.

"It's not far in advance at all," Theophane disagreed. "It's because of your competent actions in the fight," he said, giving me a light rap on the ear. I immediately covered my head. "And because of your progress in learning difficult techs. Not all warriors can do that," he finished. "And stop taking that tone with me," he said, raising a lecturing finger. "At least in front of strangers. Outside the grounds of noble estates, such a teacher-student relationship isn't remotely accepted. A student is supposed to be silent and heed his teacher's wisdom with all respect."

"That *is* how I acted back at the hotel. I was quiet and listened to everything you said," I said with a somewhat offended tone, and added: "How do you like that, you save someone's life and he gives you a smack on the ear! Please tell me you went over the security camera footage and saw me trying to slap you awake."

Theophane smirked at my attempts to goad him.

"What are we planning to do next, anyway?" I decided to ask after a bit. "How far do we have to go before we get to these Wastelands?"

Theophane thought about it.

"In two or three hours we'll get to Kvilich — that's a regional city. New documents and a new car registered to me are waiting for us there. After that, we have two more days of driving ahead of us, and then we'll arrive at our destination."

"I hope the people buying our Mountain won't be like our friends from last night," I said.

"No." Theophane shook his head. "The buyer is one of my oldest friends — he forged us the new documents and registered the new car."

"Man, I was just getting used to the Mountain Commander," I said, running my hand along the comfortable leather seat. "It's a nice car. I hope the next one isn't any worse."

"You'll see," said Theophane promisingly.

"By the way, I'm kinda hungry," I said after a bit, rubbing my stomach a little.

"It's all in the trunk," said Theophane. "Put the back of the seat down on the driver's side, and you'll see the bag."

I climbed into the back, quickly found the button I needed, and gently folded the seat down. The car immediately smelled like food.

The first thing I did was take out the box with juice in it and take a couple of big sips.

Lovely!

After that, I reached in for the leftover smoked meat and was surprised at Theophane's wild appetite — this morning he'd annihilated a good half-chunk of it and all the sandwiches.

I started searching for the knife in the bag and realized that was pointless, since the only knife was the same one I'd killed the bandits with.

I'll eat it like this, without cutting it! I decided.

While I was eating, images of last night's fight came to my mind.

Hitting my first enemy in the groin, throwing my knife into the other guy's eye, and doling out more injuries later.

Why did Theophane put that there? I thought, looking at the knife. Was this another test of my psychological stability? Or was there really not another knife?

Despite my slight bravado in front of Theophane and my awareness that I'd done the right thing, it still hadn't been easy for me to take human lives.

I'd still grown up in my own world as a perfectly ordinary, average person. I wasn't on the special forces, I never killed people or animals. So last night's fight had been very unpleasant for me, although it had been needed experience.

I understood clearly that this was a very different world. With its own laws and moral code. And if I didn't kill my enemies — didn't matter if they were humans or demons — then they'd gladly kill me.

"Have some bread," Theophane scolded me, interrupting my unpleasant thoughts. "Why are you eating nothing but meat? That's not going to be filling."

"But it's tasty," I said with my most casual expression. "Don't forget how big of a piece you had this morning! Let the child partake of the feast."

"Just make sure you don't get sick later," Theophane warned me somberly.

"I won't!" I replied. I finished my meat, grabbed the package of sweets I hadn't opened yesterday, and climbed back into the front seat.

For that I immediately got another light rap on the ear and a wet wipe for my hands. Apparently they had those in this world too.

We got to the city we needed to fairly quickly. I found it very interesting to look at the cars, the people walking along the side of the road, the gas stations, and the small hamlets we passed along the way and compare them to the everyday things of my world. So I barely even noticed the time passing.

For the most part, there weren't that many differences.

It seemed like everything here was the same but just a little bit different. Like being in our world but in a different country. That was the feeling I got.

Overall, I wasn't bored.

The city of Kvilich didn't impress me at all. As it turned out, it looked like a typical, average city. Just like in our world. Except, of course, for its slightly unusual design and for how clean it was.

I didn't even know what I'd been hoping to see. I guess something futuristic and totally out of the ordinary. This was another world, after all. But everything was entirely what I was used to.

The outskirts of the city were predominantly

a residential sector dotted sparsely with multi-story apartment buildings. Then came multi-story concrete buildings with all kinds of institutions on the first floor. In the center of the city, several historical districts and parks had been preserved.

Ordinary three-colored stoplights shone on the streets, typical white paint marked the roads.

"How many people live here?" I asked curiously.

"Fifteen hundred, I think, maybe slightly fewer," answered Theophane after considering.

That wasn't much for a regional city. But like Theophane had said, it was a small city.

The city-dwellers' clothing varied greatly.

It was impossible not to notice that the women and girls preferred bright-colored clothing — clearly the latest fashion. The men preferred more subdued colors.

I also noticed that there were almost no overweight people on the street. Really! On the contrary, absolutely everyone was slender and in shape.

What was this? A peculiarity of this world? Or, more likely, a sensible government policy aimed at raising the youth for warriorhood? Because needless to say, if an infernal Wasteland made itself at home in your territory, like it or not, you'd be a country at war that could suffer a demon attack at any moment. It was probably that.

We drove into the residential sector, where

Theophane's friend's house was, and stopped at the gate of a lovely two-story house surrounded by a tall brick fence.

"We're here," said Theophane, then started briefing me. "Don't get out of the car unless I tell you to, and keep your mouth shut — it would be best to try not to talk at all."

"Got it." I nodded. "I'll be a statue."

The gate didn't open, so Theophane signaled a few more times. When even that didn't get a response, he frowned.

"Wait here — I'm going to go see what's going on."

He got out of the car and cleared the six-foot fence with one unbelievably high jump.

Whoa! I was thunderstruck by his acrobatic feat. Who was this guy, that he could do stuff like that? And this after he'd passed out from exhaustion last night? Something was wrong here...

But I wasn't able to pursue the thought that had come to my mind.

The driver-side door opened, and a guarded-looking young man of about twenty in stylish skinny jeans and a dark t-shirt dove straight into the car. He wordlessly pointed the barrel of a gun at me and froze.

Are you kidding me? I screamed internally, begging for help from who only knew what. Should I expect new adventures every day now? Or what? What the hell?

The guy holding me at gunpoint clearly couldn't read my mind, and I obviously wasn't of interest to any higher powers, so I didn't get an answer to my question.

Instead, the back door of the car opened.

"Clear!" barked the voice of a man to someone as he sat behind me.

"There's a boy in the car," said the guy with his pistol aimed at me, his hand cupped to his ear, and I noticed a miniature headset that he was talking into.

"Are you good or bad?" I asked quietly, addressing the man sitting behind me and simultaneously trying to punch with Shiki-Cho by gathering my spiritual energy in my fist.

Despite last night's adventures, I still couldn't get used to the idea that someone could just pull a gun on me so easily. So I braced myself for the worst, giving in to the terror seeping through my body.

"Be quiet," said the man behind me kindheartedly.

The guy in the driver's seat got distracted listening to something in his earpiece. He deflected his gaze and turned his gun slightly aside.

This was my chance! I'd take him out first, then the other guy right after! I just couldn't overdo it and blow all my spiritual energy in one punch.

All of a sudden a wicket gate directly adjacent to the bigger gates opened. A perfectly calm

Theophane, in the company of some elderly man, appeared before my eyes.

"They're friendly," said Theophane's companion, and the guy holding me at gunpoint put the safety on. Then he winked as if nothing had happened and got out of the car.

The gate started moving aside, and Theophane resumed his place in the driver's seat and took the Mountain into the driveway.

"We're switching cars and getting out of here right away," he said to me. "Abraham — " He nodded towards the old man returning to the driveway. " — is having some slight problems with a criminal sect. I don't really want to come into the sights of the local law enforcement or any similar organizations."

"I see. But I'm also having a slight problem," I answered in a bit of a strained voice. "When that guy pointed a gun at me, I started gathering Shiki-Cho in my hand, and now I don't know how to get rid of it. I can't make it go away."

"A lot of energy?" said Theophane, narrowing his eyes.

"I think it's a lot more than in the woods," I said, my voice tense. I added angrily: "Maybe we can do something about it? Otherwise I'm going to wreck the car! And I'll get shrapnel wounds, and we'll lose the car. What'll we exchange for the documents and the new car then?"

The door opened on my side.

"Is this your student?" Abraham asked

Theophane, squinting. "When you said my boys were in grave danger, I pictured him a little differently."

A few of the men who were with us on the driveway laughed quietly.

"Do you have a target range in this house?" Theophane asked instead of responding.

Abraham nodded.

"Then let's go there and I'll show you a little something — otherwise everything here might get destroyed."

A curious Abraham headed towards the house along the comfortable, tile-paved path. The armed men in the driveway and I followed after him.

The target range that Abraham had at his disposal was a sixty-five-square-foot rectangular area covered in yellow sand.

"Strike in the center," suggested a smirking Theophane. I quickly walked to the middle of the area and unleashed the energy from my fist with great pleasure.

When I struck, I felt the Shiki-Cho come out of my hand not in one powerful stream, as it had seemed to before, but in a thousand little rivulets of energy that turned into something more powerful when assembled together.

By some instinct I imagined those thousand rivulets wrapping themselves around clockwise and becoming a whirlwind of energy. There was something unpleasant about it — spending such energy in vain. I wanted beauty.

At the last second, I closed my eyes and held my breath. I did it just in time — yellow sand flew away from me on all sides at high speed. I could hear muffled cries and frantic coughing from several people.

When the dust settled somewhat after a bit, I opened my eyes and saw that I was waist-deep in some kind of pit.

Now that wasn't too bad! I thought, climbing out of the deep hole.

The face on the guy who'd been holding me at gunpoint was a sight for sore eyes.

In a rush of childish pride, I winked at him and went back to Theophane's side.

"Well, Theophane." Abraham shook his head. "You know how to pick your students. This one's even better than the last — "

Abraham didn't get a chance to finish his sentence — he was cut off by a pointed cough from Theophane.

What students is he talking about? I thought, curious. And why didn't Theophane want me to know about them? What terrible thing might Abraham blurt out in a random conversation? Interesting...

"Now that we're done confirming your student's capabilities, can we get on to business?" Abraham remembered abruptly.

Our new car was a tough-looking black off-roader.

My verdict was "not bad." Simpler than the Mountain, that went without saying. Clearly not as expensive, but it was definitely good.

"Abraham," said Theophane with a tone in his voice I didn't understand, "I asked you to find a good-quality, inexpensive car.

"It wasn't expensive." Abraham smiled slyly.

"Was it stolen?" Theophane clarified immediately.

"How could you say that?" Abraham feigned outrage, then calmly added: "You Changeling-demon, you."

"And what about the inspection?" asked Theophane, who couldn't resist and sat in the driver's seat. He adjusted the seat under himself and started the ignition.

"Everything is as you requested," said Abraham, walking up to the window. "The inspection has been passed, the tank is full, all the car's paperwork is in the glove compartment, and there's money in a bag on the back seat."

While the men discussed various topics — like how the quality of work for document forgery specialists was getting worse, how passport office functionaries were taking too many bribes, and how young people were too unruly, I stood like a statue next to the car and listened to their conversation attentively.

What if Abraham suddenly said something out of place again?

While that was going on, the young men

unloaded our car's trunk and transferred all our things to the new car.

When that was all finished, Theophane got out of the car and embraced Abraham, and they clapped each other on the back a few times.

"I can't stay and help you," said Theophane unexpectedly, frowning.

"Don't worry about it, my friend — it's not such a big problem that I need to ask for your help," said Abraham with a smile. "I'm just teaching some arrogant brats life lessons, that's all. Although..." He thought for a moment. "I wouldn't mind borrowing your student for a few days."

"You take care of yourself," said Theophane, laughing. "We old-timers have less and less time left with each passing year."

"So *you* take care of yourself," said Abraham, shaking his head, then shot me an unexpectedly sharp glance. "You're mixed up in dangerous business, kid, and on top of that, you're going towards what I ran from in my time. Make a good warrior of yourself, and don't get yourself killed."

Theophane narrowed his eyes.

I felt somehow ill at ease on hearing those words.

What did that mean — *don't get yourself killed?*

"You've always been such a jokester," said Theophane in some kind of heartfelt voice. Putting his hand on Abraham's shoulder, he gave him a last friendly farewell. "I want you to remember: if anyone finds out about this, I'll come back and slaughter your whole family."

"I know, my friend, I know," said Abraham with a nod, and they laughed and embraced tightly again.

A young girl in a formal dress came out of the house and thrust a large bag at Theophane.

"This is for you for the road," said Abraham. "So you don't have to live only on store-bought food."

Once we'd gotten in the car and driven away from the local Mafioso's house, I breathed easier.

Right up until the end I'd been thinking that something would go wrong and we'd have to fight again.

"You were joking when you said you'd slaughter his family, right?" I decided to confirm anyway.

"No," was all Theophane said in response.

I figured there was probably something in this life that I just didn't understand.

Chapter 6

SERGEI DIACHENKO — a tall, handsome, dark-haired man of middle age — strode confidently through the halls of the Temnikov estate to his new study.

Servants who happened across him along the way lowered their eyes or tried to hide unobtrusively so that his gaze wouldn't fall on them.

Sergei smiled. He liked that — that power, that carefully hidden fear in the eyes of most of the estate's residents. He knew it wouldn't last long — he'd soon get used to being seen that way and start to view it as something he was owed, if he continued to pay attention to such trifles at all. Sergei wasn't a vain man — rather, he was ambitious. He knew that his monetary compensation depended on the height of the position he'd assumed, as did his chance to resolve several personal matters. Thus, he saw his ambitions as a virtue and not a shortcoming.

However, even he couldn't have imagined how much he'd surpass his past self in one paltry week.

Though there had, of course, been hints that he might move up soon. How could he not, when his superior was a senile old man who'd been in his position for far too long, entirely failing to fulfill the duties of his position and understanding nothing about his field — although perhaps, once, he'd been capable of something. But his time had come and gone long ago, and power needed to be transferred to younger hands.

If someone had told him a week ago that he, Sergei Diachenko, would be taking a position as head of security for a prince's family, he would readily have laughed in that person's face — or perhaps instead he would have considered it a veiled insult.

He hadn't been on this family's security team for very long at all, only for a year, but in that time he'd been able to accomplish a lot. He'd investigated the way the service operated, the duties of the people in charge, and the organization of the types of resources. He'd exposed weak points where it could be attacked so that they'd have a chance to report on the flaws he'd discovered in a timely manner. He'd established communication with many of the house's servants and staff, and even with its ordinary soldiers, turning them into his informants. He'd carried out tasks given to him personally by Princess Galina Temnikov and established a close working relationship with her, making her want to work specifically with him due to his professionalism and executive talents.

In reality, he was by all accounts an ordinary man, not remarkable in any way. A man of the common people with roots in an ordinary working-class family, who'd been lucky enough to be born a mage gifted with mid-level strength. The painstaking work he'd taken upon himself had borne fruit — now he already had a second-level bachelor's degree. That was most likely as high as he could go, but he knew well that if he had the chance, he could get an incredibly exotic potion from the Wastelands that would increase his magical strength a bit.

After he'd finished school as a young man, he'd gone to the Academy of Public Security, which prepared personnel for law enforcement. He'd expected to choose the department of police studies — he'd never expected that he would break into the elite, prestigious study of special services. But that had given him its share of hardship, not least because students there worked with their feet and not with their brains.

After six years of laborious but fascinating service in the Internal Security Department task force, which served as the police, he'd found himself with priceless experience in the field.

During that time as a young officer, he'd established connections to the criminal world, many representatives of noble families, and their security officers, since his official position let him do that.

His unprecedented stroke of good luck was the very rewarding collaboration that had arisen between him and the representatives of the Belov family's security service. He'd even done some favors for one of the contenders for the title of Prince Temnikov's wife.

After that young woman had ascended to her new place, she hadn't forgotten about the help Sergei had given her, and she'd helped him get into her personal hierarchy — that was how the matter of the previous head of security had been settled. Still, a typical supervisor never likes to lose an experienced operative who's resolved a large number of difficult problems.

The department of the ISD where Sergei had served specialized particularly in criminal offenses.

Sergei's job had been to conduct interviews of victims and witnesses, inspect crime and accident scenes, collect material evidence, and search for the guilty parties. In his time as a young policeman he'd caught many thieves, bandits, and murderers. During his service, he'd not infrequently run into demon worshipers and other disciples of forbidden cults. However, to his great delight, such tasks were handed over to other competent organizations: the one and only Department of Imperial Security or even the Inquisition.

Overall, he'd taken a lot of beatings in his day, but he'd gained distinct experience from it, as well as a touch of unscathed cynicism. If one took into account that he still had a great number of agents in criminal environments and many friends in powerful departments, then one could say that he'd become a very valuable asset to the Temnikov house's security. Which, to his surprise, had not been in the best condition.

At the suggestion of the young princess Galina, Sergei hadn't let his connections from his previous place of service slip away from him uselessly — he'd taken every possible opportunity to suggest interesting activities to his acquaintances and generously paid for it all.

Despite this, unfortunately, he'd remained one of the house's ordinary security operatives. But he hadn't despaired — he'd prepared for change, knowing that his moment of triumph was still yet to come. He'd waited, hardly daring to think that his wish would be granted so quickly.

In the fallout from the recent tragic events, the house's former head of security had been personally put to death by Prince Temnikov for his carelessness. He'd been replaced with Sergei, who had taken up his task with zeal.

After that night's raid on the estate, the experienced Sergei had immediately studied the scene of the crime — or, more precisely, what was left of it after the servants and other unauthorized personnel had gone tramping through it.

He was different from the other security officers in that he had information about what must have happened, but what remained unsolved was at which point an operation carefully premeditated and planned down to the smallest details had turned into a bloody slaughter-fest.

Without additional commands from his mistress, Sergei went around to all the locations of of the incident and tried to form a picture of what had happened. But he was completely unable to do this. The immediate authorities were also trying to raise morale and set to work on this incredibly important task, but in doing so they'd frankly interfered more than helped.

Meanwhile, Sergei's colleagues had found some weighty, obviously planted evidence. However, they had purposely ignored this so that they would have something to present to their supervisor and the prince himself as an excuse.

Sergei, despite his comrades' "success," kept digging persistently. The evidence they'd found gave rise to very contradictory ideas. He'd even confirmed the accuracy of his own information many times over with various informants, so he knew for certain that theirs was a false trail.

When Sergei began searching for answers to his questions with his "proof by contradiction" method, he started to put the fragments of an unbelievably convoluted picture together like a jigsaw puzzle.

He founded the structure of his logic on a clear interrelationship between the three major occurrences from that night. The attack itself, the killing of Ivan — the head of the family's son — and the death of the Morozov prince, Yegor Temnikov's elderly father-in-law who'd lived far past his time.

It was exactly then that Sergei found the very thread that, by tugging on it, he was able to unravel the tangled knot of confusing events and determine what each specific interested party had wanted, as well as what each had gotten in the end. Once he did, of course, he didn't share this information with anyone.

First of all, it was life-threateningly dangerous. Second, he hadn't worked this hard to hand out pieces of his work to others just like that. And third, he needed to finally begin putting his plans for his own ascension to power into action. Sergei's stance on life was simple. If you don't take your success into your own hands, no one will do it for you.

Once he'd worked through the plan, for the first time up until then, he got in touch with the princess and presented his carefully retouched version of the events. Of course, he didn't give the slightest hint that he knew about her significant role in the tragic events. There had been gossip that day that had turned the life he'd gotten used to upside down...

"Are you ready?" Galina asked him, looking him over carefully again.

"Yes," he answered with confidence in his voice that he didn't have in reality, internally praying to the Savior and earnestly hoping for something good to come of the upcoming conversation.

"Let's go," said Galina curtly, striding down the hallway with the gait of a woman who knew her worth.

She approached her husband's study, opened the door without knocking, and entered. In this house, only she was permitted to do such things.

"Wait here," she said over her shoulder, closing the door.

Sergei exhaled quietly.

He understood clearly that in a few minutes his fate would be decided.

Today, either he would get the promotion he deserved or he would die, if the Temnikovs suspected even for a moment that he knew a small part of the truth.

"Come in," said Galina, opening the door.

Sergei entered the room and stood before the prince's desk as his wife studied him.

Yegor Temnikov — a sturdy, short man of fifty years with a thick, luxuriant mustache and raven-black hair without a single streak of gray despite his age — looked younger than he was, in spite of his regular and profuse bouts of drinking. He was sitting at his desk with a glass full of amber liquid in his hand and staring intently at Sergei as he walked in.

On a passing inspection of the desk, Sergei's sharp eyes caught the label on the alcohol bottle, and he wanted to let out an impressed whistle.

It was a plain-seeming bottle at a first glance that cost as much as a year of Sergei's salary while he'd been serving in the ISD, and that was despite ISD officers making a fair amount more than other civil servants.

Yegor continued to remain silent and regard Sergei as he stood before him at attention. When the silence became oppressive, he proclaimed:

"Speak."

His quiet voice conveyed no emotion. It was neither threatening, nor displeased, nor cheerful, nor angry, nor even remotely interested. It was simply quiet and incredibly powerful.

As disconcerted as he was by this, Sergei used all his strength to keep his composure, so as not to go spilling all of the information he had.

His experience serving in the ISD proved beneficial. He'd often crossed paths with people in high positions in various structures, many of whom had even been notable members of noble families.

Most of the highest-ranking police officers were just such behemoths, with great magical power and an ingrained belief in their hereditary right to rule.

Sergei got a hold of himself, gave a dignified nod, and began to speak confidently.

"Prince Yegor, while studying the aftermath of the attack on the estate, I took the liberty of identifying the burnt bodies. This investigation revealed that two of the bodies had no relation whatsoever to your family. My colleagues believed that they belonged to the servant Theophane and your son Ivan, but based on their medical records I can say with certainty that they do not."

Yegor didn't react to this news in any way, so Sergei continued.

"I'm certain that the purpose of the attack was to abduct Ivan. Because in any other case, there would be no need to exchange the boy's corpse for another. It's worth noting that the servant Theophane, who was tasked with Ivan's education, also went missing, and there was also an attempt to cover up his disappearance with a burnt corpse of the same build. From this I can conclude that he was the one who found out the patrol schedule and gave the enemy forces all the information necessary for the success of the mission."

"Are you certain?" asked Yegor with doubt in his voice. "Ivan's body was also switched?"

"Beyond a shadow of a doubt," Sergei answered confidently.

"That's interesting." There was still doubt audible in Yegor's voice. "Were you able to ascertain whose bodies you actually found?"

"Yes." Sergei nodded, although that information was actually in need of additional clarification. "The corpse of a boy with a similar build went missing from a regional morgue two months ago. They still haven't gotten back to us on our inquiry into the second body."

"Two months," said Galina slowly and thoughtfully. "That means the attackers began preparing that far in advance."

"Exactly," Sergei agreed. "This scheme was not devised simply — it was meticulously planned."

"And our security saw nothing," said Galina in a kind of strange voice, looking at her husband.

He answered her with the same look and asked Sergei his next question.

"Have you found out how these bodies came to be on the grounds of the estate?"

They were driven in on something, how else? thought Sergei, surprised at the strange question. But from his time serving in the ISD, he knew that a subordinate must always have an answer to any question, even the stupidest question, from a superior.

"They were probably brought in hidden in a motor vehicle and stealthily placed in the room before the fire was set. As I already said, the burned bodies must have been meant to mislead us about the victims' identities, and they fulfilled their purpose. Despite the knowledge that we've gained about the missing bodies, the time is past.

Even if we exhausted all our resources searching for Ivan immediately, finding him would be unfeasible. The element of time is working against us."

"And why would they need my son?" Yegor clarified in the meantime.

"In order to seize the Morozov fortune," Sergei replied with no uncertainty. "Ivan is the official heir of the bloodline, and he inherits it after his grandfather's death."

Yegor nodded.

"And what do you think about me? Why wasn't I able to sense the attack with my magic? In my own estate?"

"After you spent all your magical strength trying to save the dying Morozov prince," said Sergei, "it was no surprise that..."

A malicious, unpleasant laugh from Yegor interrupted Sergei, making his whole body break out in goosebumps involuntarily.

Well then, it seems I was right, and the prince had a hand in his father-in-law's death, thought Sergei, not surprised in the least.

Based on the information Sergei had obtained, after the death of Yegor Temnikov's first wife, Yegor had begun sliding headfirst down a slippery slope, drinking alcohol and using narcotic substances in vast quantities.

Such pastimes made even ordinary people prone to instability, to say nothing of a very powerful mage and a prince with generations of the purest pedigree! Yegor Temnikov had become simply unpredictable even to those in his closest circle.

How much had it cost him, his wild and — as many saw it — perfectly illogical decision to marry Galina Belova, a woman from a viscount's family?

He'd faced the public criticism and the community's dissatisfaction with truly aristocratic scorn. As things had progressed, it had turned out that he had not erred in this decision. For his newfound wife didn't just run around between balls, receptions, and beauty parlors — instead, with a zeal characteristic of her youth, she'd occupied herself with the family's economic dealings and proved excellent in that field.

Maybe wasn't as drunk as he wants everyone else to think? Sergei thought unexpectedly.

"What did you discover about the attackers?" Yegor asked Sergei when he stopped laughing and calmed himself.

"Judging by how many ruses there were, and by the fact that they simultaneously point to several families that are hostile to us, we can conclude that this is a blatantly false trail. The organizers of the attack probably didn't have enough time to put a more typical cover strategy into place. And in their hurry they decided to throw a few false clues together, hoping that at least one of them would appear genuine to us. But that doesn't preclude the possibility that one of the families we'd suspected could be involved with what happened."

"That is to say, you have no concrete results?" said Yegor, frowning slightly.

"Only various versions of events," Sergei was forced to repeat. "Unfortunately, I'm working alone in this respect. There's not enough time to confirm everything objectively."

"Then give me your view of the situation and how everything happened," ordered Yegor, and Sergei tried not to disappoint him.

Now was when everything would be decided!

"Because our enemies succeeded in their plans, we can conclude that they began preparing relatively far in advance. The enemies knew the positions of the patrolmen, their movement schedules, weak points in the security systems, and the location of the video surveillance premises and staff. That is, they had all the information they needed. This indirectly confirms Theophane's involvement with the events, because he had the opportunity to remain on the grounds of the estate freely for an extended period of time and learn all of it thoroughly." Sergei paused for a bit, then continued. "Having all the necessary data, the enemies took measures to weaken a critical part of our ability to fight back."

Sergei was hinting at Yegor, without groveling — just laying out the facts.

"But you went a long time without leaving the estate, so they decided to weaken you to the greatest degree in another way. The servant waited until the right moment and poisoned Morozov, and you spent all your strength trying to save him. You were unable to do so, because an incredibly rare and unusual poison was used. So, after you left to recover, they planned to attack. All of the other casualties, aside from the guards, were incidental."

Yegor gave a satisfied smile.

"And why did the attackers try to hide the servant's involvement?" he asked. "What was he to them after it was over? Just an unwanted witness!"

"Probably so that we would waste resources on trying to find him. But I don't think that will be necessary — they'll most certainly kill him."

"That means you think they got rid of him in the end?"

"Most certainly." Sergei nodded. "Who would need an ordinary servant, let alone one with information about the attackers? He's already served his purpose, so now he's a dead man walking."

"Well said." Yegor nodded, thought for a bit, and added: "I'll accept that."

After that, he paused for a long time and declared:

"On that night, before the attack, Ivan died. That I know for certain. So I don't understand why someone would have needed his corpse."

Sergei also knew this. But he hadn't thought that Yegor would confess to it.

"No one must know that my son's corpse was exchanged for another," said Yegor sternly. "But investigate why someone could have needed to do this."

Sergei nodded.

"You're free to go."

Sergei gave a shallow bow and silently exited into the hallway.

Success! he thought, breathing more easily. They hadn't suspected that he knew more than he said. The prince himself had given him the task and decided to put a few cards on the table. That could mean only one thing: his long-awaited promotion was coming soon.

* * *

"Do you think he understood everything?" Yegor asked his wife.

"Yes." Galina nodded. "We still have some work to do on him, but he's a smart and promising man — much smarter and more ambitious than the entirety of your old guard. And he'll hold his tongue and do everything as best he can."

Galina was satisfied. This man she'd pulled from the ISD was beholden to her personally and could take a high position in the Temnikov family's security, which would necessarily ensure his full loyalty. The most important thing was not to forget to remind him whom he owed his promotion to.

"We've needed to cut down on security staff

for a while now — all they do is loaf around," said Yegor, interrupting Galina's thoughts.

She gave him a sour smile and put an obviously insulted tone into her voice.

"I told you long ago that we needed to do something about them!" Those leeches! How easily they earned their keep!

"Their work used to satisfy me," Yegor disagreed.

"Right! Straight up until they 'cut down on' your family!" Galina said with anger in her voice. "What if I'd been home and in my bedroom at that time? Would I have been able to defend myself from them, or would the fate of my maids have awaited me?"

"Calm yourself," Yegor cut her off. "What's happened has happened. Now we need to think of the future, and not what could have been. So we should make use of this situation. Now we have full justification to give the security staff a nice little clean-out, just like you wanted. Before, we couldn't have done that — no one in my circle would have understood why we were doing it. But now it's clear to everyone who's being punished and why. Besides, after Morozov's funeral, I'll be able to withdraw money from his account and transfer it to you. You'll have the necessary assets for the further development of our projects."

"Are you serious?" Galina nearly jumped up in glee, ecstatic that everything was going according to her plan.

"Yes."

"And the funeral will be grand?" she said.

"We can't have it any other way." Yegor shook his head and took a big, hearty swig of whiskey. "Though I didn't love Morozov, he was an important man in the empire. So we have to arrange his send-off as is customary, so that no one can find fault with anyone over it. And you'll be in charge of that."

"Me?" Galina pretended to be surprised.

"Of course," said Yegor. "We're going to build an image for the residents of a noble young wife sincerely grieving over the death of a worthy man. I think it'll be good for business."

Galina looked at her husband with feigned admiration and jumped into his lap.

She always let him explain trivial wisdom to her so he'd feel smart and important.

Covering him with sweet kisses and showering him with affectionate words, she slowly began to lower herself so she could do what her man liked most of all...

"Good girl," said Yegor, putting his hand on her head.

"All of this is strange," he said thoughtfully after a minute, feeling the waves of approaching pleasure. "Why exchange the boy's body for another, if he was dead?"

After another moment, all his thoughts disappeared from his head.

Chapter 7

"GET UP, IVAN!"

I heard Theophane's deep voice and slowly opened my eyes.

Had I slept at all? The sleepy, fully perplexed thought flashed through my mind, and at that moment I was yanked from my bed by my leg with a sharp jerk.

"Gah!" I cried angrily, getting up off the cold floor and looking at Theophane with irritation, for which I got a slight and barely noticeable clip round the ear.

"It's already five in the morning! Why is my favorite student still asleep?" said Theophane with a smile on his face and an unbelievably contented tone as he looked at me.

"Because you didn't tell me I was supposed to get up at five!" I noticed with annoyance after thinking back on it.

"That's too bad!" Theophane threw up his hands. "But now you know that if your teacher says 'Get up!', you'd better get up right away or you'll end up on the floor."

There was nothing to be done about it — I realized I couldn't escape this unbelievably early workout or my very cheerful teacher, so I went into the bathroom to wash up.

"I'll be waiting for you downstairs in five minutes!" Theophane called cheerfully and threateningly, leaving our hotel room.

Why was he so cheerful and smiley? What happened? I was at a loss for answers as I brushed my teeth.

I quickly made the bed, put on the workout clothes that were lying on a chair, and hurried outside.

I found Theophane not far from the hotel where we'd stopped last night. He was inhaling the fresh morning air with a dopey expression on his face — there was no other way to say it.

I walked up to him and just stood next to him. I didn't want to interrupt him — let the man enjoy life's little pleasures. That wasn't so easy for him. An old, slightly embittered killer who'd been saddled with caring for an adolescent aristocrat.

"Follow me at a light jog," Theophane commanded when he sensed my presence, and we jogged along the street at an unhurried pace.

The sun rose.

All the better that I hadn't sprinted forward at full speed, I thought, glad for Theophane's occasional moment of good sense. I would have gotten lost, one hundred percent!

While we jogged, I had a lovely opportunity to get acquainted with the city we were in and its architecture.

We were in the small town and military outpost of Morshansk, located on the border of the Gorbovich Wasteland, which we'd finally reached yesterday. The town was built mainly of three- and four-story brick houses with narrow windows and — the thing I expected the least — firing points on the roofs of the buildings.

What was that for? Were they always warding off demon raids here or what?

The ground floors of the buildings were devoted to all kinds of shops, bars, and inns where a lot of residents were hanging out despite the early hour. I could hear drunken howling, singing, laughing, and heated squabbling.

But despite the heightened activity, I didn't notice any fighting or disorder. Probably because the streets were being patrolled by a large number of military detachments equipped with guns, melee weapons, and even magical weapons. Generally better not to kid around with guys like that.

Theophane started to pick up speed a bit as he ran ahead of me, and I had to speed up too so I wouldn't get left behind.

After a while, we reached the thirty-foot-tall wall that surrounded the perimeter of the city.

Was this much material really necessary? I was staggered. Yesterday when we'd driven into the city, I'd been sleeping and hadn't been able to see this behemoth!

There were turrets with firing points every fifteen feet.

So they could shoot down demons from the walls. Very smart. I had to give credit to the architects.

Obviously, this was a permanent defense intended to prevent demons from entering.

Interesting — did they attack the city often?

We jogged for a fairly long time, and Theophane didn't even think about reducing our pace — just kept getting faster.

We ran into a good number of "athletes" like ourselves, among them several platoons of strapping young men and women equipped military-style.

After a long jog, we switched to walking and finally got to a big open sportsground tightly packed with all kinds of exercise gadgets.

I was once again glad for the excellent physical condition that had been passed on to me in this body. If it weren't for Ivan's training, I simply wouldn't have been able to run such a long distance at a fast pace.

We stretched a bit at the sportsground and practiced a few sets of combat exercises, and then

I tortured myself at Theophane's instruction — that is, I worked out on various high bars and exercise machines.

After that, the run seemed like a nice leisurely stroll. At Theophane's suggestion I had to do a lot of chin-ups, push-ups on the parallel bars, squats, leg lifts, and a bunch of other stuff. It wouldn't seem too hard if I'd only done a few of them. But when Theophane got down to business, the number of exercise repetitions went up two or three times, and yes, that was very difficult.

In the moments when I was having trouble getting through an exercise another time, he would whip out a needle and threaten to jab me with it in a tender spot. A few times he actually did it.

You ancient, decrepit, barbaric old fart! I thought angrily. And I'd been feeling sorry for him earlier! I knew that he was doing this for me, but at times it seemed like he was just bullying me!

After that, we switched from the strenuous exercises to all kinds of stretches and tests of my agility.

Ivan hadn't slacked off on this either in his day, but all the same I winced unpleasantly and wiped off the tears coming from my eyes after Theophane "helped me stretch a little better" a few times. If my ten-year-old body hadn't had such good muscle plasticity, he would simply have torn me in half.

Obviously, it wasn't like that at all, but

thoughts just like that and all other kinds of insults were running wild through my head.

"Assume the meditation pose," said Theophane after making me do the splits yet again, then sat across from me.

"Finally!" I exhaled very slowly in relief, trying not to strain my muscles more than they were already strained, and assumed the position he'd instructed.

We were in an empty part of the sportsground, so there was no one keeping us from talking.

"Ivan, we need to talk seriously," Theophane started to say, then continued after a short pause: "We've finally arrived at our destination. We'll be hidden from your family's potential pursuit of us, and now the time has come for me to set your new task before you." Theophane went quiet, gathering his thoughts, then sternly looked me in the eyes and continued. "As the one responsible for you, your education, and your life, I consider it my duty first and foremost to teach you to defend yourself and be strong. Well, I'm not so young anymore, as you know. It could be that I won't wake up tomorrow — my heart could stop for mundane reasons. I want to die knowing I did everything for you that I could. That's why I believe I can demand full exertion to the limit of your abilities from you, and the fulfillment of all my demands."

"You're being too dramatic," I disagreed. "Remember how you jumped over a stone wall without so much as a running start not long ago? You didn't seem to have any intention of dying then."

"I admit, I can do much more than that." Theophane shook his head. "But that doesn't mean I'm going to stop being old."

I observed his silent figure skeptically.

After a moment, I got scared again — what would happen if he really didn't wake up tomorrow? What would I do? Where would I go? Who would I turn to? Who could be bothered to care about me? All other things aside, I was stuck in a child's body and couldn't get a job or anything. And how were the boarding schools in this world? Where would they send me? Overall, it would be better if Theophane could live another ten or fifteen years — otherwise things would be really bad.

How strange, I thought unexpectedly. Just a few minutes ago I'd been cursing Theophane with all kinds of insulting words, calling him barbaric, a bloodsucker, a scoundrel — I'd even thought about ways of running away from him. And now I didn't want him to die.

"What are you thinking about?" asked Theophane.

"I'm thinking that even despite your barbaric teaching methods like poking a needle in my butt and mocking your helpless student, I still don't want you to die," I answered honestly.

Theophane burst into sincere laughter.

"You're not the first to say that to me."

"That means the first ones got lucky," I pointed out. "You were only honing your personal experimental teaching methods on them, and you're unleashing the full force of them on me."

"I'm glad that after everything that's happened you've grown up instead of breaking down," said Theophane, smiling.

And I was glad he thought that was what had happened instead of suspecting that some kind of intruder had made his way into Ivan's body.

"How about this," said Theophane after a bit. "Since we've established that we need to intensify your training, let's set a goal. Let's say that after two or three months you should start to feel confident in the Wastelands."

"What?" I exclaimed, forgetting about the respect-my-teacher thing. "Those muscly gray Nocer things are everywhere there! And I'm supposed to feel confident there?"

Theophane gave me an indignant look and smiled impudently.

"Oh, I've known people who've beaten those demons thanks to their mastery of their skills. And here we have you, who learned to use spiritual energy and immediately became several times more dangerous."

I took a painful breath in, realizing that arguing with this crazy old man was just useless. If he got an idea in his head, that was how things would be, and that was that.

And I couldn't help admitting that every so often he was annoyingly right. The time had come for real, full-fledged training and hands-on battles in the Wastelands. I hoped they would make me stronger instead of killing me once and for all. I'd try to listen to Theophane. He was my teacher, and I was his student. Besides, it seemed I had no real choice. Either grow stronger alongside my mentor or run away and remain alone. Which would lead to the Temnikovs finding me someday, and that was going to be very, very painful. Because they thought I had information about where the Morozovs' money was. I had no naive belief in their familial love. I'd learned quite well from my history lessons how brothers could turn on their brothers and sons could turn on their fathers over far smaller sums of money — some not even over that, over just the idea of it.

Despite meditating and regaining my strength, I didn't remember returning to the hotel. Up until then I was very tired, and I had no time to stop and smell the roses.

After standing under supple streams of hot water for a while, I recovered my senses and got out of the shower with unstable steps.

A big bowl of stewed vegetables and meat was waiting for me on the table.

I got dressed quickly and practically threw myself at the food. After that morning's workout, I was as hungry as a wild beast. I suspected that hunger would become my constant companion after drills like this.

"Here, take these," said Theophane, placing two large pills in front of me.

"What are these?" I asked suspiciously.

"Vitamins," he replied. "After working so hard, your body needs its building materials — all the essential vitamins and micronutrients."

I swallowed the big pills with difficulty and washed them down with water. With that, my breakfast was complete.

"Come over here," Theophane called. He'd seated himself comfortably on the soft couch in front of the big screen TV.

"In the near future, we'll be going on constant excursions to the Wasteland," he said after I sat down comfortably next to him. "So it's time for you to become more familiar with your likely enemies and the Wasteland itself — I think you'll find it interesting."

I nodded in agreement, then asked right after:

"Can I ask just one question before that?"

"Go ahead." Theophane gave me an encouraging nod.

"Why will we be going on constant excursions? What if we maybe focused on my training first? Waited until I'm a little older and more skilled? Can I at least get more familiar with spiritual energy? Why do we have to storm the Wasteland at this exact moment? It'll only be another chance for me to get hurt, be traumatized, or just die."

"You'll be safe as long as I'm with you," said Theophane weightily. "But as to why we'll be going on a lot of excursions, I can say this. We simply and mundanely need something to live on. Paying for living accommodations, buying food and clothes and other things we need."

"Is our money situation really that bad?" I exclaimed. "There must be at least something left! We could even withdraw something from my bank account if it's that bad. I know it's not much, but I think it'll be enough to tide us over."

"Hah." Theophane looked at me like I was an idiot. "We withdraw anything from your account and we'll be shouting out to the world that you're alive and where you are."

Oops — stupid of me! I thought, but all the same, I continued:

"What about the car? It's valuable. We could sell it and buy ourselves some time until I'm ready for the excursions."

"You're already ready now," Theophane disagreed. "I would even say that you're very well prepared for someone of your age and skill. Personally, I started going into the Wastelands at exactly your age. But I knew much less and was able to do much less then.

"Besides, I don't like how desperate you are not to leave the city. You must understand that for people without a stable place to live, a car is an unbelievably important thing. We could spend the night in it if worst comes to worst, and you want to sell it."

I took in a painful breath.

I agreed with Theophane's conclusions — what he was saying was logical and correct — but I just really didn't want to head into the Wastelands so soon without any serious confidence in my skills. I didn't feel deep down that I was prepared to fight, let alone to kill. Even demons. I could consider what had happened at the hotel as the exception that proved the rule. Everything had been simple in that case: either I died or the bandits did.

"So that means our situation is even worse than I thought?" I said anyway. "If you're anticipating spending nights in the car?"

"No." Theophane shook his head. "It's not that bad. We have money, and it will go towards buying a house. I'm planning to set us up here long-term. Other questions?"

It was clear that he was itching to jump into a lecture.

"Of course." I disappointed him. "What did you mean by 'We need something to live on?' Is there something to make a living off of in the Wastelands? Or do the authorities pay people to reduce the number of demons?"

"Oh!" said Theophane with a dreamy look. "There's always something to live off of in the Wastelands. They've provided for many generations of people and families, but more about that later."

Theophane turned on the TV, and a photo of the planet I was already familiar with from the local Internet came up on the screen.

"Look — see the black patches?" He started to show me on the image.

"Those are Wastelands territory?" I asked.

"Yes," Theophane confirmed. "You can see that the demons have seized two continents, several small islands, and a fairly large amount of land on the other continents, and the two most extensive Wastelands are located on our continent.

"Here's ours," said Theophane, pointing to one of the most significant black patches.

"Is that the Gorbovich Wasteland?" I asked thoughtfully, trying to compare the size of the Wasteland with the size of the continent, and I noticed — "It's pretty big."

"That it is," Theophane agreed. "It's a very big Wasteland — that's exactly why we've come here. We'll be harder to find here, though there are also a lot more demons."

"Can we get a closer look at it?" I asked.

Theophane pressed a button on the remote, and the picture switched over. A satellite photo of the Wasteland appeared.

"Why is it impossible to see what's going on down there?" I asked. The entire surface of the Wasteland was covered in thick, dark reddish-purple clouds with greenish lightning running through them in various places.

Theophane was silent for a bit, choosing the words he needed carefully, then started to speak:

"That question isn't so simple to answer, so I'm going to start in a roundabout way. Long, long ago, before anyone can remember, only humans lived on our planet.

"There were many different nations with their own armies and leaders, which at that time were in a state of constant, mutually destructive war. Everyone was fighting each other, and the world wasn't going through its best time.

"At a certain point, for reasons unknown to this day, demons arrived in our world. Who exactly opened the path to them, and how that happened, is unclear. Many scholars study this event today, so many years later, but they've had no substantial success. They believe that the demons' access would need to have been at the center points of the biggest Wastelands and the demon-occupied continents. They'd be able to say more, but enough on that for now."

Theophane paused for a bit, remembered who he was telling all this to, and kept going.

"So here's the thing. Demons appeared suddenly, all at once in different places, and they started to destroy everything around them with great pleasure and delight.

"Our continent was saved by the tense political atmosphere between the nations and the fact that the leaders somehow managed to agree to form an Alliance and combine forces against the demons. Our neighbors on the continent Arentica were much less lucky, since human foolishness and greed have no rational boundaries.

"The demons would destroy countries, and their neighbors would take that as a convenient opportunity to seize their territory, and rather than helping them they'd stab their neighbors in the back. Later, the smug scoundrels would be slaughtered by monsters that had only grown stronger and gathered more strength.

"At that time, mages — masters of the art of combat and holy war — were true heroes, entering into battle with their strong and dangerous foe. Normal armies of people with no such talents had simply no chance of taking on such unusually treacherous enemies. This was precisely when the sciences of magic and warriorhood took their first steps forward. The demons continued waging war to the point of annihilation, slaughtering entire villages and cities of people. Nations gradually lost resources and people, and they died out.

"It was right then that humanity discovered the possible military uses of gunpowder. The first muskets, guns, and cannons appeared.

"This allowed humans, if not to stop the demons' advance, at least to slow it down considerably. As firepower technology improved, humanity was able not only to stop its enemies, but even to push them back a bit. Day by day, month by month, year by year.

"At the same time, the world's population

began steadily growing. The Church of the Savior furthered that by calling for an increase in the number of children within families.

“By and large humanity grew stronger, got back on its feet, and started to conquer its enemies.”

“And what then?” I said, curious. “If humans got so strong, then why didn’t they beat the demons?”

Theophane scratched his head.

“Because the demons turned out not to be quite the stupid, heartless, blood-loving brutes we thought they were. When they learned of the danger posed to them by firepower and the technology of the time, they — as our scholars tell us — conducted a large number of rituals.

“One of the results of which you can see on the screen.

“The ability to see into the territory from outer space, fly aircraft, and use firearms are all blocked in the Wastelands. In general, there are a lot of other limitations like this that I’ll tell you about during our excursions.”

“How’s that?” I exclaimed. “What, so — gunpowder doesn’t ignite, or something?”

“Exactly,” said Theophane. “It doesn’t ignite, and many other chemical processes don’t work.”

“That means demons can change the laws of physics?” I said, unable to believe what I was hearing. “How is that possible? How have they not won yet, in that case?”

“You’re right.” Theophane confirmed my thoughts. “They’ve changed the laws of physics in that territory, at any rate — so our scholars believe.”

I shook my head in astonishment.

“And what happened after that?”

“Well, mostly, the advancement of human armies has come to a halt on the borders of currently existing Wastelands.”

“Why didn’t humans keep attacking? We could have come up with something else! I’m thinking another type of weapon that would let us kill demons just as effectively! Did the demons really plug all the possible loopholes so we can’t create a new kind of weapon?”

I immediately thought of tasers, air-powered weapons, and the laser swords from the universally popular *Star Wars*.

“I know of government plans to destroy the Wastelands once and for all,” replied Theophane. “But apparently, no one’s going to go for it.”

“Why not?”

“Probably because it’s advantageous to humans for the demons to be here,” said Theophane with a kind of sadness. “A strong enemy keeps humanity in good shape and prevents them from rebelling against the acting powers, while they impose more and more new taxes and turn a blind eye to an aristocracy drunk on laissez-faire. Plus, it supports numerous private armies and the interests of large pharmaceutical companies that directly depend on the supply of valuable raw materials from the Wastelands for their income."

"What was that? What were you talking about just now?" I said. "What kind of raw materials are they, if big companies are based around them entirely?"

"Oh!" Theophane grinned. "There are so many. Different kinds of flowers, herbs, and berries, unusual and very valuable little creatures, many crystals of all sorts, and of course the demons themselves."

"What can you get from the demons?" I asked in surprise, remembering the Nocers. "Their weird axes?"

"Those too," said Theophane. "But I'm talking about something else — pieces of their bodies. Horns, tails, claws, hooves, chitin, wings, and mucus in particular are valued highly at various workshops and spoils collection points."

And you have to take all those things off their bodies? I thought, making a face as I imagined that.

Was it just me or I was I turning a little green?

"Don't worry, don't worry," said Theophane, clapping me on the back, "you'll get used to it. We have a lot of work to do in the near future."

"For some reason I don't exactly feel like it," I admitted to him. But, all the same, I asked him about the details I was interested in. "What was that about chitin? Do insect demons exist?"

Theophane smiled a bit unpleasantly, and I imagined the most frightening thing possible.

"Not only do they exist — they go around, jump on people, and eat them."

Now I really didn't want to go to these Wastelands.

Meanwhile, the image on the screen changed, and Theophane continued his lecture.

"Now that you have some general knowledge of the Wastelands, let's move on to our second educational point. Types of demons, how they look, and how they differ from each other."

"Don't you think this is too much new information for today? I won't be able to remember all this."

"It'll be an introductory lesson," Theophane reassured me. "I'll tell you about some general points so that you'll understand what's in store for you."

Theophane pressed a button on the remote, and an image with a large collection of all kinds of creatures appeared on the screen.

"At the moment, humans know of two types of demons: greater and lesser. It's too early for me to talk to you about the greater ones," he said with a smirk. "Those are encountered very rarely. So for now we'll talk about the lesser ones.

"There's a great number of varieties, and completely new and previously unknown ones are constantly turning up. In order to systematize this incredibly vast bestiary in some way, they're divided into two main categories: humanoid and insectoid.

"First let's talk about the humanoids, since we've already encountered them," Theophane reminded me of the incident on the road. "In general, there are four common types of humanoid demons."

"Why humanoid?" I asked just to be sure.

"Because they look very similar to us humans. They walk upright, they move primarily on two extremities, and they have a similar internal organ structure."

A small green demon with a long, extended head and a face with fully human proportions appeared on the screen. It stood out for its large upturned nose with a narrow slit, huge number of curved teeth that seemed sharp even by the look of them, and small pointed ears.

There was no hair on this specimen's head. In its place were four horns arranged one after the other like a punk hairdo.

On its four-fingered hands were black talons of a corresponding size.

"That's a Dwarf Saw," said Theophane, referring to the demon. "Despite their small size of one meter, they're no joke to fight. Very fast, maneuverable, and dare I say slippery. It's very hard to hit this kind of demon. And if you get closer, they can easily bite into your flesh and tear off a chunk of it in just moments. Swift and unpleasant death is guaranteed.

"They usually hunt in packs of up to seven individuals, inclusive. Run into these in the Wastelands and you'll be lucky to make it home alive."

The screen changed over.

"Anthro." Theophane gave me the name of a light red creature.

This demon's face looked less like a human's. Probably because there was a long, thin, unpleasant-looking horn coming out of its forehead, and its eyes were positioned close to it. Its large black nose was covered in scales. The demon's beastly grin showed off big fangs and teeth. Its ears were small, almost unnoticeable.

Its stomach and chest were protected by hard yellow bone plates. Its feet were goat-like, and it looked like it was walking on two hind legs.

"This specimen is a bit larger than a Dwarf Saw," Theophane continued. "They're closer to two meters in height. Not quite as mobile as the former, but much stronger. They have a large number of bone layers that can take a lot of damage from weapons."

The image changed again, and a Nocer appeared on the screen.

"You know this one, so let's move on."

After that, I saw a picture of a very tall, thin demon with two twisted, bull-like horns on its head. Its skin was bright red with nasty yellow splotches.

Slits for eyes, a small nose, and a wide —

almost clown-like — mouth left me a very bad impression.

Jerrax was written at the bottom of the picture.

I didn't feel so good.

"And you want to go into the Wastelands and fight these things?" I asked again, sinking into the back of the couch.

It seemed like Theophane had gone out of his mind!

"If we see them," said Theophane.

I cursed internally.

Theophane looked at his watch and got up off the couch right away.

"Time really flies! We've been planning to do a Shiki-Cho training session for a while now."

"Great!" I was happy that the lesson on these abominable creatures was over, and we could move on to one I knew better and was already used to.

Chapter 8

PUNCH, PUNCH, punch again...

My work with Shiki-Cho was going just great. Every day I felt the spiritual energy better and better.

As I punched again, I willed a stream of energy to surround me, coming from my palm and spinning on its axis.

The concentration of Shiki-Cho in this limited space grew dense enough to be seen even by the average person's eye. Manifesting itself as a flash of bright blue light, the energy hovered in the air for about a second, then vanished without a trace as if it had never been there.

At one point I raised my fist, keeping the rapid flow of energy going in a measured spiral, and started to admire its unusual, unbelievably beautiful light.

Incidentally, during the final drive of our fascinating journey towards the Wastelands, Theophane had shed some light on this for me.

I was actually not the first person who'd guessed how to twist my power in a spiral — it was all too easy for a warrior who was capable of sensing spiritual energy. I would be very surprised if it were any other way.

So what did I have to be happy about, in that case?

It comforted my soul to know that I myself, without my teacher's prompting, from my own inspiration, had intuitively figured out that I could control spiritual energy. That it was fit to be used not only for brute strength, but also for something else...

What? I didn't know yet. But after what had happened at the target range in Abraham's house, I realized that the study of spiritual energy was my path to strength, freedom, and independence. Only after mastering this incredibly promising course of combat arts could I be at peace with my own life and safety. The most important thing in that regard was not to forget to use my head and to remember I could always improve my skills more than my brute strength.

I really wanted to practice and develop my skills — even when I was practicing my ordinary punches, my hands itched with a desire to try something out. That whirlwind, for instance. But I knew I shouldn't do that in the car. My bodies (the physical one and the spiritual one) weren't synchronized yet, and obviously nothing would work in the real world. Even if something did, I'd just smash our new off-roader to bits, so I had to run around in my internal world.

It was there, during another of my experiments, that it occurred to me it probably hadn't been an accident when Theophane let slip about my success in independently mastering the simplest warriors' techs. I figured by doing that he'd wanted to inspire me to train independently even more. Nothing motivates you to action like success you've already achieved.

Manipulative old man. Although on second thought, he hadn't done anything wrong. He was just doing his job, trying to make a worthy man of me — worthy by his own definition, but still.

Besides, I was even a little grateful to him for those words. Because as we'd been driving, I hadn't been sitting with my head down or staring at this new world's countryside sailing by out the window — instead, I'd been occupying myself with something interesting and fascinating.

I hoped this thirst for knowledge and experimentation boiling in my veins would stay with me a while longer and not disappear after some time.

And sure, maybe in the beginning stages of my familiarity with spiritual energy, instead of fully mastering the tech, I was reinventing the wheel in a way that was already boring and cliché to everyone. But this first understanding of Shiki-Cho that had awoken in me at that moment opened broad horizons for independently developing and testing new ideas.

Besides, as it turned out, the tech I'd come up with had a fully official, well-known name — the "Simple Power Whirlwind" or just the "Power Whirlwind."

What did I think of that name, if I could be honest? I would rather have called it something more poetic and threatening — I'd even say something epic.

More likely than not, I got that impulse from watching dozens of old Chinese martial arts films as a child. With unbelievably strong and cunning swordmasters, epic battles, and the age-old tale of "my kung-fu is better than yours."

From a lack of anything better to do — or, more accurately, just for fun — I'd thought up two of my own names for the tech, but I hadn't decided yet which one sounded cooler: the "Divine Whirlwind of the Light of Truth, Punisher of the Godless," or the "Cascading Stream of Untold Power, Destroyer of Evil and Injustice."

The names I'd come up with were really funny, so when I came back to the real world to chat with Theophane and remembered them, I had a goofy grin on my face, after which I noticed Theophane giving me suspicious glances.

He asked: "Why are you constantly smiling like a moron?"

I had to answer that I was thinking about the dumbstruck face on the guy from Abraham's house who'd held me at gunpoint.

After that, even Theophane allowed himself an understanding smile.

But anyway, according to the universal laws of unfairness, in every cask of choice, sweet mead there's always a small but very foul-smelling spoonful of tar that spoils the whole thing.

In my case, the spoonful of tar was my inability to pace myself skillfully when using my energy in the real world.

Simply put, when I punched with Shiki-Cho, I involuntarily spent all the power I had in reserve and was left with nothing. I couldn't restrict the amount of energy I used.

Sure, a punch like that would be one hundred percent lethal to almost any enemy, but even so, it would be that lethal to just one enemy. Theophane said that ten times less spiritual energy was definitely enough to take out a dangerous enemy, so that meant I should be able to get at least five punches out of myself. Just to be on the safe side.

However, even though I wanted to, I couldn't do it yet. I had one hit in my arsenal, and that was how it still was.

So it was my spiritual and physical bodies I'd been working on developing — you could say I'd been doing it night and day, since Theophane had seemed somehow preoccupied this week.

He only had enough time to spend with me in

the early morning and late evening. On his breaks, he roamed around the city sorting out some sort of unbelievably important problems of his own, which he didn't elaborate on. The only one he deigned to tell me about was that he was looking for a suitable place for us to live. We couldn't keep hotel-hopping, after all.

He decided to compensate for his absence in the flow of my day with even more vigorous morning and evening workouts (or at least they seemed much harder). I came back from them either walking like a drunk, wounded, selflessly dedicated buffoon or just plain draped over Theophane's shoulder. To be fair, it was worth noting that the second one only happened once.

Even though I clearly wasn't loafing around, he gave me independent assignments for practice in mastering my warrior techs. As if I wasn't working on that myself already. I constantly — a few times a day — practiced that Eyes of the Wolf tech. Some positive changes had started to happen already, which I was very happy about.

I'd already managed to figure out how to rest properly through meditating. Half an hour in the lotus pose and I already felt more or less energetic. Better by a long shot, at least I could move on my own...

I finished a workout in the internal world and came out of my meditation, intending to continue training in the real world.

I hoped today I could divide my energy into at

least two punches!

I didn't have the chance, however. My energetic mood was curbed by a group of little boys talking to each other not far from me.

"He moved, he moved!" I heard them whispering quietly, and I cursed in my head.

Fully aware of the dangers of practicing with spiritual energy in a closed space as a neophyte, I'd decided to practice in the open air.

A walk around the areas surrounding the hotel had allowed me to discover a small, convenient park nearby.

There, incidentally, there was also a sportsground with horizontal bars and other outdoor exercise machines, which a few people were always using.

"Gym bros" — I remembered the name of the Earth subculture that preached about hitting the machines.

There were plazas fitted out like this in a lot of places on Earth, but in this world they were practically on every corner.

It was clear to see that state policy was geared towards propaganda about self-improvement and the pursuit of physical activity. The Empire needed well-prepared soldiers who would defend it both from demons and from other countries' aggressive actions. And, of course, even a fool would understand that a fit young person was easier and cheaper to make into a soldier than one who was out of shape.

This particular park had a playground where a bunch of kids were jumping around. Obviously, this was where the little boys had come from.

"Look, he moved! Give us candy! Give it! You lost! Or we'll punch you in the face!" I heard the boys' voices talking over each other in unison.

Argh. It seemed they'd taken an interest in me. I got up from the ground. I really didn't want them focusing on me like this. So it would be better to get out of here as fast as possible. Otherwise they'd surround me and start asking questions. Like: "Who are you?" "What are you doing here?" "Why are you sitting here in weird poses?" "Who are your friends?" "You think you're cool?" And so on. No, I just didn't need that.

For that matter, I'd had children myself not long ago, and I knew well that they didn't really like people who particularly stood out or somehow differed from them, for better or for worse.

And I admit, in case of unforeseen circumstances, I really didn't want to get into a fight. Beating up children was thoroughly unpleasant, even though I was in a child's body right now.

There were exceptions, of course. Those three jerks in the cafe parking lot had fully deserved that beatdown, and I was sure it would be good for them.

Moving further away from the boys, I set up next to two burly men in khaki combat pants who were working out.

"What, are they bothering you?" asked one of them very loudly and threateningly, fixing a point-blank stare on the noisy group of kids.

The boys, hearing this, immediately scattered.

"No, I just think it's much more comfortable to work out over here than over there," I replied.

"All right." The man nodded understandingly. "Then work out over here as long as you like."

I nodded gratefully — he'd driven away the kids who'd been bothering me, after all — then found my way to a little round platform free of machines and other people and started practicing my combat sets.

Giving myself over to my instincts, I thrashed the air, jumped around, and avoided blows with pleasure. I got onto the right wavelength and concentrated again, just like when I was coming out of meditation. With this attitude, I started to very slowly gather spiritual energy into my hand...

"Oh, demon hellspawn!" I roared, clenching my fist in fury after once again not managing to limit the amount of energy I wasted when I punched.

All the better that no one was nearby, and it rushed out in no particular direction.

"Now I believe you." I heard a somewhat stunned voice and turned around.

The men who'd been working out nearby were looking at me with clear astonishment, like I was some kind of strange beast.

"Who are you?" one of them asked immediately. "Who's your teacher?"

"That's not important," I shot back sullenly.

"It's very important," he replied. "Someone needs to tell him his student is very committed but out of control."

"Exactly," the second one chimed in. "What's your name?"

I didn't want to talk about myself, or Theophane either. But I had to tell these soldier types something, distract them somehow, or they'd really box my ears and force me to take them back to Theophane — ostensibly because "it takes a village" — so they could acquaint themselves with this extraordinary teacher. I'd be in even more trouble then. And Theophane would have a blast during my next workout. No, we did not want that.

"Well?" said the man with a threatening frown. "What's your name?"

"You'll find out for yourselves soon," I said to them, turning around and leaving. I was happy to see that they didn't try to stop me — probably because there were a lot of people in the park. Well, that was good.

When I got back to the hotel, I found Theophane there lounging on the sofa watching the news and eating a huge sandwich.

"What are you doing back so soon?" he asked immediately. "I thought you were going to work out for longer than that. You decide to blow it off today?"

"No, I just caught the attention of some local kids at the park, and then some men started asking me who my teacher was. I barely got away from them."

"Ah," said Theophane understandingly. "Next time memorize this and repeat it: 'I have already gone to the local authorities and confirmed my warrior rank.' Say, why do you look so grumpy? Still no luck?"

I sighed heavily.

"That's no good." He frowned. "I'm planning an expedition to the Wastelands soon, and you simply don't want to make progress!"

"What? I don't *want* to? I'm blowing my blood vessels! Especially after your lectures on those humanoid demons!" I fumed in response.

"You wouldn't know it from watching you," said Theophane even more angrily. "I gave you a whole week, and you've had no results! This conversation is over!"

I wanted to fly into a rage and tell him again that I was training diligently, but I couldn't. Theophane wasn't interested in my pathetic excuses.

"And how's it going with with the Eyes of the Wolf?" he asked. "With that, I hope, there are no questions or problems? Or can you not do that either?"

Instead of responding, I just used the tech — I looked around the room with sharpened eyesight a few times and then deactivated it.

I was used to my eyes itching afterwards, but I didn't give in to my hands' desire to scratch them — as I not infrequently did when practicing on my own.

"All right, at least there are no problems with that," said Theophane in a slightly gentler voice, then noticed: "You're not even fidgety after deactivating it."

I didn't say anything.

"If you keep training in the same spirit," Theophane continued, "then soon you'll stop feeling any discomfort at all."

I couldn't disagree with that, since that was essentially what had happened. If I compared the first time I'd activated the tech to the most recent, the difference was simply colossal — my eyes hurt several times less.

Clearly, I had to adapt little by little.

"I have good news for you," said Theophane, not waiting for a response from me. "It seems that I've found a perfectly suitable place for us."

"That would be terrific," I said, and admitted, "This place is already really getting on my nerves."

"Why's that?" asked Theophane, surprised. "Nice hotel rooms, a TV, a shower, good food, all the necessities — what's not to like?"

"Lots of unwanted eyes," I answered. "People looking at me and asking 'Who are you? Where are you from? Why are you out walking alone? Where did your grandpa go? Are you staying here long?'

The list goes on."

"Such curious souls." Theophane frowned. "If it's all right with you, we'll get out of here today or tomorrow."

We went to inspect our potential new home together. By some miracle I managed to get Theophane to take me with him, even though he repeated up until the last minute that he wouldn't be taking any knuckleheads with him and I needed to work out more.

We drove, to my surprise, rather far.

"The city seemed a lot smaller than this to me," I said.

"That's because you slept the whole ride, and while we were in the city you only occasionally opened your eyes, took a look around, and went back to sleep. Morshansk is a fairly big city."

"Then I don't understand this at all," I said. "Whose idea was it to build a heavily populated city next to an incredibly dangerous Wasteland? And why don't the civilians move away from here?"

"Oh, you're asking me?" Theophane shook his head, but he tried to answer all the same. "In the early days, as you know, there were no settlements around the Wastelands, and certainly no cities — it wasn't possible. The demons destroyed everything without a trace — people were killed, cities and villages were razed or burned...

"When the Wasteland borders were defined, which was fairly easy to do — you'll learn why later — the emperor dispatched military units to set up outposts around it, organize reconnaissance and patrol services, and prevent demon hordes from getting into our land as it revived itself after the slaughter.

"For greater protection, the decision was made to construct defensive walls and military posts. It was clear that maintaining such a large number of troops on the border would require many, many resources.

"Provisions became an especially important question. They had to be transported a long distance, and there was no way they wouldn't spoil on the road. So the emperor needed to resolve this problem urgently and get peasants to settle there, to begin cultivating the land and feeding the armies. But how to do that? Simply order them to? If a man doesn't want to work, it won't do any good to try to force him to — he'll even run away from a 'good' position.

"But the emperor needed results — he needed people really working, earning wages for their labor, and being happy to be allowed to live there. Maybe even recommending that other people come settle there.

"Long story short, the emperor promised a large allotment of land, a cart, a horse, farming tools, and a cow to everyone who wanted to move to this new location, and he also exempted them from taxes for the following thirty years.

"People, of course, were frankly terrified of going. Chasing demons out of your land, getting to enjoy peace, and then settling a new area from scratch while packed together like sardines?

"But being exempted from taxes and receiving a lot of land and assets helped many people adjust to the new life — not to mention that the land near the Wastelands is excellent for harvesting.

"The first caravans set out for the Wastelands, and then workmen and other city-dwellers moved in. Cities started to grow.

"Even later on, when alchemists came into the mix producing useful elixirs and drugs from Wasteland ingredients, places like this were flooded with easy-money lovers and a new generation of adventurers — people who started running around on the other side of the gate and cutting down on the number of demons. Either that or they got cut down themselves." Theophane smiled as he finished his story.

As we talked, we passed the center of the city and entered a large residential sector that had beautiful, high-quality brick houses with red-tiled roofs.

"Nice neighborhood," I said, looking around with interest.

From my conversations with Theophane I'd concluded that our assets were limited, and we couldn't allow ourselves more than a lousy little apartment with them. But if he decided to buy one of these houses, I wouldn't be against it.

"Yes, definitely a nice neighborhood," he agreed.

The wall came into view some distance away, telling me that we were approaching the edge of the city.

"What, are we going to live near the wall?" I decided to ask.

"Problem with that?" Theophane answered my question with a question. "People have lived here for centuries, and nothing's ever happened to them. Besides, we're pretty close to the Wastelands here — little perks everywhere you look."

He stopped the car in front of a short brick fence with blue wicket gates and a sturdy, one-story house beyond it.

The wicket gates opened, and on the threshold stood a stocky, very thickset old woman of about sixty-five years. She was already fairly elderly, but judging by her fiery eyes and ruddy cheeks, she was still full of strength and energy.

She was wearing a white linen blouse with some kind of embroidery on the collar and the sleeves, a luxuriantly colorful skirt that went all the way to the ground, a brown leather vest, and a red shawl around her head. The shawl was tied up in a very unusual manner. The knot was tied not under her chin, like I was used to seeing, but at the top of her head. The ends of the shawl stuck out boldly over her forehead. I'd seen something similar at a screening of an old film set in the deep country.

The old woman had a heavy, homemade cane

in her hands that she was leaning on.

"Who are you?" she asked in a resonant voice that didn't sound old at all, narrowing her eyes menacingly.

"Your future tenants," said Theophane cheerfully. "I'm the one who called you."

The landlady looked him over, then looked me over, then cast a glance at our expensive car and smiled tenderly.

"Oh, yes. Dear guests, why don't you come in?" she said in an extraordinarily kind voice.

"Thank you," said Theophane, getting out and walking into the yard with me shuffling along behind him.

The house had seemed high-quality at a first glance, and it was the same at a second glance.

The bricks were fitted together perfectly, the roof tiles were lovely, and the yard had flat ornamented tile pathways and a few fruit trees. Everything spoke to the owners' good management.

"There's a place to park the car," said Theophane with satisfaction, looking around. "And what about inside the house?"

While I examined my possible new home with Theophane, the landlady — with surprising dexterity for someone of her age and build — climbed up onto the small porch, opened the door, and beckoned welcomingly.

It'll be fine, I commented mentally as I saw it had been cheaply and recently repaired.

The house had a full-sized bathroom with a shower, a kitchen with an electric stove, and three other rooms.

I shot Theophane a covert thumbs-up out of the landlady's field of view, then left to go look at the outside of the house again.

Let him take care of the lodging situation — I could see he liked it here too.

Outside, I found three more old women near the car.

They were sitting on a bench I hadn't noticed earlier and talking amongst themselves angrily.

"She's swindling people again..."

"That good-for-nothing..."

"How do people like that walk the planet..."

I pricked up my ears.

What did she mean, swindling?

Theophane and the landlady came out into the yard and walked unhurriedly in my direction. I opened the wicket gate next to the bigger gate.

"Hello!" I greeted the three old women.

I knew from all my experience that it was best to be friendly to such representatives of the residential sectors, otherwise unpleasant rumors about you would spread through the whole neighborhood and you'd never be able to wash your hands of them.

"Hello," said the old ladies after a bit.

"So what's going on, you planning to live here, or what?" one of them asked me in a hostile voice.

I suspected that something was off about the

house, and Theophane was already outside, so to get his attention I said loudly: "The house is really nice! I think we could live here."

Theophane came out onto the street, noticed the old ladies, and greeted them as well.

When they saw him, they immediately smiled.

Of course, I thought, laughing internally. A mature, strong, single man (although the ladies were old and couldn't see well, they were throwing him persistent glances) of their age. They had to snatch up a guy like that. Make him soup so he'd do household tasks like chopping wood and digging gardens.

The landlady followed Theophane onto the street and immediately received scornful glances.

"What are you doing, Marissa, cheating people?" One of the ladies immediately went on the offensive.

"What have I done to cheat anyone?" said Marissa indignantly.

"You can rent a place like that for fifty thalers! And you're asking for a hundred fifty!" the second old lady on the bench said to her.

"What do you know about this house?" replied Marissa in outrage. "Is it anything like your pigsty? Because I could rent that out for twenty!"

"Pigsty?" the second lady fumed.

"What else would you call it?" Marissa glared at her insolently. "Seeing as pigs live there!"

I went and hid behind Theophane. What the hell, these grandmas were going to start a brawl!

Life hadn't prepared me for anything like this!

The squabble continued in the meantime. New characters entered the scene as they heard the shouting match.

I was frankly glad for our new friend — she was mercilessly destroying her opponents and doing it so adroitly that everyone around her was just laughing.

"Enough! Quiet, everyone!" bellowed Theophane when he got tired of the show. "This is chaos! Who's still selling a house here? And for how much?"

"Dearie, what are you doing? Are you leaving me?" Marissa looked at him in surprise.

"Your place is noisy," he said, frowning. "And expensive compared to the others."

"One hundred and forty thalers and you can move in right now."

"One hundred and thirty, and I'll pay for six months upfront," Theophane countered.

"One hundred thirty-five for three months."

"Sold," replied Theophane after thinking for a bit, then addressed everyone around us. "The concert is over, ladies and gentlemen. Please return to your homes."

Chapter 9

I SLEPT SURPRISINGLY WELL at the new place. The fresh air, the smell of mown grass, the lack of so many people and cars passing by outside the windows — it all created an unusual feeling of peace and quiet.

I suspected that the reason for my sound sleep wasn't the splendid atmosphere of the new house, but rather my chronic exhaustion from my harsh workouts. After those, my weakened body collapsed into an abyss of serene rest. All the better that Theophane was busy with errands and housework, so he didn't summon me to do an evening workout.

The next morning, he came into my new room with a glass of water in his hand and an incredibly nasty smile on his face.

What made me think that? Because I'd seen

all this before with my own eyes. I suspected that at first he'd had the vilest plans for my wake-up call, but once he came into the room he stumbled upon me staring at him attentively. By that time I was already awake and had even managed to change into my workout clothes.

"Ah, you're already up? Good morning," he said, his smile fading, then took a big gulp of water from the glass — probably so I wouldn't suspect his ghastly hidden intentions. "Then let's go, time for our workout."

The morning workout was as I expected — that is to say, very difficult. A long run around the residential area (which was surprisingly big), then a workout at the local stadium — where there was a pretty big area with horizontal bars — then some tough strength training, meditation, and tech practice, and then we went home.

Maybe I was starting to get used to working so hard, or maybe the key was that I'd finally gotten a proper full night of sleep, but I felt much better than I had during the past workouts and even ran home cheerfully.

I earned a few approving glances from Theophane for that in moments when he thought I wasn't looking.

The return home was fairly interesting. The neighborhood was already awake. One person was feeding livestock, another was leading cows to the pasture, another was simply standing and looking at the street curiously to see what was going on there. All of them were united in one way: they were staring at us with curiosity.

We had a big surprise waiting for us at home — Marissa the landlady was in the kitchen.

Theophane frowned and seemed to want to get angry at her willfulness — we'd paid for the lease honestly, after all, and it was logical to assume that we didn't want to see outsiders in here. However, when he sniffed the air, he shut his mouth.

"I'm just here making you a little something to eat," said Marissa in a sweet voice. "With two boys in the house, how will you ever cook yourselves proper meals? So go get changed and have a seat at the table."

I took a quick shower, changed, returned to the divine-smelling kitchen, and found an interesting scene there.

Theophane was sitting at the table with a stupid expression on his face, opening and closing his mouth like a fish and trying to find the right words for the situation.

What situation, incidentally? What had I missed here?

I moved a chair, took my spot in front of a plate of unbelievably delicious-smelling food, accepted a cup of fresh milk offered to me by Marissa, and dug into my breakfast with pleasure. At the same time I decided to find out what exactly was going on.

It turned out that while she'd been loading

our plates with fried potatoes and homemade cutlets, Theophane had decided to ask Marissa why exactly she'd been so generous as to provide us with this banquet. She'd gotten up early, she'd brought us groceries, she'd even made us food.

It turned out the answer was mundanely simple.

This banquet was in honor of new, good, and generous tenants moving into the house. Marissa always got up early, since she wasn't a city person — she had her own housekeeping to do, and it needed attention. And as for bringing us groceries and cooking for us, it wasn't quite that simple. Food cost a lot of money these days, and organic food was even more expensive, and utilities cost a lot of money these days too, so Marissa had suggested that Theophane should pay her for her work. She said the groceries she'd bought were very good, and she was a splendid cook — she'd been doing it all her life.

"Yes," said Theophane, choosing his words slowly. "You Avtiukians have a great sense of humor and enterprise."

"You think you're funny!" Marissa pretended to be indignant. "I cooked for you and it was good, so I want fair payment for my work!"

Then I understood why Theophane was so speechless. The prices she was asking for her services were simply astronomical.

"I could eat at the best restaurants in the city for that kind of money!" he exclaimed.

"Oh, come on now!" Marissa wagged her finger at him. "You'd go broke on gas! I'm no sort of fool, I added it all up properly! The nearest proper establishment would be ten kilometers from here — your car needs twelve liters of fuel per hundred kilometers with a three-point engine. That is — " She smirked impudently in his face. " — you'd be wasting ten liters in two days! That would add up to a hundred fifty a month! Are you prepared to pay that much? Hmm? After five months you'd have to take your car in for an inspection, an oil change, and a new filter. How many months will it run before you have to replace it? Ten thousand? And that's another additional expense! If you add the cost of eating at a restaurant and the traveling expenses together, you'll see that I've named a better price all along!"

I had to admit, I was astounded at how streetwise this ordinary-seeming old woman was. She'd calculated everything, she'd thought of everything, even the price of gas in this town. Really, I was blown away!

"So true, my good woman, so true!" Theophane shook his head.

"So how about it, dearie? Do you agree to my rate?"

"No," said Theophane. "Thank you for the food, of course, but I'm going to look into cheaper and better places of getting it! Our gratitude for today's breakfast!"

The last remark clearly offended her. She

frowned right at us.

"Better?" Marissa hissed.

"Much better," said Theophane, not the least bit afraid.

"Then in that case, pay me for what I cooked for you this morning!" she raged.

"Oh, please." Theophane threw a piece of a cutlet into his mouth, washed it down with milk, and smiled insolently. "This turned out to be an expensive breakfast! Lower the price and maybe I'll pay, but you said yourself that it was a gift so we'd appreciate your culinary talent. We appreciated it!"

"It was meant for good people! But it wasn't long before I took a good hard look at those 'good people,' and realized it's better to have nothing to do with Wasteland-vomit like you! So pay me what you owe!"

I looked at Theophane — it was like he was slowly starting to boil over. He reeked of a thirst for death, as if he was planning to kill the poor old woman. I retracted my head into my shoulders completely involuntarily, but Marissa didn't even blanch.

"Right, listen up, you old hag," said Theophane, saying each syllable slowly. "I leased this house from you for three months, and I don't want to see you here again until the end of that term! If you come here again and say such insolent things, I'll simply strike you dead without a thought."

"You wouldn't dare..." Marissa whimpered.

"I would," said Theophane, as if he were cutting her with his words. "Oh, yes... I would."

Once he'd finished speaking, he finally started to calm down a little, and much less of the thirst for death radiated from him. Eventually it went away completely.

Once she'd recovered from the shock, Marissa was in a bad temper from the fright; she put her hands on her hips, slowly raised her voice, and began to speak.

"Who do you think you are, you louse — you're not planning to pay for either the food or the cleanup? Let me tell you!" She raised her hand with a towel in it, like she was going to hit Theophane, but she didn't get any closer.

"The cleanup?" he and I said at the same time.

"It only makes sense, doesn't it?" Marissa narrowed her eyes, then added with great menace: "If you're going to fight with me, I'll set my old man on you — he'll thrash you!"

"Taras?" Theophane confirmed just to be sure, then gave a booming laugh.

This was a scrawny and drunk but cheerful specimen with a stylish white beard, a nose red from drinking, and a huge straw hat; we'd had the honor of seeing him in our yard yesterday, where we'd met him.

Old man Taras had come over with a bottle of homemade liquor in his hands and offered

Theophane a little bit.

I'd seen the way Theophane's eyes lit up and the interested glances he threw at the large bottle, but Marissa had put a stop to all the fun by showing up with a towel in her hands and chasing her husband back home.

"Or does this beauty have other admirers?" added Theophane in the meantime. "If so, I'll tell old man Taras everything!"

"But have you thought of the child?" Marissa changed her tone. "Are you going to feed him sandwiches and sausages and that carbonated garbage? Or restaurant food, so he'll die from ulcers at a young age? Or proper home-cooked food? My potatoes, cucumbers, radishes, onions, eggs straight from the chicken and milk straight from the cow?"

"Stupid woman — you already know," said Theophane with conviction, "that I actually was planning to find myself a housekeeper from among the locals who could feed us and do the washing and cleaning. We're warriors, it's not convenient for us to do that. I even took the cooking you did for us today as a blessing — I thought, here's the homemaker I was looking for. But you've ruined everything with your boundless greed. I've never seen such prices for such services even in the capital city."

"It's my hard work, and I want to be paid for it accordingly." Marissa stamped her foot.

"Why are we even fighting with her?" I asked

Theophane, chewing a piece of meat. "Let's offer a housekeeper position to one of the ladies we met on the street yesterday — what were their names?" I tried to remember the unusual name of one of Marissa's opponents from the street yesterday. "Oh! That was it! Thestoffe! I'm sure she has chickens too, and cows, and potatoes, and all those things! And she won't ask such a high price — five times less, at least!"

"What?" Marissa threw up her hands, crestfallen at our baseness. "What are you saying? How could you suggest such a thing? Inviting that shriveled hag into my house? She'll ruin everything she touches!"

"So what?" I shrugged. "You are, of course, a very good cook, Mrs. Marisa, that's true. But we just have no intention of paying that kind of money. I think you planned it that way from the start, so you'd have something significant to bargain with. So let's drop the theatrics — how much money were you really planning to make?"

Marissa looked at me with curiosity.

"Is the boy one of us?" she asked Theophane. "He's so little, but he's got a cleverer head than yours!"

"What do you mean, one of you?" he exclaimed.

"He's quite the Avtiukian!" Marissa couldn't help but notice. "Smart, quick-witted, and bright! Unlike you!"

"I'll be outside if you need me," I said to

Theophane and got up from the table.

I hoped Theophane understood what a weak case Marissa had and would be able to talk everything through with her on reasonable terms. Because she was a great chef, and I'd never breakfasted so well anywhere else in this world.

* * *

That same night, Theophane and I had a serious talk.

"Well, Ivan, you and I have finally settled down properly and adjusted to this way of life." He grinned happily. "Now it's time to think about our main goal. Are we ready for your very first excursion into the Wastelands?"

"You might be ready, but I'm not," I said to him in exhaustion, not even trying to be subtle.

Today had been yet another day in the saga of my grand fiasco. I still couldn't use Shiki-Cho in the real world while controlling it. I was making progress, of course — now I felt something like a stream of power circulating through my body before each punch. As if I had a second circulatory system, only instead of blood it had energy flowing through it.

"Why wouldn't you be ready?" said Theophane, surprised.

"Because I still can't fully use spiritual energy."

"That can be remedied," he brushed me off

thoughtlessly. "The most important thing is that you can do at least one full-power punch. You'll perfect that ability in time — it's vital that you retain that desire to work on yourself!"

"I like working on myself," I decided to say, "but I have no desire to go into the Wastelands unprepared."

"Then you're going to have a hard time!" said Theophane harshly.

"I think my desire to go there is already growing," I replied in an overly cheerful tone. "If only because of your rude threats."

"I'm glad you realize that." Theophane nodded. "And since you agree that we need to go, I expect full-fledged work from you. We'll head out in two days!"

"In two days?" I exclaimed. "Isn't that a little soon?"

"No," he answered me, "because we're switching to a light workout regimen. The usual exercises and meditation. Your body needs to rest and gain strength before the upcoming excursion."

That evening we set off on a shopping trip so we could buy what we needed for the excursion.

The big shopping center that we visited, Hit-It, was almost no different from the ones I was used to in my world like Pyaterochka, Magnit, Eurotorg, Auchan, Vitalur, and others. I think everyone understood the concept. A typical shopping center.

Theophane grabbed a cart, and we headed

into the aisles.

I curiously examined the unfamiliar labels and the names of various products. Like a real child, I was running through the aisles and looking at stuff I thought was interesting.

For the sake of my curiosity, I put a couple small bags of chips and a couple chocolate bars similar to Snickers in the cart. Well, "a couple" in a loose sense. There might have been a dozen others. This body wanted its sweets!

Theophane smirked when he saw this, but he didn't say a word. He remembered that I was a child, after all.

Once we'd checked out, we brought the cart back to the car, and in the meantime Theophane happily started eating one of my candy bars.

"What do you think you're doing?" I cried. Reaching my hand between the bars of the cart, I claimed the delicacy for myself.

"What do *you* think *you*'re doing?" he asked, smirking. "I forbid you to finish that."

"If you need some, you could've bought more," I replied. "Money's not as tight as all that. We didn't buy a house. On that note, why was that? I seem to remember that you were originally planning to do that."

"I decided it would do us no good to rush at the moment," said Theophane. "Say we suddenly have to run, and we have no money because we invested it in a house. We can't take the house with us in the car. So it's better if we save that money for a rainy day. We'll always have time to spend it."

Smart enough.

"Are we going home now?" I asked after we'd loaded our purchases into the trunk.

"No." Theophane shook his head. "First we're going to make one very important stop."

"Where's that?" I asked, unwrapping a second candy bar.

"The Free Hunters' Exchange."

"What's that? And who are the free hunters?"

"Free hunters are people who constantly venture into the Wastelands and aren't employed by any departments of the government or private companies."

"That is, people who work for themselves?" I confirmed.

"Exactly."

"And the Exchange?" I asked, already imagining roughly the answer I'd hear.

"The Free Hunters' Exchange, or the FHE, is an area where all kinds of individuals, companies, or the state itself can place orders for hunters to bring back loot from the Wastelands. The hunters assess the offers and take on what they can handle. Novices take simpler orders, and those who are more experienced — appropriately — take more difficult ones."

"Hmm... I see." I scratched my head. "So you want to find out what they'll buy and at what price? So then we'll know what we should prioritize collecting and what we can walk past because it goes for peanuts?"

"Exactly." He nodded. "The prices may not be stable — they might change, and some ingredients might go up in price significantly."

We pulled out of our parking spot and made for the address Theophane had in mind.

"What did you mean by departments of the government?" I remembered a question I'd been curious about. "What, they go out into the Wastelands?"

"Of course," said Theophane. "And they do it constantly. Because despite the large number of free hunters, the demon population isn't decreasing. And if we let the demons join ranks, they'll become a threatening force and storm the city."

"So that's why there are firing points on the roofs of the buildings!"

"Exactly. Besides, government agents who go out hunting also aren't squeamish about collecting expensive ingredients. Some of it they give to the state, and some of it they bring to the Exchange."

"Interesting." I shook my head. "But it's probably much safer to go into the Wastelands in such big groups than as a group of two."

"Not entirely." Theophane shook his head. "When you have a large group, a large band of demons comes together against it. It used to be the case that when large groups of seasoned fighters would go into the Wastelands, not one would return. How that matter stands today, I don't know."

"Incidentally," I asked Theophane, "is there no way to make orders online or something?" I wanted to confirm, not entirely understanding why we were going to the Exchange. "Go to a webpage, choose a task, fill out your info, and claim it for yourself. That's it, go, get to work."

Theophane looked a little surprised.

"There's logic in what you're saying," he agreed. "It's possible that might happen — new technology is swiftly entering our lives, after all. But I'm not so young anymore, I'm used to doing it old-school. It never occurred to me that it could all change."

Theophane thought about it.

"No," he said after a bit. "The FHE operates and is located right where it always was! Let's go and find out if there's an Exchange website or not."

The mercenary Exchange was an entirely commonplace bar. It wasn't far from the main gateway to the Wastelands and took up a full two stories of a fairly large building. From behind the doors we could hear drunken laughter and loud music.

"Are you sure this is where we're going?" I asked Theophane with uncertainty. "Seems to me like there are more suitable places in the city to find work."

Theophane didn't answer. I looked at him and realized that he was nearly in ecstasy.

Was it nostalgia or what?

“Okay,” was his irrelevant answer. “Let’s go.”

It wasn’t too bad on the inside. The place was fairly bright and comfortable, although a fundamentally dark atmosphere dominated the interior. Its feeling of pleasantness was corrupted by the smell of large quantities of alcohol being drunk and cigarettes being smoked — I couldn’t endure it for long. The local contingent primarily consisted of men dressed in military style and scantily clad women, all living it up.

It was still early in the evening and they were already getting drunk. I shook my head.

“Let’s go up to the second floor,” said Theophane, making for the stairs.

It was much quieter on the second floor. A soft, pleasant melody was playing, and the people there were behaving themselves fairly well.

Taking a seat at the counter, we ordered some ice cream for me and asked for all the latest on hunting assignments.

The waitress stepped away for a minute and brought us a large tablet.

“Here, take this,” she said to Theophane. “You can see all the current requests here. By date and by ingredient type. You can also use the searchbar to find the types of things that interest you and read about who’s ordering them and selling them.”

“What do you mean, selling?” said Theophane, not understanding.

“It’s very simple,” replied the waitress,

smiling. "That's our newest feature — if you have extra things, you can sell them. That's all."

"I see." Theophane thought for a minute, then asked: "And where can we see the prices for ingredients?"

The waitress left, and Theophane took to studying the prices carefully.

"What in the world are Cross-Spider fangs?" A nasty photo caught my eye.

Theophane glanced at me.

"I completely forgot that we never studied insectoid demons. Truth be told, they're sometimes much more dangerous than the humanoid ones. At least because they have a completely different body structure and movement mechanisms we don't fully understand."

He tapped something on the screen and pulled up a picture of an enormous white spider with huge fangs.

The next photo had a top-down view that showed a distinct, nasty-looking red-orange cross on its back end.

"What is that abomination?" I asked, wincing. "A Cross-Spider?"

"Yes." Theophane nodded. "An extremely rare type of demon. The weakest Cross-Spiders can jump ten meters forward and weave very sticky webs. They're very quick and dexterous creatures."

"And the strongest?" I asked, breaking out in cold sweat once I'd had a chance to carefully examine the next photo.

There was a small village in it. A huge Cross-Spider had woven a web across its main street. And what's more, on either side of it, there were two other demons just like it, only smaller and without the clearly visible crosses.

"And the stronger ones can create minions for themselves."

"What?" I said, thinking of the little yellow guys who loved bananas. "Helpers?"

"Yes, these right here," he said. "You see the smaller spiders?"

"Yes," I said. "Those are its minions?"

"If you look really closely, you can see that they're a little smaller than the main one, and their crosses are almost invisible."

"But what do you mean they can create them?"

"Exactly what I said. They have this..." Theophane thought for a minute. "...let's call it an ability to 'give birth' to these minions. Eggs come out of their abdomens, and the minions hatch from them. They don't need to adapt to the surrounding environment like newborns. They rush into fights after just a few seconds."

"And can one Cross-Spider have a lot of minions?"

Theophane thought about that.

"I've heard it can be up to seven, but I've only encountered three myself. Incidentally, large Cross-Spiders that are ready to create minions are known as Queens."

I looked at top-down view of the Cross-Spider again. And I compared it to the car parked nearby. I gulped.

I didn't want to meet one, not even one of the minions.

Meanwhile, Theophane found pictures of two other types of demons right away.

"Waskors and Moskors," he explained. "Small demons. About as tall as a grown man's knee. Not very smart and not strong at all."

"Wasps and mosquitoes?" I said, looking at the little demons.

"Well, essentially, yes, they look like those insects."

The Waskor looked like a very big wasp. It had a fluffy black-and-yellow torso, a sharp stinger on its rear end, conspicuous wings, and net-like eyes.

However, instead of the legs I was used to seeing on insects, I saw it was covered in scaly, three-toed limbs that looked a lot like the ones on the little Dwarf Saws.

The Moskor, in turn, looked like a mosquito, only instead of a proboscis it had a huge mouth studded with sharp teeth.

"What do they do, fly around in big groups?" I asked, trying to figure out why these small demons were dangerous.

If that was the case, then I certainly wouldn't want to meet a dozen of the little creatures.

"Groups of three to six," replied Theophane.

Just as well, I thought, then asked: "And do

they break into the city often?"

"No, but it happens, and if they manage it, they're much worse than even Nocers."

"Why? Are they hard to find? Something like that? Because they're small and can hide anywhere they want?"

"Not just for that reason," replied Theophane. "Rather because their weapons aren't the standard elemental spells, but curses. They're bringers of harm. Their spells can provoke heart attacks, numbness in the limbs, loss of eyesight, diarrhea, and many other things."

"How do they do that?" I said, astounded.

"They influence people's auras."

"And how do you escape that influence?" I was immediately anxious.

"Amassing more magical or spiritual energy within yourself. Its circulation provides a particular kind of defense. Well, we can keep talking about this later — it's a big, complicated, and interesting topic. The point is, these demons are dangerous because they can curse the Earth and turn it into a Wasteland."

Not what I'd expected!

The last insectoid demon picture was of a Betlor. It was an enormous demon that looked like a rhino beetle. It couldn't fly, despite its huge wings, but it could ram like a pro and let off poison gas.

"Bon appetit," said Theophane when my ice cream arrived.

After seeing such things, I had no desire to eat, but I tried a small bite anyway. The ice cream was really not bad, so I kept eating with pleasure.

"Thank you," I said to Theophane.

While he continued to study the menu, I thought to myself that after what I'd learned, I wanted even less to enter the Wastelands.

Chapter 10

THE MORNING OF THE EXCURSION was warm and placid. I got up early.

It seemed like I was already starting to develop a habit of waking up at five in the morning, I thought with a wide yawn.

I got dressed very slowly, but to my surprise, Theophane's typical reveille wasn't lying in wait for me. He, by the way, had never lost his stupid desire to wake me up with that glass of water he so lovingly brought in with him.

We'd finished collecting everything we needed for the Wastelands yesterday evening, so we wouldn't have to bother with it this morning. I'd fit my things easily into a small backpack — all that was left to pack was the food from the fridge, and we could go.

There was more than enough time to have a

bite to eat and prepare ourselves. So I let myself relax and not hurry.

As I had some curd cheese with raspberry jam for breakfast, I looked at the table where the sword Theophane had given me was lying.

It was a small two-foot saber. For those who don't know much about weapons, I'll explain — it's a very sharp, curved sword with a reinforced edge (for harsher, more powerful blows), a wide guard (to protect the hands from injury), and a comfortable asymmetrical hilt curved in the opposite direction from the blade that ended in an iron pommel (which was convenient for poking enemies in the head with).

Theophane justified my needing precisely a weapon like this because it was much more practical than a typical sword.

First, a saber was a less heavy weapon for a trained fighter.

Second, its curved blade had more cutting power than a sword.

Third, because of the blade's curvature, a direct blow delivered by a saber both pulls and cuts at the same time, which has a damaging effect on enemies.

Fourth, Theophane had ordered me to use it, and it was no good asking my teacher all kinds of inappropriate questions.

Fifth, Theophane's "Steel Autumn's Death" style was based precisely on chopping and cutting blows. He himself also preferred a saber, though he'd taught me to use a variety of weapons from a young age.

I'd worn the saber around in its sheath without taking it off for the past two days — I'd even been running with it in the mornings. I'd done this so I'd get used to its weight and shape, and so I'd see it as something perfectly natural on a subconscious level.

Remembering that overexertion was unacceptable, I did a light workout, practicing some combat sets Ivan knew and trying to get a feel for the saber I was so unused to.

If I'd been a little worried at first because of my long break from working with bladed weapons, I felt calmer after the workout.

I managed each part of Ivan's known combat sets first satisfactorily, then pretty well, then just splendidly.

The saber felt like an extension of my arm. I know that sounds pompous, but that's just how it was. It was like the sets I'd learned up till now had been invented specifically for someone who used this weapon.

Once I was done playing with my new toy, I imagined hordes of evil demons rushing me and — without straining at all — carried out a fairly complex chain of blows, chopping down hordes of enemies right and left. At a certain point I started to feel heat radiating from the lower part of my stomach through my whole body. It seemed I had a second wind — I even started hearing harsh and rather loud noises as the saber cut through the air.

It was precisely because of these noises that I was discovered by Theophane, who reminded me that he'd forbidden me from doing any serious training right before our excursion to the Wastelands.

"What serious training?" I said, and then realized at that moment that my shirt was covered in sticky, unpleasant sweat.

Overall the weapon Theophane had given me was excellent and felt good in my hand, and I was unbelievably pleased that holding a saber didn't make me look like some kind of Pinocchio-esque marionette.

But I had to admit all the same, it put a mental strain on me...

The idea that I had to go somewhere independently to learn how to kill things was somehow irrational to me.

I couldn't even believe this was happening to me specifically, and that instead of refusing to commit mass slaughter I was preparing for it diligently.

The second idea that brought me discomfort was that I wasn't ready for this trip to the Wastelands yet...

Theophane had been going there to kill demons at my age with fewer skills? Raise the flag and play the fanfare! Good for him! What was I supposed to say? But it seemed to me that I personally wasn't ready yet for demon hunting, morally speaking. Not just morally speaking, but physically too.

I'd had some success in mastering spiritual energy — I'd finally managed to use my Shiki-Cho three times before the energy ran out, but I still knew that would be nothing in a full-fledged fight. I needed at least a month of full training, but I hadn't been able to get through to Theophane.

My attempt to appeal to him had ended in complete disaster. For some reason, instead of an ancient, unbelievably wise master of combat arts who was duty-bound to silently listen to his only student's doubts and respond with something smart and inspiring, I'd gotten a stubborn geezer despot who was constantly clipping me round the ear and not even wanting to hear me out when I had reasonable ideas.

So after I'd gotten a good dressing-down, I'd realized that there was no worming my way out of this excursion, and I'd continued my independent training sessions.

Actually, there was another reason I was a little angry at Theophane...

See, it seemed like if you were an experienced guy who'd decided without hesitation that you were going to drag your student into the Wastelands, and that his weapon would be a saber you had in your possession... why wouldn't you give it to him earlier? So he could get used to it at least a bit? And train up a little?

But no, of course not! He'd given it to me two days before we left. Huge thank-you to him for that! Although there was a possible situation that was even worse — he could have given it to me right before we left.

What was his problem? Did he think he was teaching me something this way? Or what? Would he say I had to be independent in everything, and if I didn't take care of myself, then no one would take care of me? Something like that, or what? I didn't even know.

Once I'd changed into the clothes I'd set out in advance, I headed outside. In the entryway, I glanced in the mirror.

Looking good! I thought.

A black-haired, blue-eyed boy of ten or twelve years with standard facial features was looking back at me.

He was dressed in a camo tunic and pants, a cap with the same color scheme, and thick-soled boots. On his hands were leather gloves with the fingers cut off. I'd wanted to refuse those, incidentally, but Theophane had explained that weapons could slip from sweaty palms, and gloves helped prevent that.

From behind that boy's right shoulder could be seen the wooden hilt of the saber with its metal pommel.

On his left thigh was an extra weapon and at the same time a useful instrument for working — a tactical combat knife that was fairly pleasing to any adventurous boy's eye.

The frosted color of the blade, the shape of the iron, the crescent-shaped cavity on its cutting edge, its comfortable guard and hilt. I only saw things like that in Arnold Schwarzenegger movies and special unit demonstrative performances. In short, a very entertaining toy!

"Looking good! Looking very good!" Theophane, never failing to tease me, broke into my thoughts when he noticed I was admiring myself in the mirror. "You'll get all the girls, I tell you — just don't forget to put on your backpack."

"Thanks! I'll keep that in mind," I said confidently, picking up my backpack and heading outside.

If he thought his teasing was working, then he'd keep doing it over and over again.

"Don't forget your water bottle!" shouted Theophane, so he could get in the last word.

"I have it with me," I shouted in response, not letting him.

"Then don't forget to hang your saber from your belt! Pompous boy! Otherwise you won't even be able to sit in the car properly!"

I took a deep breath in, recognizing that he was right, and started to unfasten my sheath. Because unfortunately, I could hardly somersault around with a sword on my back, even though it looked so cool like in movies!

The car was already parked on the street, and Marissa was standing nearby waiting for us. She had her palms laid out in front of her and was earnestly reciting prayers — whispering something quietly.

Theophane came out onto the street after me, closed the wicket gate, and got into the driver's seat.

"Thank you for the prayers, Marissa," he said with some kind of warmth in his voice, then added: "We'll be back tonight."

The car lurched forward, and in the rearview mirror I saw her staring after us and old man Taras approaching her with his wobbling gait.

Would you look at that! Six in the morning, and he was already drunk! What a professional!

* * *

For some reason I'd believed that anyone who wanted to could get into the Wastelands if needed. That the gates to "the other side" were open during the day, and one could enter freely. However, after studying information on the local equivalent of the Internet, I'd once again discovered that life was as always much more complicated than it seemed.

It turned out that passage to the "demons' land" was open only via special customs points.

Rightly, I supposed. The state always strove to keep everything under its control. And this was a dangerous place, and an incredibly profitable one at the same time. Because it was always possible to drag taxes out of the various people who wanted to earn a living in the Wastelands, and judging by the info I'd found on the Internet, it was a lot of money. Several countries that didn't have a great number of useful mineral resources and other ways of reinforcing the budget were farming the Wastelands with full confidence.

It was just a shame that Theophane very rarely gave me a phone, and even then only for about half an hour a day — otherwise, I'd have a lot more info I could use to analyze the situation in the Empire and the rest of the world. I hoped that when summer vacation was over and I went to school, that situation would change fundamentally. Since I'd at least need a phone to keep in contact with him...

The customs point was a fairly large complex of buildings closely adjacent to and forming a part of the defensive wall. Its fundamental tasks were to keep the established Wastelands visiting procedure in place and prevent demons from getting through into the city. I hoped no one there had forgotten that some of these creatures could turn themselves invisible. And that the demons sometimes gathered in massive ranks themselves and stormed the walls, if they weren't mowed down quickly.

We approached the customs point and left the car at a fairly large parking lot. Surprisingly, there were quite a lot of cars parked there.

"Interesting," said Theophane, running his hand over the incredibly dirty hood of the nearest car, and added thoughtfully: "This one's a goner."

After that, we headed for the customs point. They let us in without any unwanted questions.

The building we found ourselves in looked like the inside of a train station. There were sturdy, high-backed benches lined up directly in a row. Big screens were posted across the ceiling with general information, and along one of the walls I could see ticket windows of the typical variety, where no one was standing in line at the moment.

That was exactly where we headed.

"Passports," said the pretty young woman at the register in a bored and tired voice, not even looking at us.

Theophane put his hand into his chest pocket and produced the requested documents.

According to him, our passports — even though they were fake *de facto* — weren't fake *de jure* because they'd been drawn up in compliance with all the needed requirements.

"Theophane Gavrilovich Elizarov and Ivan Yegorovich Frost," the young woman read out, hammering the keys as she entered the passport data into her computer. "Reason for visiting the Wasteland?"

"Tourism," answered Theophane, perfectly calm.

The young woman raised her head from the computer and looked at him skeptically.

"What other reason could there be?" Theophane asked.

"Hunting or collecting, for example," she prompted him.

"Let's say a little of both."

"How long will you be gone?"

"Up to forty-eight hours."

"Weren't we planning to go for one day?" I asked quietly.

"Yes, but why not reserve an extra day in case we suddenly want to head back later than that?" Theophane answered me just as quietly. "In that case, let's not tell her the wrong thing."

I frowned. I didn't like his ideas. One day was more than enough for my first time.

"Will you be paying now or after you return?"

"Let's do it now."

"In that case — four thalers."

Once she'd taken the money, the woman gave Theophane a receipt and explained:

"The number of your assigned group is written here. When you hear it announced over the loudspeaker, you'll know it's your group's turn."

"The documents stay with you?" Theophane confirmed, with regards to our passports.

"Yes." The woman nodded. "In compliance with the twenty-third mandate of the Imperial Council, to prevent the loss of information or damaging of documents, the passports of those who enter the Wasteland remain at registration. They'll be given back to you immediately on your return."

"Understood," said Theophane thoughtfully,

then thanked her and went to sit on one of the benches. I sat next to him.

I had time to look around a little. There were a few groups of hunters in the hall with us, waiting for their numbers to be called.

The biggest group, which had about ten people, was settled not far from us. It was made up of young men who were clearly bored of waiting for their turn, and they didn't know what to occupy themselves with. Without question, no sooner had we come into the hall than had their attention shifted to us.

It was worth noting that Theophane was dressed exactly the same as I was. The same tunic (only with the sleeves rolled up to the elbows), the same pants, boots, fingerless leather gloves, and cap. He also had a saber fastened to his belt — bigger than mine, of course.

"Hey, look! They're twins," said one of the guys. "But one of them grew up, and the other didn't."

"Hah! And all their clothes are new," added one of the others. "It's their first time, clearly!"

"Rookies," said a third scornfully.

A fourth didn't contribute any commentary and turned to us.

"Hey, grandpa, where did you think you were going, all dolled up like that?"

"On a sightseeing trip, or what?" said another one, and the whole company laughed merrily.

"You could say that," answered Theophane

calmly, settling against the back of the bench, although it seemed like this was a situation that could make him fly into a rage.

We'd see how this turned out.

"Then you shouldn't be going to this place!" said another one of the guys. "Go check out the parking lot, not the Wasteland."

"On the contrary, we like our trips to the Wasteland," said Theophane. "Mutilating and killing demons, and other bloody revelries. Right, Ivan?"

His voice was completely calm — I'd say even a little bit friendly — but there was such a chilling aura of terror coming from him that everyone in the hall sort of braced themselves.

A few customs officials carrying machine guns showed up. The young men let out fake laughs, realizing that they'd stupidly messed with the wrong person.

"Right, I see," one of them quietly squeaked.

"Good morning!" A young, lean man of about thirty years cheerfully greeted Theophane.

His hair was cut short, he was clean-shaven, and he had an obviously soldier-like bearing, but judging by his uniform he wasn't customs personnel.

"Morning!" said Theophane, scrutinizing the man's outstretched hand before shaking it.

"Sergei Polivoda," the man introduced himself.

"Theophane Elizarov," said Theophane.

"What are you stressing out my boys for?" Polivoda asked Theophane with mild reproach, nodding towards the now-silent group of young men.

"The Web of Fear isn't considered a big deal these days, is it?" said Theophane, raising an eyebrow.

"It is to some people," Polivoda answered evasively. "Not to others, but to some very much so."

"In that case, they need to spend more time on self-improvement, instead of wasting time picking on strangers with stupid questions and advice."

"Thank you," said Polivoda. "I'll take that recommendation into account in their next lessons."

"Groups seven and eight, please come to the exit point," we heard over the loudspeakers.

"That's us," said Polivoda to Theophane, then added: "Please forgive my boys for their lack of restraint. They're young and hot-blooded — I'm sure you understand."

Ah, the customs people had gotten wind of this and didn't want a fight breaking out, so they'd let the young men go first.

"I understand," replied Theophane. "When a man is afraid of something, he attempts to suppress his fear with forced jollity and tries to seem much more confident than he truly is."

The young men heard Theophane's words

and were clearly aggravated, but for some reason not one of them decided to say a word. Evidently, the "Web of Fear" was a really scary tech.

I absolutely had to ask Theophane to teach me how to use it!

"Yes, young people are weak today," muttered Theophane once the group of hunters had left the hall. "If they weren't going with someone of Veteran rank, they'd die, one hundred percent."

After about twenty minutes, our turn to head out into the Wasteland came.

We went into a small area with high ceilings and thick walls. We were met by gun barrels sticking out of firing points. I didn't feel too well, seeing as they were pointed towards a massive door.

The door leading to the Wasteland opened.

Lord help us! I thought, and strode forward decisively.

"So this is really the Wasteland," I said, looking around at the land overgrown with grass that stretched to the horizon. Puzzled, I asked, "Is it all like this, or what? Just grass and nothing else?"

"No, this is just an optical illusion," Theophane explained. "In about a kilometer you'll see the mirage dissipate, and patches of green will appear at first, then a forest."

We moved forward unhurriedly, carefully looking around on all sides, since from what Theophane had told me I knew demon attacks could happen even right next to the wall.

He was right — after a while, the mirage became covered in blurry green patches, which in the end turned out to be the tall trees of a forest.

"You see the footprints?" Theophane pointed to a wide path leading into the woods. "Those are the footprints of the hunters who went in before us. They took the main path, and they're hardly likely to find anything interesting. We're going to do things differently — let's walk a few kilometers along the edge, and only then will we head into the depths of the woods. I think we may run into something very rare."

We walked in silence for a while, but then I decided to ask a few questions.

"Theophane, why don't people use horses in the Wastelands?" I was genuinely interested in the answer now that we were walking around on foot — I even found it strange that I'd only thought of it just now, after apparently being "fully trained." "Sure, cars don't work here, but why doesn't anyone use horses? They'd be good for maneuverability and speed."

"For a lot of reasons," said Theophane, lazily brushing away a midge that flew in his face. "But the main reason is that it's very easy to inflict different types of magic on horses that cause panic and fear — the panic and fear that makes animals lose their minds, foam at the mouth, and rush in whatever direction their eyes are pointing. Do you know what happens to the rider in that case?"

“There are only a few possibilities. Either serious injury or death.”

“Right. Unless the rider turns out to be an experienced warrior and jumps out of the saddle first. Riding a frightened horse is a very difficult task. You’re trying in any possible way to hold onto an animal that’s rushing at full speed and doesn’t notice anything around it. In a moment like that, you have no time at all to look at your surroundings, and your frightened horse could carry you straight towards an enemy.”

After he said that, Theophane sort of slouched, and it was like he wasn’t himself. I got the impression that someone close to him, or he himself, had had to live through something similar.

I didn’t say anything for a bit, deciding not to interrupt his unpleasant reminiscing. After that, I asked,

“And why hasn’t anyone thought of finding some kind of special amulet for horses that would protect their minds from being impacted like that? Because I’m sure something like that exists, right?”

“And no one would have thought of it without you,” said Theophane with a smirk, looking at me askance. “No, unfortunately, amulets like that are still very ineffective. They’re weak — they’ll hold out for about five minutes, and then their defensive effect goes away. And to be honest, the cost of such amulets is incredibly high. Sometimes it's a shame just to put one on a person, and here we're talking about a horse."

"That's too bad..." I said, disappointed — my hope of traveling through the Wasteland on something other than my own two feet had been mercilessly destroyed. "I think if we could get them to lower the price, we could travel in comfort."

"I don't think so," Theophane disagreed. "I said that was the main reason, but there are other secondary reasons."

I didn't say anything, waiting for him to continue telling me, but instead of answering he asked me a question.

"Remind me, where do demons get their power? What helps them evolve?"

"Well," I said, "they become more powerful when they kill living beings and do torture rituals on their victims. Those actions allow them to evolve. But," I suddenly remembered, "you haven't told me about that yet. I got that information off the Internet."

"Of course you did," said Theophane, smirking. "If things were different, I would never have given you a phone. A student who can't find the answers to the simplest questions on his own is positively useless."

"Then why do I have such a lazy mentor?" I said indignantly. "Who hands me a phone instead of answering my questions. And only for half an hour a day, at that!"

"If you find the answer to a difficult question

on your own, you'll remember it for a long time, but if it's handed to you on a silver platter, you'll forget it in a few days."

"That's not true," I said angrily. "You've 'handed' me plenty of information about demons — ask me something and I'll answer."

"I'm glad that you're not a completely lost cause," said Theophane, not wanting to expand on this topic. "But now let me answer your other question. What would happen to a horse if it was captured by demons?"

"First they'd torture it for a long time, then they'd kill it."

"Right," said Theophane with some bitterness in his voice. "A horse, especially if it's a war horse, is a strong and fierce beast packed with firm muscles and lots of blood and flesh. A lot of energy can be reaped from that. No, horses aren't intelligent beings and don't grant demons the same power as humans, but they're suitable for qualitative strengthening."

I felt a little sick when the images of torture entered my imagination. I had even less desire to hang out in the Wasteland, but now that we were already here, there was no going back.

Besides, I'd set an immediate goal for myself — to become stronger so that in the future I'd be able to defend myself from humans as well as demons. And I could do that only by looking fear itself in the eyes — that is, going into the Wasteland and fighting. Even despite the possibility of getting taken prisoner. If I didn't, I'd have to spend my whole life being weak and dancing to everyone else's tune, and I didn't want to do that at all.

The conversation died down on its own. After a while, Theophane stopped.

"Go," he ordered.

Hearing that command, I activated my Eyes of the Wolf tech and carefully looked around at the surrounding area. Everything was quiet.

"Coast is clear," I reported, deactivating the tech and blinking furiously in an attempt to escape the unpleasant feeling in my eyes.

Theophane nodded, corroborating my assessment of the area.

Another thing he'd done before the excursion was carefully instruct me on the commands he would give and my tasks in the Wasteland, so that I wouldn't have any unnecessary questions.

We'd been walking along the edge of the woods for a fairly long time when Theophane, finally, decided to turn towards a particular place that only he knew about. I had no idea what the difference was between this specific acre of the forest and the other hundred just like it. It seemed no different at all from the forested areas we'd been walking near.

Walking further into the woods turned out to be more interesting for me. We quite frequently stumbled across strange types of shrubs, herbs, and mushrooms. Theophane gave me short descriptions and told me what kinds of poisons they could be used in and how much they cost. We hadn't come across anything truly valuable yet, so we decided not to take anything.

Every so often Theophane would command: "Go!", forcing me to use Eyes of the Wolf constantly, which wasn't hard but was getting more and more painful with each usage.

We'd been walking for a very long time through potentially dangerous territory, but to my surprise, we hadn't met a single demon yet.

"Here's a nice surprise," said Theophane unexpectedly, then commanded: "Go!"

I wanted to say "The coast is clear!" after looking around, but upon analyzing Theophane's behavior I decided to look around again.

Aha! There it was, I thought, noticing a little shrub with about a dozen berries in a small hollow to our right. To the naked eye it didn't stand out at all, and I'd hardly paid any attention to it, but when I used my Eyes of the Wolf tech I was able to notice a distinct, bright light coming from it.

"There's some strange plant over there," I reported to Theophane, pointing in its direction.

"All right, that's what I was talking about," he said, taking his knife out of its case. "We're incredibly lucky today — we found a snowy cessbush."

"And why does that make us lucky?"

"Well, if nothing else, because it's a very rarely encountered plant, so it's worth quite a lot.

The raw berries can even be a powerful stimulant for spiritual energy."

Theophane got out a small plastic jar, showed me how to properly cut off the bright white berries so that they wouldn't lose their valuable properties, and suggested I finish the rest of them. Once I was done, he put the lid on the jar, and we kept moving.

"And why were the cessbush berries glowing?" I asked.

"You don't get it yet?" Theophane raised his eyebrows slightly.

"I would guess that they can accumulate spiritual energy."

"If you know the answer to your own question, why take an unnecessary opportunity to annoy your teacher? Get in the habit of thinking before you ask me something," he lectured me.

I wanted to retort that my mentor's answers were different from my conjectures because they gave me real, true information, but I suddenly sensed something's cold gaze watching me and my lowered guard with anticipation.

My Eyes of the Wolf tech spoke for itself, and not far from us I noticed three motionless Dwarf Saws — those short green demons.

"Go. On your ten," said Theophane, his intonation not changing, and at that moment one of the demons darted out of its position and rushed in my direction.

It was small, fast, and unbelievably

dexterous.

I realized clearly that I would have to fight much better than usual to beat this thing!

My body felt like it was burning from the inside with hot, blazing fire.

I waited until the demon got closer and then dealt it a swift blow, leaving a long, deep wound on its chest and shoulder as it jumped to the side at the last moment.

Warm red blood instantly gushed from the wound, and it let out an unexpectedly loud screech.

So you can feel pain just as much as us, hmm? I thought, feeling unexpectedly bloodthirsty. *Get over here!*

But I wasn't able to enjoy my first success in dealing it short-lived pain, because another demon threw a fireball at me.

Oh-ho-ho! I thought, dodging to the side to avoid that hazard and then immediately leaping upwards to escape a blow from the approaching demon's clawed hand.

With a cutting downward blow from above with my saber, my first enemy lost a hand; with my next move, its head flew off to the side.

Meanwhile, another Dwarf Saw flew towards me on clawed wings like a bat, summoning a few more fireballs mid-flight and hurling them towards me and Theophane.

My knife appeared in my hand as if by itself and hurtled straight at its target. The demon folded its wings, dodged to the side, got a powerful kick from Theophane, and fell to the ground with a somersault.

A quick movement of my saber, and the second demon found itself headless.

I looked around to the sides a few times.

No one was left.

While I was looking around again, I noticed the corpses of three more little demons next to Theophane.

“Well, congratulations on your baptism by blood!” Theophane glanced at me with a smile.

“Thanks,” I said, picking up the knife I’d thrown at the winged Dwarf Saw off the ground.

“My pleasure. Clean your saber, and we’ll start the most interesting part.”

I gulped. What lay ahead was probably going to be harder than just killing them.

“While you’re busy tending to your sword, remind me — how many groups are humanoid lesser demons divided into?”

“They’re divided into three groups,” I answered. “Number one: tailless demons. The weakest and least intelligent of their kind. They act only on instinct, and they’re not particularly sharp-witted — you could say they’re feral. Number two: long-tailed demons. These are former tailless demons that have grown into greater strength and become smarter. They, unlike the first group, can use weapons and are more quick-witted. Number three: winged demons. The most dangerous kind of demons, because they're pretty smart and can use magic."

"And can all of them fly, too?" Theophane asked.

"No, only Dwarf Saws can fully fly — all the rest of them move along the ground. They're easy to tell from their compatriots by the so-called 'cloaks' on their backs."

"So you do remember something after all," said Theophane. "Now go and have a look at that long-tailed Dwarf Saw's weapon."

The weapon was a small, all-metal spear that was now sticking out of the trunk of the nearest tree.

How hard had the demon thrown it, if it had pierced the tree like that? The thought came to me involuntarily, and I made a mental note — I had to be more careful interacting with even the weak-seeming Dwarf Saws.

Incidentally, at that moment I started to feel like the feverish passion of the fight was dying down, and I was beginning to shake a little.

Theophane laid out the five demons in a row and started to dissect the first one, explaining all the while which parts of them were especially valuable at the market.

When he started to gut the first corpse, showing me what was located where, my composure took a sharp turn for the worse. Walking off to the side a bit, I said goodbye to my tasty breakfast from this morning.

Throughout the course of the lesson, I went off to the side another two times, even when there was nothing but bile left in my stomach.

After Theophane had dissected the third carcass, I took to the task. It was much worse than watching from the sidelines, especially taking into account that the corpse wasn't cold yet.

We took the hearts, kidneys, ends of the tails, and certain parts of the wings from these demons. After that, we placed them neatly in special containers from Theophane's backpack.

Once we'd finished the sordid task, I washed my hands and undertook yet another attempt to clean out my stomach.

The next hour went by as if in a fog. I moved my legs mechanically and saw nothing around me, even though Theophane was constantly calling out "Go."

After some long reflection, I arrived at the conclusion that I shouldn't let what had happened bother me. I had to see it as experience that I just couldn't manage without. It was allowing me to come into my own and continue learning more about the Wasteland.

After a while we came across another small group of Dwarf Saws, which preferred to retreat, and later on we found a company of three long-tailed Anthroi — the medium-sized demons.

At least they're not Nocers! I thought.

Playing around with those guys was no joke, and I think if it wasn't for Theophane, he would've been down one cocky heir of an ancient bloodline.

Why cocky, you ask?

Because when I came face-to-face with yet another enemy, I once again felt that heated passion inside me. My movement became much quicker, and I felt like I could use the specific amount of spiritual energy I needed at any moment. So I faced a joint attack from an Anthro and a Dwarf Saw with full confidence in myself.

Easily dodging a slow-flying fireball, I deflected the blow of the Anthro's sword and chopped off its leg. Thirty seconds of dancing around with the saber, and the taller of my opponents fell to the ground dead. The winged Dwarf Saw, which had only taken a partial hit on the sidelines, flew away in fright.

Right at that moment, I noticed a punch coming in my direction from yet another demon, and I thrust my saber in front of myself. The powerful punch literally knocked me to the side.

I didn't know how, but at the last minute — by some kind of miracle — I managed to concentrate a whole bunch of spiritual energy in front of me and turn it into a sort of way of defending myself. I think that was the only thing that saved me.

Getting up from the ground, I hurriedly passed under the demon's outstretched arm and punched it in the side with Shiki-Cho.

I looked around — there were no more living demons nearby.

"You let one of the Dwarf Saws get away," Theophane immediately criticized me. "It'll be back with reinforcements soon. So we need to leave quickly."

"It would've been amazing if it *didn't* get away," I snapped in response. "With my experience in the Wasteland, I should've predicted this!" And then I added, "And my very experienced mentor almost let one of my enemies kill me! How do you like that? If I hadn't accidentally gotten that tech to work, I could've gotten seriously injured."

"That, my inexperienced student, was an ordinary Spirit Shield! It typically adapts itself to warriors' needs in cases of mortal danger, because Shiki-Cho techs are based fundamentally on your intellect and the strength of your spirit. You needed defense urgently, and you were able to create it. You can thank your teacher for standing by to protect you at that moment. You're now in possession of your first defensive tech."

Has he gone completely out of his mind? I thought angrily. Letting me almost get hit for the sake of teaching me some tech? So certain that he'd be able to save or protect me? From a thing like that?

I was incredibly angry and felt like there was a wave of cold energy coming off of me.

Theophane's expression changed.

"Ivan, calm down," he said, lifting his hands. "We're not in a place that's suitable for childish hysterics."

My hand went to my knife.

The fury gripping me was otherworldly.

"How dare you risk my life?" I said in an unearthly voice, and — not expecting it myself — added: "Me! The heir of the Morozov bloodline!"

The idea that arguing with the guarantor of my safety in such a dangerous place was really stupid did, of course, enter my head, but I forgot about it instantly. Because, as it turned out, Theophane himself was the biggest danger to me.

I started to shake a little from the rush of negative emotions coursing through me. I wanted to rave and scream. Tear apart everything in my path.

A wave of burning heat rose inside me

Fire on the inside, cold on the outside, I thought.

At that moment, the first of a pretty big group of various demons hurrying towards us flashed by between the trees.

A slight smile flickered on Theophane's face.

I heard the pounding of hooves, and it leaped forward, throwing out a huge axe in front of itself.

I knew it right away — a Nocer!

After the first axe came a second, but Theophane caught it by the end of the handle, turned around cunningly, gave it some momentum, and sent it in the opposite direction.

Oh, demon-spawn! I cursed. Despite my emotions' grip on me, I could still think to some degree. This was a whole army, and Theophane clearly wouldn't be able to protect me. I'd have to get out of this one myself.

"This is the end for you, devils!" I bellowed, feeling like I had no strength left to hold back my emotions. I rushed into the fight, trying to spill this concoction of fire and ice brewing inside me.

Chapter 11

I WAS WOKEN UP by a bright ray of sunlight piercing through a small slit in the closed blinds and hitting me in the face. I screwed up my face, rolled over onto my stomach, hugged my pillow, and tried to go back to sleep.

I heard a loud *ding!* from the kitchen, then a wheezy curse from the landlady — Marissa. My second attempt to sleep was unsuccessful.

All right, time to get up for my workout, I decided — otherwise my personally appointed tyrant would come in here and begin the water-based proceedings. After all, since Marissa was in the kitchen, I couldn't have much time left.

I rolled over onto my back, looked at the clock, and froze in surprise.

Twelve o'clock? *Twelve?* Holy crap, I'd slept a really long time! And no one had woken me up?

Not even Theophane with his glass of water? What in the world was happening?

Sharp pain suddenly pierced through my shoulder, right arm, and stomach.

“Mmm...” I whimpered from the unexpectedness of it, unsuccessfully trying to assuage the very unpleasant feeling in my body and trying to figure out why it had appeared so suddenly.

The sharp pain passed just as suddenly as it had appeared, giving me a chance to sort out what exactly the problem was.

A quick glance at my forearm alerted me to the presence of a very thin, old-looking scar that stood out plainly on my lightly tanned skin.

I didn’t remember having a scar like that! I was shocked as I noticed it.

I saw the same mark, to my great surprise, on my hurting shoulder. And my stomach was covered in a whole grid of scars of wildly different kinds.

What’s happening? I thought, bewildered.

The block of ice in my internal world responded with a burst of cold. The sharp pain flared up again, allowing me to remember the details about how I’d gotten such unusual markings. My brilliant subconscious was hiding an entire day from me so I could avoid worrying about what had happened and rest properly.

Was that the fault of my “frozen emotions”? What if this wasn’t the first time they’d concealed reality from me, and there was more hidden in my mind than I would have liked?

A chill ran up my spine, and my thoughts turned to the previous day.

As luck would have it, on my first excursion to the Wastelands, we'd been "fortunate" enough to encounter a pretty big group of humanoid demons.

I remembered my body, as a reaction to the mortal danger I was in, lighting on fire from the inside, filling me with a ton of spiritual energy. Meanwhile, the cold from my internal world had started to look for a way out and scattered around me in invisible waves.

I shook my head, chasing away the vivid memory.

Was I tripping, or what? Apparently, a lot of adrenaline had been pumping through my bloodstream, and my mind had taken it upon itself to create these incomprehensible feelings and hallucinations. Or had I just inhaled some kind of hallucinogen in the Wastelands, and it was having this effect on me? I mean, all sorts of unusual things were more than likely to happen there.

My memories brought me back to the fight, the very heart of the battle with the demons. I'd slashed, slashed, and slashed at the soft flesh of my enemies... using Shiki-Cho, I'd defeated my very dangerous, massive opponents... I'd evaded the blows of their weapons and magic... I'd put up my Spirit Shield and attacked them in return...

But after a certain point, my memories were like a blur. I only remembered the sweat covering my face, my enemies falling to my blows one after the other, the death I sowed with my saber and my Shiki-Cho, my leather gloves refusing to let my sweat-soaked and bloodstained hands release the handle of my weapon.

Then I remembered one of the demons wounding my hand… and another right after him wounding my shoulder… how I'd torn them apart with my spiritual energy and gone on fighting…

The last memory that came to me was feeling an ocean of pain flare up in my stomach, falling, and seeing Theophane burst through the circle of enemies and literally tear the creatures to pieces.

Obviously, he had a very high rank as a warrior…

Hmm, interesting — so why, instead of deep nasty wounds, had I been left with thin and seemingly years-old scars? I thought about it as I got out of bed and got dressed. Had I been treated with some kind of healing potion? And was I feeling psychosomatic pain at the sites of my former wounds because of the unbelievably quick regeneration? Was the pain manifesting itself psychologically, because my wounded body wasn't used to healing itself so incredibly fast yet and was generating pain impulses from the injured areas? I figured that was probably it.

After washing up and brushing my teeth, I went into the kitchen feeling completely cheerful and satisfied and sat at the table. Hot porridge topped with baked chicken and a big glass of milk were waiting for me there.

Marissa had clearly heard me washing up and set everything out on the table.

The porridge, like everything else she cooked, was incredibly tasty. I threw myself at it like a starving man and asked for seconds right away. I ate my second helping slowly — you could say I savored it — although my appetite was ruined by Marissa's sighs and clucks, and the mournful glances she cast in my direction.

"How are you feeling, Ivan, dearie?" she eventually decided to ask, coming to sit on the chair next to me.

"Thank you for your concern, but I feel just great, especially after that delicious breakfast," I replied, shrugging. "Do you know where Theophane is, by any chance? I'm surprised he didn't wake me up for my workout."

"For what workout now?" exclaimed Marissa. "You just got home from the Wastelands yesterday! All covered in blood! Covered in it! I helped your dolt of a grandfather wash you off and get you into bed! And he just wanted to put you to bed in your bloody clothes and call it a day! I was worried what kind of state you'd wake up in! And here you are, worried about him! And thinking about your workouts! You need to rest!"

Marissa was visibly agitated. But what was there to do about it? There was no fighting nature.

She was a grandmother, and I looked like a child. Her maternal instinct was manifesting itself in all its glory. She had grandchildren my age, after all. It was understandable why she was worried. I needed to make use of this and ask her a few questions.

"And when he brought me home, did I have a lot of injuries?" I asked her. "When you washed the blood off of me, I mean."

"Well..." She froze for a minute, trying to remember. "It seemed like there wasn't a single one."

Aha — that meant Theophane had treated me with his potion while we were still in the Wastelands. The stuff was clearly pretty effective, if the healing process had worked so quickly.

"Well, then, why were you telling Theophane off? I didn't have any injuries, I just worked a little too hard."

"Ah, worked too hard..." She made a wry face. "Like after your morning workouts, when you come back scarcely alive!"

"What's tough in training is easy in the fight!" I parroted the truism I knew well, but I didn't wait for an answer — Marissa retreated into her own thoughts.

"But how can that be true?" she asked herself. "Clothes all torn and covered in blood! And the bloodstains in such specific places. Could it have been the work of potions?"

"It wasn't my blood," I reassured her. "So you

don't have to be too worried. I was just very tired and passed out on the road. What kinds of potions are you talking about?"

"Healing potions," Marissa replied. "But they cost a lot of money."

"No, I definitely didn't drink any potions like that."

Marissa narrowed her eyes and stared at me attentively, but she didn't say anything.

"So where's Theophane? Did he leave a while ago?"

"He doesn't report to me," snapped Marissa. Frowning, she continued, "He's tired of life himself, so he wants to bump you off in the Wastelands. What a scoundrel!"

"Aren't we kind of done talking about this?" I said, tired of this. "Believe me, if I hadn't wanted to go there myself, I wouldn't have gone. And Theophane is a very experienced warrior — I feel safe with him."

As I said those words, I remembered how easily and casually he had scattered the horde of demons closing in on me.

He was indeed a very strong warrior. Sometimes he seemed like a real character, but he'd proven his professionalism. No matter what his temperament, he'd have my back without even thinking twice about it, and as practice had shown, he would drag me out of any nasty situation. He'd even had a special potion in store! Prepared in advance, which was very important!

That meant he really did care about me, and going into the Wastelands with him was something I could — and even needed to — do. I fully understood his teaching method. Put an impossible task in front of someone, and you'd get the best results.

I automatically created a Power Whirlwind in my palm and immediately extinguished it. It was all coming to me easily and naturally, and I didn't need a lot of spiritual energy for it because of that. Yesterday I couldn't even do that, and now I could produce it without even trying.

Okay, though, that wasn't true — I had to try a little bit. I was able to admit that to myself. But any kind of progress was huge.

After I used the tech, my chest ached slightly and my arm hurt just a tiny bit. Like I'd given it a heavy load just after overworking it badly. But apparently, that was just how things were. Yesterday I'd done very good work with Shiki-Cho, I'd taken a big step forward, and today I was trying to use that energy. That wouldn't do — my spiritual system needed to restore itself.

It wasn't that one sane action on Theophane's part in the Wastelands had allowed me to trust him completely — that wasn't what had happened. He would have to provc to me at least a few more times that I could count on him.

But it seemed to me that after a few more of these mortally dangerous excursions to the Wasteland, where I had to really give my all, I'd become strong enough to stop fearing for my life.

"By the way," said Marissa, interrupting my thoughts, "here — this is for you." She produced a ten-thaler banknote. "Your bloodsucker said that you're not to occupy yourself with anything today — you're simply to rest."

Not much, but not too little either, I thought philosophically, putting the money into my pocket. At least enough to get my hands on a few helpings of ice cream.

Once I'd finished eating, I decided to take a stroll around the city. I'd been wanting to do that for a while now.

Heading outside unhurriedly, I walked in the direction of the nearest grocery store. I hadn't been able to go there yet, but I knew very well where it was. Theophane and I had run past it many times during our workouts. Incidentally, those runs had allowed me to study our neighborhood back to front.

In the store, I ran into a fairly attractive middle-aged woman who looked at me funny when she saw a little boy no one knew, but she couldn't even tear herself away from her device. She was giggling and smiling dreamily every so often.

She's texting back and forth with some beau, one hundred percent! I thought.

I didn't hide my curiosity as I — in no particular rush — studied the whole assortment of groceries available, took note of the prices, and decided to get myself one ice cream for starters.

I wasn't particularly hungry — Marissa had outdone herself — but why not treat myself to something tasty? All the more so since it was hot outside — perfect for a cold, sweet treat.

While walking past the bus stop, I came across a small company of children roughly my age, who judging by their conversation were planning to take the bus to a city park.

Oh, now that was a great idea! Why not join them and explore with them a little?

I stood not far from them in the shade of a tall oak tree and got on the same bus as they did — memorizing its number in advance, since I'd be returning alone.

The children, four boys and five girls, kept glancing in my direction curiously — clearly they recognized me as the morning runner, but no one decided to approach me. And thank the Savior! I couldn't begin to imagine what I could talk about with children, and I awaited with terror the day when summer vacation would end and I'd go to school.

We weren't on the bus for long, and in fifteen minutes I found myself in a big amusement park full of people. There was a ferris wheel, all kinds of slides, a haunted house, a shooting gallery, and a whole lot of other interesting things.

Like in our world, they were selling popcorn, sweetcorn, ice cream, and some other particular kind of treat — something like a sweet potato sprinkled with powdered sugar. Unfortunately I didn't find any cotton candy, even though I'd wanted to try it at least once.

I walked around everywhere and investigated every nook and cranny of the big park, then sat down on one of the empty benches with a content expression and and started observing the passersby.

In the epicenter of happiness and fun, looking around at the happy faces of people walking by, I felt more sharply than ever before that I was alone in this world.

I remembered how I used to stroll through parks just like this with my family back on Earth and enjoy myself without a care in the world.

I shook my head.

I had to drive these destructive thoughts away. There was no use dwelling on what I couldn't change — it was better to think about what I could do in the future! I'd be fine, just like my family.

A little girl — about five years old and wearing a bright pink dress, sandals of the same color, long white stockings, and puffy bows in her thick brown hair — sat down on the bench next to me. With curiosity she watched the people walking by and the other kids enjoying themselves, occasionally throwing side glances in my direction.

"Hi! Why are you bored? Where are your friends?" I heard her curious voice — she had very good pronunciation for a child of her age.

I didn't want to upset her by not saying

anything, so I answered her.

"I'm not bored — I'm just hanging out here by myself. I like doing that. Why are *you* alone? Where are your parents? Are you lost?"

However, to my great surprise — seasoned with a pinch of embarrassment and awkwardness — someone else answered the little girl. I looked around and was surprised to notice a boy I didn't know. I had no idea how, but it turned out he was sitting on the same bench.

I didn't understand it at all! I could have sworn that he hadn't been there a few seconds ago! How had he managed to walk by so quietly? And why hadn't I noticed him at all?

The boy was roughly my age. He had typical features, short hair, and loose-fitting dark blue clothes in a style that reminded me of my black ones — the clothes that descendants of aristocratic families wore. There was some bewilderment on his face as he looked at a little girl with astonishment.

"What the — can you see me?" the boy finally asked.

"Of course I can see you," said the girl, barely turning her head.

For a second it seemed to me like she was looking at the guy as if he was a mental patient, and I couldn't help laughing.

The boy turned a shocked stare to me.

"Don't tell me you can see me too?"

"Of course I can see you," I replied, in the

same words as the girl. Laughing again, I asked with curiosity, "What's the matter with you?"

"You shouldn't be able to see me!" he insisted, shaking his head. He grabbed an amulet that was laying on his chest and checked something. "That's right, you shouldn't!"

"Sorry to disappoint you, but I can see you just fine," I said, grinning. This guy had my curiosity. "That's not an invisibility amulet or something you have there, is it?"

"Where are you?" we heard a man's voice.

The boy went white and froze, but the little girl grinned.

A strong, slender man came up to the bench and took the brown-haired girl by the hands.

"I told you never to leave my side," he scolded her in a somewhat tense voice. "What if something had happened to you?"

"But Dad!" said the girl angrily. "You're boring! I met some boys over here!"

The man gave our bench a careful look, focusing his gaze on me and seeming not even to notice the other boy.

"Say goodbye to him, and let's keep going — let's not keep Mom waiting," he said, nodding in my direction.

"Bye, Ivan! Bye, Godimir!"

The other boy and I stared dumbstruck after the little girl.

We'd never told her our names! I knew I hadn't! How did she know?

"Oh, you and your imagination!" said the man. "There's only one boy there, and you haven't seen Godimir yet. He's at home now — you'll meet him later."

They walked a bit in the other direction, and I stopped being able to hear them.

"Your name's Ivan?" the boy asked immediately.

"Yeah," I replied, not recovered from the shock yet.

"Godimir," he said, extending his hand.

"How did she know our names?" I asked in astonishment. "Because I definitely didn't introduce myself to her."

"I didn't either," said Godimir, shaking his head. "But I've seen her father a few times — he knows my father. And if she convinces him that she wasn't just imagining things, I'm going to have problems."

"Then let's move to a different bench, or just walk around," I suggested. "Honestly, it's kinda boring over here."

I was curious about him. I wanted to know who he was, where he'd gotten an amulet like that, and why he was using it. Of course, I also wanted to shed light on that little girl character. That was mainly what I wanted. After all, she might have known my last name along with my first name. And anything she said about me could have more frightening consequences than whatever was threatening Godimir.

"Let's go," he said, nodding.

"So what is that artifact on your chest?" I asked as if in passing.

He immediately laid it out in his hand, then thought for a few moments before he finally spoke.

"This is an amulet that diverts the eyes. It allows me to go unnoticed. At least, it did until today. Nobody except you and that girl could see me."

"Oh-ho! An amulet that diverts the eyes! So things like that exist? And why do you think we noticed you? Did it run out of juice? And stop keeping you hidden?"

"Why would it?" exclaimed Godimir indignantly. "Do you have any idea how much it cost? There's a self-charging unit inside it! I've been walking around with it for ages! And not one person has seen me yet!"

"Why can't you just walk around?" I asked. "Without it? Is something stopping you from doing that?"

"Ummm..." he said, then confessed, "See, I'm not allowed to walk around by myself, only with a bunch of people escorting me around, and that's hardly relaxing, now is it?"

"Really? And that man," I decided to ask, "do you know his name?"

Godimir thought for a bit before answering.

"His name is Artem Kuznetsov — some long-time friend of my father. I've seen him a few times, and I honestly didn't know he had a daughter."

"Kuznetsov," I said, committing the name to memory.

I'd have to tell Theophane about the unusual girl who'd somehow known my name. This could be really important.

"And this Kuznetsov doesn't happen to be a marquis?" I remembered there being some people with that surname among the Empire's mid-ranked noble families. I had to admit, the old Ivan would never have thought that his knowledge of heraldry would ever come in handy.

"Yes, he is," said Godimir, nodding and looking at me suspiciously. "How do you know that?"

"I'm a good student," I answered him vaguely — and it was true. In his time, Ivan had had to memorize the coats of arms and surnames of all the Empire's noble houses, plus a few foreign ones.

"Huh." Godimir shook his head.

When we walked past some ice cream stands, Godimir gave them a depressed look and let out a sort of melancholy sigh.

"Do you want ice cream?" I asked him, getting my money out of my pocket.

"Hmm? What?" he said, giving me a surprised look.

"I'm saying I want to buy some ice cream, and if you're not against it, I'll get you some too. It's no fun to eat it alone."

"You want to buy me ice cream?" He pricked

up his ears.

"I just want to treat you."

"And you're not going to ask anything from me?"

"No, of course not," I replied, though I was lying a little bit. This guy had some link to that little girl from that influential family and was clearly not as ordinary as he might seem at a first glance, so I wouldn't be opposed to getting to know him a little better. He was also most likely from an influential family. Even having him as a passing acquaintance was better than nothing. Plus, I felt bad for him. His sigh had sounded so depressed.

"Well, if you're sure, then I'd take a scoop of chocolate," he said, sort of embarrassed.

Our conversation was a lot more fun with tasty ice cream.

Godimir told me that he had a dimwitted older brother and a terror of a younger sister, that he worked out a lot and was already a second-level Soldier, and even that he was already able to sense spiritual energy — but that was a secret for now. I congratulated him on his progress and told him that I was also training with my mentor, and that according to him only strong fighters with great potential could sense spiritual energy at our age.

This unskilled flattery — which was actually true — gained me more of his favor.

By then, we were already sitting on the grass not far from one of the main paths. Godimir was telling me with great excitement that he'd soon catch up to his older brother in terms of strength, and he was going to absolutely smash his face in for always picking on him and fighting with him.

Right at that moment, two guys started to approach us, walking like they weren't entirely sober.

I realized they were the same young hunters who'd been making fun of Theophane at the Wasteland customs point, and I screwed up my face. My eyes had fallen upon them too late.

"Well, hey there!" said one of them in a slurred voice, squatting down in front of me, then asked menacingly: "Why are you sitting here being bored all on your lonesome?"

"I'm waiting for my teacher," I replied, hoping that would scare these guys away from me. After all, it was one thing to pester a little boy, but it was quite another to pester a grown man with a high rank as a warrior.

"Don't lie, kid," said one of the guys, smirking. "Your teacher's not here and never was — you've been walking around alone for a while now."

Godimir continued to sit next to me and watch what was happening with curiosity.

"What do you want?" I asked, standing up and preparing to take a fighting stance.

"We just want to talk," said one of them with a cough. "Your old geezer insulted us. If it weren't for our teacher, it would've gotten real painful for him."

"I'm amazed at your self-confidence, but what's that got to do with me?"

"Your teacher isn't here, but here you are, and someone needs to pay for the insult. With blood!"

"Are you right in the head?" I said, wincing, upset that I wasn't allowed to exert myself much today. "Are your brains totally out to lunch, or what? Two burly guys, and you're going to beat up a kid? Have you no shame? You're warriors! Besides, if you have questions for my teacher, you can ask him personally, but don't come asking me."

My attempt to put them to shame amounted to nothing — they just got even angrier.

All right, if I fought these guys today, then Theophane would have to ban me from exploring the city. Couldn't go anywhere without a fight, couldn't make it a day without an adventure!

"I really don't feel like fighting you," I said as the guys took a few steps closer to me. "But it seems I'll have to."

"I'll help," said Godimir, getting up and taking a stance.

To my surprise, they didn't even hear him.

At that moment, two more of their tipsy friends came up to them. Things didn't look good. However, as it happened, the new guys were perfectly right in the head, and they apologized to me and dragged their friends away. Incredible luck!

"Where do people that petty come from?" I asked rhetorically.

"I don't know." Godimir shook his head. "But my brother is a lot like them."

"Then you really drew the short straw," I said with a smile.

"That's for sure," said Godimir, then looked at his watch. "It's already time for me to go," he said, sounding disappointed.

"Let's go, I'll take you to the park exit, and then I'll head home myself. I have a feeling I could run into those idiots again, and if that happens I won't just turn away."

"When are you planning to come out here again?" Godimir asked casually.

"I'm thinking of swinging by periodically on weekends," I said to him. "So I hope we'll meet again."

"Me too," he admitted.

We exchanged a firm handshake and went our separate ways.

As I returned home, I wondered curiously what noble family he might be from.

* * *

"So you're saying she called you Ivan, but you yourself never gave her your name?" asked Theophane, scratching his head thoughtfully.

I nodded.

"That's not good," he said. "In that case, I

can't understand at all how she was able to do that, although..." He thought about it. "Could that be how her family's magic manifests itself? There's nothing new under the sun..."

"Her family's magic?" I repeated.

"Yes," said Theophane. "It's believed that ancient bloodlines have unique aptitudes for certain kinds of magic. A bloodline of fire, for instance, has a predisposition towards fire magic. If someone has to work up a good sweat to master the simplest of fire spells, then such an ability will manifest itself. The Temnikov side of your family can somehow manipulate darkness, control shadows, and become stronger at night. I haven't seen their abilities for myself, but there are rumors going around. There's also the Golikov family — their power is being able to raise up the strongest shields in the Empire. I think you understand exactly who defends the emperor and his family, right?

"In general, here's what I'm getting at — each ancient bloodline has its own aptitudes. There might be one per family or there might be more. No one knows for certain. So I'm not ruling out the possibility that the Kuznetsovs might have some unique family talents, and one of them somehow allowed that little girl to know who you were. Although, of course, their main ability is controlling metals."

"So that means I must have family magic too?" I said, curious.

"Yes," said Theophane. "I think it's somehow connected to ice and the cold."

So that was the significance of the ice slab in my internal world! It was a subconscious visualization of my gifts. Hmm... So maybe the pitch-black darkness in my internal world wasn't what it seemed on the surface?

"I believe it, but now that there's a pretty big chance of something like that being the case, we need to insure ourselves against it somehow. What are we going to do?"

"Nothing." Theophane shrugged. "I'll try to find out how long the Kuznetsovs will be in Morshansk, and until then you're not to go out into the city. We can't take any risks."

I frowned. There was nothing actually wrong with that rule, but I would have liked to keep getting to know my new friend. When I went back to using my family name, I would need allies, and the fact that we'd met long before that happened would become very valuable.

This thought was very unexpected. Because at first, when I'd only just arrived in this world, I hadn't seen myself as a real Morozov — just a substitute for one. But some time had passed, and I'd started to think about the day when I'd grow up and restore that family name to myself. For now I was just reflecting on the possibility. I wondered — what would happen in the future?

For sure, when I became a Morozov again, I'd immediately have a bunch of enemies and ill-wishers who would constantly be testing the waters with me, I thought with unexpected calm.

My usual desire to hide in my shell and blend into the background was already gone — instead, I had aspirations to become so powerful that I could drive foul words back into those ill-wishers' throats, and preferably their teeth too.

A crooked smile came to my face.

I wondered — was our excursion in the Wasteland responsible for this, or my realization that I could rise to a certain level? Because sakes alive, I'd killed demons with my own hands! That meant under my mentor's supervision I'd get stronger and stronger every day. I could handle anything!

"By the way," said Theophane, "I've already started looking for a proper school for you, and I've found a few promising options. True, there is one big 'but' — we'd need a lot of money for you to study there."

"So that means we'll have to gut the Wastelands real well?" I said.

"Precisely." Theophane nodded. "We can't let ourselves skimp on your education. Back at home, you had great specialists tending to your education, and they laid a certain foundation. We can't let you regress below that level — it'll be very useful to you in the future."

"So that means we need to increase the number of our excursions to the Wasteland," I said, telling him what he wanted to hear.

And why not? Our goals were fully aligned. Theophane would get enough money for my education and a lot of practical training for his student, and I'd only get stronger every day.

* * *

George Temnikov was sitting on a soft, comfortable couch, drinking young red wine, watching the hot flames burning in the fireplace, and thinking.

His thoughts had been melancholy and a little anxious for a few weeks now.

What was there to say, when so many horrible things had happened in such a short space of time? His home had been attacked, his little brother had been burned up in a fire, and his grandfather had died.

It was frightening to realize that all of this had happened to members of a prince's family in their own estate, and no one had any idea who was capable of carrying out such a thing.

What George found most unexpected was that his father, the head of the family, had been at home during the attack and hadn't sensed outsiders infiltrating his territory.

It was really quite strange. Heads of families were several times stronger and more powerful on their own turf than outside its borders. Home is where the heart is, as people said, and those were certainly not empty words.

The official statement — that his father had

been poisoned and miraculously survived — was also a little embarrassing. True, he hadn't been looking too good recently, but that was less likely related to being poisoned with a rare substance and more likely to his exorbitant abuse of alcohol and various psychotropics.

George cursed in his head.

No, he didn't believe the official story. On the contrary, this situation smelled really fishy, and he was trying to understand what exactly was out of place. A few ideas had occurred to him in secret. No one would answer his question about what specific poison had been used on his father — they just talked about his grandfather's treacherous servant.

Right, right, thought George, smirking. *They'd just tell me again that he was the one who killed everyone.*

George's life had gotten pretty hard after his mom had died. His father, who'd hardly spoiled him and the rest of his children even before that, had lost interest in them entirely and overloaded the servants and tutors with caring for them after that tragedy. Even George, the heir to the bloodline, could count on all of one or two personal lessons per month from him.

Precisely for that reason, George didn't have especially fond feelings for his father, who apparently had stopped being concerned with what was happening in his family and society. All he did was waste money and lie around constantly.

When George had realized that he had no particular hope in his father, a former poster child for spoiled rich brats — no, he'd started actively studying and preparing to take over the family's assets. His father had washed his hands of this task, so George had never doubted that he'd succeed. However, as always, at a certain point everything had completely changed.

His father had unexpectedly started keeping several mistresses from less deep-rooted noble families, and then — to the great surprise of everyone around him — he'd gone and flat-out married one of them!

No, I get it, thought George angrily. *The old man wanted young flesh.* That wasn't something high society would condemn him for, and hadn't been for a long time — besides, he was officially a widower. But why take one of his mistresses... as a *wife?*

George felt furious again.

Not just because his father's new wife was no fool and an active schemer who used all the resources she had at her disposal, but also because the family's affairs — which he'd been planning to take over himself — had been handed over to her.

It was precisely because of her that George had stopped living at the estate long ago and preferred his own home in the capital city.

The darkness behind him grew thicker, took

on solid form, and hung over his shoulders like a giant cloak.

No. It's not time yet, he told himself. *It's not time yet. But how I want to...*

His mind jumped to a recent conversation he'd had with his father.

According to him, all the Morozov assets had been transferred to George as the next heir, since both his grandfather and Ivan were dead. And now he, George, was supposed to share them by combining the families' bank accounts.

It was precisely after hearing those words that he'd started to become even more anxious in his thoughts.

He'd studied all the materials related to the attack on the estate, and he'd realized that the deaths were beneficial to only one person: his father.

His brother and grandfather dying opened the way to the Morozovs' money, and the deaths of all of Galina's staff (the attackers hadn't even spared her maids) had severely limited her capabilities. The number of Temnikov staff who'd been killed that night was actually very small.

Or... from a different perspective... thought George unexpectedly. *The death of all of Galina's staff — it could be Father's answer to the deaths of his son and his father-in-law. Interesting idea.*

Whatever the case may be, George didn't want to share the money, and he was looking for ways to avoid becoming the cash cow.

Perhaps he could abdicate from the bloodline? But what was the point, if he couldn't fully become the Morozov heir? The talents he'd inherited were closely linked to the Temnikov bloodline, and if he lost the magical support of his heritage, then he'd become the most ordinary of weak mages. And did he want that? Absolutely not.

He had no ideas for how to prevent his father from taking possession of the Morozov money.

A knock at the door interrupted his thoughts.

"Come in," said George authoritatively.

Sergei Diachenko, the family's new head of security, came into the room and bowed his head in greeting.

George frowned.

"Is there something you require?" he asked politely.

He and Sergei had already had a chance to be introduced to each other, so Sergei didn't find additional formalities necessary.

"Mr. George, sir, I have grave news for you."

What kind of game are you playing? Or is this all coming from your puppet-mistress? thought George, carefully scrutinizing Sergei's face.

According to his sources, the family's new head of security was a trusted proxy of his father's wife.

"Please, sit down." George gestured to the neighboring couch.

Sergei sat as suggested.

"Wine?" George offered him.

"No, thank you," replied Sergei. "I'm only stopping by for a few minutes, because I believe that the information I have is very important to you.

"Go on."

"Here's what I was able to discover," said Sergei thoughtfully. "Your brother's body was replaced by the burnt corpse of another boy."

"What?" said George, dumbstruck. "You're sure of this?"

"More than sure." Sergei nodded. "Here are the forensic results."

In his hand, as if by magic, appeared a sheet of paper that he held out to George.

"Before I was appointed head of security, I was an ordinary operative, and I've personally verified this information — so I can guarantee its authenticity."

When he'd read the document, George returned it to Sergei.

"Why doesn't my father know about this?" He directed a harsh gaze at him.

"He knows." Sergei showed no signs of agitation, but he turned a little paler upon saying those words. "He's confirmed that despite the swapped corpses, he knows for certain that Ivan is dead."

"Hmm..." George thought for a moment, feeling less tense. "That's very interesting information. Is there anything else?"

"Not yet, but if I learn anything, I'll definitely tell you."

"Why?" George asked him simply.

"Because I swore an oath to your family," said Sergei, correctly catching the drift of George's question. "The heir to the bloodline and the bloodline itself are one and the same, no matter what. Besides, I hope that you won't forget to ask this humble attendant for help. I may still be young, and I admit it was pure happenstance that I came into this position, but I'll do my best to show you that I wasn't put here in vain. I'm a professional who's capable of resolving the greatest variety of situations and achieving the goals set out for me."

Sergei left, and George said thoughtfully out loud:

"What kind of game are you playing, Father?"

* * *

While Sergei walked to his office, he took in deep breaths and smiled internally.

Everything had gone as it should have — he'd let George put pressure on himself. He'd let him think that he knew Sergei was weak and that he now had some power over him. A head of security who was so predictable and easy to understand was very convenient and useful. He could control and manipulate him — he wouldn't want to part with him and exchange him for someone new whom he didn't know or understand at all. So Sergei believed that his position in the household was even more secure.

The only thing he'd found troubling was the enormous shadow that had sat quivering over George's shoulders and almost attacked Sergei when George had gotten angry. It had been very frightening, though he'd tried not to give that impression.

That was the way of things with ancient bloodlines! Their family magic and their ability to wield it without a staff… however, he thought after a bit, he'd established contact with George, and all that was left was to slowly and unobtrusively strengthen it. Today's task was nearly complete — now it was time to talk to Prince Yegor.

Chapter 12

"GROUP OF DEMONS AHEAD, five Dwarf Saws," I reported to Theophane, drawing my saber and leaving my position.

We'd practiced for this situation plenty of times, so I didn't wait for any additional commands — I did everything according to the scenario I was used to.

The Eyes of the Wolf allowed me to track down my enemies, invisible and standing still, and I rushed straight at them without waiting for them to make their move.

Realizing they'd been discovered, the little creatures left their spots and rushed headlong in my direction.

My body was already suffused with spiritual energy, allowing me to dodge slightly to the side as a flying spear passed me by.

A lightning-fast movement of my saber, and another spear changed course and flew by half an inch from my face.

Two long-tailed demons at once — very rare!

I reached the closest demon quickly and chopped off its head with a move I was used to. I caught the second one midair without even giving it a chance. Now I had to dodge the third and fourth demons' savage attacks. The claws on their hands only looked like they weren't a big deal, but in reality they could easily dig into the body and tear off chunks of flesh. Besides, it was those two Dwarf Saws that were long-tailed, so their fighting was pretty coordinated and skillful.

The fourth demon came up behind my back and tried to skewer me with its spear.

I met its blow with a saber hilt to the head, then sliced at it with the bloodied blade as it leaped towards me. I finished off the now-disoriented Dwarf Saw carrying the spear by throwing a knife into its back.

Not today, demons!

Five quick leaps forward, and the fifth Dwarf Saw dropped dead.

I glanced to the sides, looking for new threats.

The coast was clear. It had happened before that one group of demons turned out to be bait, and afterwards we had to deal with another group that was bigger and stronger.

I pulled my knife out of the one demon's corpse and took to the task I was now used to —

dissecting the demon carcasses.

Doing this had stopped making me want to puke a long time ago — I'd even say that it had become habitual. Even though it would seem that something like that was impossible to get used to.

I noticed a belt around the last demon's waist with a pouch dangling from it.

Hmm, I hadn't encountered anything like that before. Might be best to not mess with it and call Theophane instead. It could be anything.

"What've you got there?" asked Theophane, seeing the pouch. "Interesting."

He cut off the belt and held his hand over the pouch, then calmly opened it.

"A Baazis crystal," he said with satisfaction, showing me a big purplish-red stone.

"Five thousand thalers?" I whistled, remembering how much those went for. "Not bad, but it's even more surprising that we found it on an ordinary Dwarf Saw."

"It's just unbelievable luck." Theophane nodded. "I'm quite curious how it turned up on this one. Finish up and we'll keep moving," he commanded as he continued to study the stone. "It's big and it's clean — I think this might even pull in close to six thousand."

I shrugged.

We'd been finding this and that, but so far this month I hadn't come across any rare stones for some reason — this was the first one. However, I didn't want to get too curious — we should get home first, and then I'd have a look at it in a peaceful setting.

Today's excursion had begun from a different customs point than the one we were used to. To be honest, we hadn't been starting from there for a week now.

The thing was, with our help, the demon population had already been greatly thinned out in that part of the Wasteland, and other groups of hunters were also trying to kill demons there. So we'd decided to play it smart and go out a little further from the city, where there was another customs point. We'd been right — there were a whole lot of demons in this direction. That was why we'd covered a pretty large distance today and come to this part of the Wasteland.

Over the course of the next hour, we had to fight three more groups of demons. At one point Theophane even had to get out his saber and defend himself from some Dwarf Saws pressing in on him.

"There are a whole lot of them here for some reason," I noticed with surprise as I finished off the last Anthro.

After spending time in the other part of the Wasteland, I wasn't used to seeing so many enemies.

"I don't know." Theophane shrugged. "I don't have enough data to analyze — maybe there are always this many over here?"

We kept walking through the woods and

heard the voices of demons chanting spells.

"Be very careful. I don't like those noises," said Theophane, and we quickly headed in that direction.

After some time, we came across a rather interesting sight. In a large clearing, there was a small group of humans defending themselves from a dozen demons.

"They're wounding them, not killing them." Theophane frowned as he surveyed the humans — two people lying on the ground between three defenders, who were using the last of their might to beat back the demons' blows with shields and magic.

Bursts of fire and wind flashed by one after the other, but they weren't causing the demons much trouble — they were damaging the demons' hides in a few places, but no more than that.

"Sort this out," Theophane commanded me harshly.

Throwing off my backpack, I rushed forward, concentrating spiritual energy in my body.

Was I afraid of such a big group of demons? Not at all. As practice had shown me, I was strong enough to deal with at least half of them. If that wasn't enough, Theophane would step in. He'd already pulled me out of the playing field four times this month, in those moments when it seemed I had no chance, so my trust in my mentor was colossal.

The demons noticed me, of course, but they

didn't take me seriously. Needless to say, they paid the price for that immediately.

The first medium-height, long-tailed Anthro that threw itself at me got a saber slice to the neck.

A long-tailed Nocer standing with its back to me found out what it meant to get a Power Whirlwind in the back. As it drenched the place with blood, it fell to the ground, squashing a little winged Dwarf Saw with its carcass.

I ducked to let a sword pass over my head, knocked another Dwarf Saw down with a kick, and thrust my knife into its ribs as it tried to hit me with the sword again.

Three down!

A rebound to the side, a somersault, another somersault, and I was already out of the reach of the nearest enemies' blows.

Several of the demons ran towards me, forgetting about the other group of humans.

I gathered a little more spiritual energy into my body and rushed at them, lightly brushing against the Anthroi as they started to get clumsy.

Lightly brushing them actually turned out not to be so harmless. There's no mistaking it when there's blood gushing from four demons.

With my spirit shield in front of me, I stopped a blow from a Jerrax — the tall and very thin demon with the red skin and the clown-looking mouth.

The blow I dealt in response with my saber didn't injure it, so I knocked it aside with Shiki-

Cho.

Yikes, their skin was really hard to cut through! I needed to hit it with more power! This was my first time running into this kind of demon, hence my little slip-up.

I cut the head off of the nearest Dwarf Saw and dodged to the side to avoid a whole stream of magic arrows slung at me by a powerful winged Anthro.

Yikes! I hadn't run into any of those before now!

Unexpectedly, the world around me seemed to turn upside down and started spinning.

An illusion, I realized! I put more energy into my Eyes of the Wolf tech.

I hadn't had the pleasure of running into enemies with this kind of magic either, so I ran to the side, trying to keep my distance.

Today was some kind of day of discoveries!

The demon that was putting the spell on me looked like a big bat standing upright.

A Night Hunter! I remembered the name I'd found on the Internet. A very rare type of fiend!

Baring its enormous fangs, it hissed and tried to throw another couple of illusions at me that looked like clusters of dark smoke.

Fighting off a couple of demons that were closing in on me, I rushed at the "illusionist," which was holding its position slightly to the side of the rest of the fighters and clearly frightened for its life. I didn't have much spiritual energy left, so

I knew I had to deal with this monster as fast as possible — otherwise, it would cast another illusion at me and it would all be for nothing.

On my way there, I killed another Anthro and another Dwarf Saw. There were only five enemies left, but two of them were magic-users, and all the others joined forces against me.

I had no hope of counting on the group of people I'd saved — they were quietly watching what was happening.

Jerks! I couldn't believe I was saving people like this!

At a certain point I found myself close to the Night Hunter, and it immediately spread its huge six-foot wings — at which, I admit, I was a little dumbfounded. I no longer wanted to get closer to it — what if it suddenly grabbed me with those wings?

It bared its teeth and took a step forward, but the next moment its head separated from its body.

Theophane had decided to step into the battle.

I cleared out the rest of the demons myself. Since they'd lost their leader, they lost their nerve, which I used to my advantage.

Once I'd killed the last demon, that very same winged Anthro, I sank to the ground with no energy left.

My heart was pounding madly, sweat was pouring into my eyes, my lungs were burning, and it felt like my limbs were filled with lead. To say I had no strength left was an understatement.

Theophane personally went around to all the demons and shamelessly finished off the survivors.

The young hunters from the group we'd saved were bandaging up their wounded companions and looking at us curiously.

"Drink up." Theophane offered me a flask with supplemented water in it.

I took a few big gulps and felt my strength slowly returning.

To my great surprise, it was Marissa who'd made this concoction. She'd used some old family recipe. It really did help in quickly recovering strength after a tough fight.

I stood, shot a hostile glance at the teenage boys and girls in expensive clothes who hadn't even tried to help me, and got down to business.

"Who are you? And why did you interfere with our hunt?" demanded one of the guys, who was holding a magic staff, in an incredibly arrogant voice.

He was tall and had a pretty face, but it was ruined by his contemptuous expression. He had several rings on his fingers, and I could see a gold chain around his neck.

What a show-off!

"Is that in place of a thank-you?" I asked him sullenly. "For some reason I got the impression you needed help. You were the hunted, not the hunters!"

"We had it handled!" said Mr. Show-Off in an assertive tone, like he wouldn't tolerate retorts. "So you can leave our catch here and get out!"

"Oh, is that so?" Theophane coughed and turned to me, holding out his knife and putting the backpacks down next to me. "Get started."

I nodded without asking unnecessary questions, since I'd already been planning to do that myself.

"What is he supposed to start doing?" Mr. Show-Off got all tense and raised his staff, trying to defend himself.

He'd probably remembered who'd just killed a bunch of demons.

I coughed. I was someone people were afraid of, and that was a nice feeling, because I'd actually become pretty crazy dangerous. Although right now, at this particular moment, I found myself incredibly weak. I'd killed all the demons, but I didn't have any strength left — I'd wasted it all, to the bottom of the barrel.

Good thing I had someone like Theophane nearby to defend and protect me if a Night Hunter got in my way along this road.

Taking a couple of containers out of my backpack, I quickly and skillfully started dissecting the nearest carcasses.

"That's our catch!" said Mr. Show-Off. "Get away from it right this second."

Theophane laughed.

Why did this guy have ants in his pants? I

didn't get it. Or had the fear of death had this effect on him? He'd been really scared when he'd known he might die soon, and now he was trying to look cool to restore his self-esteem? That was most likely it.

"When we noticed you were being attacked, two of your party were already injured, and the other three were somehow still on their feet — but the end was near, because even those three couldn't manage to kill a single demon."

"They took us by surprise!" Mr. Show-Off cried. "They cast an illusion spell on us! If it hadn't been for that, we would have beaten them easily!"

I didn't even turn to look at this idiot. Why did he want to show off? What was he hoping to get from this? What was he trying to prove, and to whom? Theophane and I had seen the whole thing. And in general, it wasn't very smart to give people who'd just disposed of a large group of demons a hard time. Had he completely lost his sense of fear? Or was he feeling reassured by the fact that one of us was a child and the other was an old man?

Mr. Show-Off's companions were trying to whisper something to him, but it was like he couldn't hear them.

I took the heart and kidneys from the nearest demon and moved to the next one.

Mr. Show-Off turned a shade of yellow and after a bit started emptying the contents of his stomach. His companions also paled, and one of the girls did the same thing.

Crybabies — they'd come to the Wasteland alone, without support, and they were afraid of the sight of blood! What had they been thinking? Probably that it would all be an adventure!

While the group pulled itself together, I managed to get through four more carcasses.

Theophane showed me everything it was possible to get from a Jerrax and a winged Anthro, and then we moved over to the "bat."

"A Night Hunter," said Theophane. "A very, very rare beast. Its wings and its hide are worth the most — we'll definitely get around three thousand thalers for one wing. So this is our most successful excursion thus far."

"I know what it is, I read about it online."

"Hmm, turns out something sensible can be expected even from those cell phones."

Theophane didn't particularly like new technology, much like the majority of the elderly — although you wouldn't know it at a first glance.

While we sorted through our spoils, the group of college kids — maybe even high schoolers — decided to return to the customs point, but for some reason they went off in the completely wrong direction.

"Want to bet they'll be back soon?" Theophane smirked.

"Do you run into these types a lot?" I asked.

"Yes, constantly — little boys and girls from rich families come here on their summer break from the magic academies and decide to test themselves in the Wastelands. They deal with small groups of demons easily — magic is a dangerous thing, after all — but with a group as big as the one they ran into, not so much. Although… if they'd been more experienced, I would've been betting on them."

"So you think mages are a lot more dangerous than warriors?"

"Everyone thinks that," Theophane replied. "And it's essentially true. A mid-level mage is always stronger than five mid-level warriors. It's a different matter when a strong warrior can level with a strong mage. It's just that there are very few strong warriors and quite a lot of strong mages."

"Was I imagining it or did you use some kind of tech on them?"

"Excellent, you noticed." Theophane nodded. "A mild version of the Web of Fear. They'll come back and ask us to take them to the customs point — we can earn a little more from that."

"It seems to me that after running into a monster like this — " I gestured to the Night Hunter. " — traveling through the Wastelands would be miserable even without the whole Web of Fear thing."

Even more so if you were completely unprepared.

Theophane turned out to be right — after a short while, the unlucky group came out of the woods and headed towards us.

"Hey, old man!" said Mr. Show-Off. "We're inviting you to join our group!"

Not expecting to hear anything like that, I started laughing in surprise.

He didn't want to lose face under any circumstances! That was just great!

"Oh, really?" said Theophane in an incredibly sarcastic tone, then continued with a taunting one: "That's a very flattering proposal, but I'm sorry to say we refuse."

"But..." Mr. Show-Off lost it a little. "We have a bigger group!"

I got the impression that he didn't understand why we were refusing, as if he'd made us a splendid proposal and we didn't want to take it for whatever reason.

"Ah, yes!" Theophane nodded. "And all of you put together were in no condition to deal with something my ten-year-old student made short work of."

"Ten?" cried Mr. Show-Off, like I'd just personally and directly insulted him.

I smiled.

I admit, I felt very flattered when Theophane said that. He very rarely praised me. It already meant a lot when he didn't scold me, and just now he'd praised me. I understood, of course, that this was how he was putting pressure on the young hunters, but it was like the smile was stuck to my face. I really had worked hard for it, after all.

"Yes indeed!" Theophane smirked. "So we

certainly don't need dead weight like you. But if you want to join our group, then you should be prepared to pay! We don't do charity work."

"Pay?" said Mr. Show-Off, outraged.

"Yes!"

"Five thousand thalers," I prompted Theophane.

"Yes..." he confirmed, going into a coughing fit.

Seemed like that was a lot of money!

"Five thousand?" cried Mr. Show-Off.

"Per person," I added. "Or do you think your life is worth less than that? You're a valuable person, after all! Are you really putting such a low price on yourself?"

"What?" he exploded. "I'm worth much more than five thousand!"

"Yes, exactly!" I grinned, catching him with his own pride. "You need to have self-respect!"

"It's just, five thousand, that's somehow too much!" said one of the other guys. "A standard agreement for an escort is around three hundred thalers, no more."

"We don't charge the standard price," I said, grinning. "I had to rescue you with my sweat and blood, and instead of a thank-you I got some kind of scolding. Besides, you definitely can't make it back without us.

"In all of one hour we've run into a dozen big groups of demons," I fibbed. "What do you think, can you take on numbers like that, if you go on alone? And for that matter, you don't even have a good sense of direction — for whatever reason, you went in the opposite direction of the customs point."

"I *told* you!" one of the girls hissed at her friends.

"Just think about it!" I added, and Theophane and I continued our bloody task.

When we finished dissecting and collecting, we got ready to go home, and the group decided to approach us after all.

"Twenty thousand for the five of us," said Mr. Show-Off, "and we'll agree to have you escort us."

"Twenty-five," I shot back.

"It's not your decision!" he barked at me angrily. "I'm talking to your grandpa!"

"Thirty thousand," said Theophane with a grin. "Or you can take Ivan's proposal."

"We'll take Ivan's proposal," said one of the girls quickly, approaching us — understanding that the price could get driven up higher because of her friend.

"Good." I grinned and took a pen and piece of folded paper out of my pocket. "In that case, let's sign a contract!"

It was no accident whatsoever that I had that piece of paper in my pocket. We'd been taking notes on the typical characteristics of the Wasteland in this area. Paths, glades, rare plants. One side of the page was covered in small handwriting, but the other side was completely blank.

I quickly wrote that each of the undersigned would agree to pay Theophane Elizarov five thousand thalers and offered the contact to the party.

"We're nobility!" said Mr. Show-Off, indignant at our distrust. "Our word is as good as gold! But I'll give you my signature anyway."

"We're people who mean business," I said, "and we understand this page is a document that can prove your words."

Our return to the customs point played out with fairytale-esque revenge, which I admit Theophane didn't really like since he didn't exactly want to attract attention.

But how could he avoid it when we were returning with so many spoils and bringing back children from noble families, whose parents had already sent several search groups into the Wasteland for them and were waiting to hear back?

I especially enjoyed the reaction of Mr. Show-Off's older relative, who gave him an expressive glare after Theophane showed the customs officer the Night Hunter's rolled-up hide and wings.

Do I even have to say that Mr. Show-Off's head sank into his shoulders?

"Wait in the car," said Theophane once we'd put the backpacks in the trunk. He took the contract from me. "I'm going to go talk to those blockheads' parents and try to get our hard-earned fee."

* * *

They say a toothache is the most unpleasant of all types of pain that a person can generally experience. However, it seemed to me that at the moment I was feeling something much worse...

It all started when in the early, sunny morning I saw one very unpleasant, arrogant young man of about fifteen years in our house's driveway.

Oh yes, you're thinking what I'm thinking. The source of the pain in my soul was the sight of Mr. Show-Off arrogantly lifting his baby-face chin.

"Why the long face?" asked Theophane, coming out onto the porch after me.

He was wearing black workout pants, a simple blue t-shirt, and flip-flops on his otherwise bare feet. He was holding a mug, which had thick steam and the lovely smell of freshly made herbal tea coming from it.

I knew that smell — I'd gotten familiar with it in my short time living with Theophane. Sometimes, after an especially successful hunt in the Wastelands, Theophane got pretty drunk with his new friend old man Taras. After these lavish celebrations, the much-experienced Theophane preferred to recover with a self-made herbal infusion, which I'd heard Taras — who used the traditional pickle juice — laughing at him for more than once. But it was worth noting that the herbal tea had proven highly effective — Theophane didn't smell like alcohol, and he even seemed to be feeling great. No headache or any other "perks" of abundant drinking. Overall good for the health.

Despite yesterday's expedition being our most successful, Theophane hadn't had a chance to drink with his friend and talk about life — instead, he'd had to celebrate his fortunate rescue of "the noble kids" with some random people he didn't know.

"Cognitive dissonance," I explained my feelings curtly.

At one point I'd happened to see that expression on the Morshansk news channel and learn what it meant here. It turned out the meaning of that expression was the same in both worlds, so I wasn't ashamed to use it.

Theophane raised a questioning eyebrow.

"He doesn't match the decor," I explained. "He looks as alien as old man Taras would at a noble estate."

"You need to stop spending time on the Internet," said Theophane, narrowing his eyes and taking a big sip of his tea. "You're crawling the web memorizing odd buzzwords when you could be spending your free time on useful things. Why, when I was your age…"

"I need it for my studies," I said, interrupting his lecture.

If I hadn't interrupted him, then we would

most likely have listened to some tear-jerker about how Theophane didn't have cell phones in his time and instead of all these websites he'd devoted all his time to training. He could go on for a pretty long time, and even if I didn't feel bad for Mr. Show-Off, I wanted to spare myself that.

I was only able to shut Theophane up so easily and naturally because he had high esteem for studies, no matter what form they took, and that was why he'd given me those devices himself so I could prepare for school on my own. After all, to my great disappointment, the school year was supposed to start soon, and I certainly didn't want to find myself among those who were falling behind.

"You're right," said Theophane after a bit. "That boy isn't dressed for a workout — all in white, and the unnecessary gold on him might be a little much, but I think that after our first lesson he'll realize he has to change."

"After our first *what?*" I got stuck on his words.

That meant Mr. Show-Off wasn't here by accident, and Theophane was apparently planning to do some kind of lesson with him? This was not my lucky day! I had no desire whatsoever to put up with this obnoxious guy. Of course, it wasn't such a difficult task, but I really didn't want to hear him constantly scolding me and saying stupid stuff.

"You calling me a 'boy?'" Mr. Show-Off tossed

his head. "Seems to me, old man, that you're forgetting who's paying you — and who you're talking to!"

"Yes." Theophane nodded, answering my question and consummately ignoring the flushing teenager. "His family thought that the amount declared on your contract was fairly high, but I was able to persuade them that if they paid only twice as much, I'd quickly get these troublemakers to realize that going into the Wasteland is a very bad idea. And next time they'll think before doing anything like that."

I shook my head respectfully. Theophane had not only resolved the issue of the debt, but also managed to score a lot of money out of the blue. Really, all we needed was to give these rich kids a few tough training sessions — take them into the Wasteland to hunt and make them dissect a few dozen demon corpses. In the end, we'd wind up with completely different people who realized for certain that their actions sometimes had consequences. The only question that remained open was of their obedience — would rich kids refuse to follow one or another of Theophane's directions? What would he do in a situation like that? I was already curious.

I addressed these questions to Theophane.

"You insult me, Ivan," said Theophane with a grin. "We have a standard contract for two weeks of teaching. Now they're fully under my control."

"You can't teach anything in two weeks,

especially to them." I doubted the effectiveness of such a short course. "You'd need at least a month for that."

"It'll be enough for them," Theophane disagreed.

"Why isn't anyone answering me?" Mr. Show-Off fumed. "My father paid you, be polite and explain."

Theophane laughed impolitely.

"My boy, you've correctly noted that your father paid me, not you. That's the first thing. Second, no one's answering you because you're nothing to me, nothing at all." Theophane gave him a crooked smile. "Just an arrogant fool who wanted to be popular at school and couldn't think of anything better than going into the mortally perilous Wastelands. And forget how much you wanted to kill yourself — you also dragged your friends into it. Idiot!"

"How... how dare you!" Mr. Show-Off exclaimed in outrage.

"Oh, I dare!" Theophane interrupted him. "Everything I just said was the truth! And you know it! But here's what I despise you even more for — you wandered around in the Wastelands for all of two hours and simply got lost, not knowing where to go, and even worse, you didn't kill a single demon! Pathetic failures and crybabies! It's precisely because of your utter incompetence that you're nothing to me — nothing at all! Meanwhile, he — " Theophane jabbed a finger at me. " — is a real warrior. Better than all of you! He managed to defeat the better part of your enemies alone! And you sorry cowards didn't even help him!"

I thought Mr. Show-Off would stop being able to contain himself and rush Theophane. But he kept it together and glared at me with hatred, like his misfortunes were my fault.

Interesting — why was Theophane pitting him against me?

We heard the sound of a car approaching.

"What kind of dump is this?" I heard a displeased feminine voice. "Is this really where we were supposed to go?"

The wicket gate opened, and the two girls I'd already met came into the yard. They, unlike Mr. Show-Off, knew where they were going, because they were wearing close-fitting exercise clothes.

Theophane coughed and went to go change, leaving me alone with the three rich kids.

"Stanislav!" cried one of the girls, swooping down on Mr. Show-Off.

So that was his name!

Mr. Show-Off assumed a dignified air and glanced in my direction with a look of superiority. Like he was saying *look at me, all the girls want me!*

The second one behaved more properly — she said hello and stood off to the side a bit.

I gloomily watched them hug each other — these individuals who'd never worked for a red cent in their lives, lived off of their families' money, and were criticizing someone else's completely hard-earned house.

After a few minutes, a few other cars drove up, and all the teens showed up in a pack.

Finally, Theophane came back out of the house.

"So, my young students," he began in a friendly voice. "Let's get reacquainted. My name is Theophane, and I'll be your teacher for the next two weeks, whether you like it or not. My goal is to teach you how to survive in the Wastelands. You have the foundation, so I don't believe this will take us very much time. Does anyone have questions?"

His answer was condescending silence.

"Great," he continued, as if he hadn't noticed. "Where are your weapons?"

"Listen, old man," said Stanislav condescendingly after a short pause. "You can cut the strict tone. Believe me, we've seen people much scarier than you, and they didn't live in collapsing shacks like this. So you'd better really keep your head down. You saved us yesterday, and good for you, you got paid for it. So take a seat in your vegetable garden, feed your pigs, and don't annoy us."

The boys and girls nodded in agreement.

"Exactly," added the girl who'd thrown herself on Stanislav, in a catty tone. "You don't have to pretend you're someone incomprehensible to mortals. We're from noble families — we're not plebs like you!"

Yesterday's fear of death had vanished without a trace, as if it had never been there. Instead of being grateful for having their lives saved, these arrogant kids were treating us with contempt just for living in this house. Maybe we were to blame for that ourselves, since we'd demanded money for saving them. Nonetheless, for their part, it seemed unwise to brag about their ancestry.

True, not all of them reacted like that. The second girl — it seemed her name was Xenia — and one short, skinny guy didn't completely agree with their friends' opinions — after those statements about their noble families, they frowned almost imperceptibly but didn't say anything.

"In my day, people from noble families didn't need to tell others who they were — it was simply obvious," said Theophane, casting a side glance at me. I nodded.

I'd absorbed the lesson. I would never become such a petty, arrogant person... it was disgusting.

"Well, let me tell you — !" cried the first girl, then took two quick steps back — as did the whole group.

Do you know what bloodlust is? I mean that infamous desire emanating from someone with an incredibly strong thirst for blood and murder?

I personally had always thought of such an ability as typical fiction. Besides, Theophane had already demonstrated one of the most complicated techs in his arsenal more than once — the Web of Fear — and I'd believed that he didn't need any other tools. But now I sensed that very bloodlust radiating from him…

A clear desire to kill… which we all subconsciously noticed…

Even I suddenly got the impression that Theophane might kill me. That he'd simply and straightforwardly tear off my head — for he was very strong. He must surely have the strength for that…

I didn't know what those teenagers felt when they got into fighting stances and turned white, but they started to set up the framework of magic spells. Just then, guards with pistols and magic staffs in horizontal position rushed into the yard.

Paying no attention to the guards as they prepared for a fight, Theophane took a few steps forward.

"You still think you can argue with me?" he asked the group of teens quietly. Without waiting for an answer, he asked the guards: "Why are you here?"

"So you don't kill them, Knight," said a guard with a magic staff.

Knight? So he'd introduced himself to them? Now I understood why the rich kids had been sent to him for training, but I personally knew that Theophane's rank was actually Hero. I figured if he told that to other people, this city would flip its lid.

And so he was letting the local administration be shocked that there was a freestanding Knight living in their vicinity. Altogether strange behavior from him... we were basically in hiding, after all! Was that not true anymore or what?

"I'll try not to kill them," said Theophane with a grin, and shot back at the guards, "Now leave this property, or I won't be responsible for what happens.

"All right, kiddos," he said, relaxing the aura of bloodlust coming from himself once we were left alone. "First let's do a short jog, and then I'll see what you're capable of and decide how we're going to proceed. Any questions?"

The teens, who'd slowly recovered their wits, did not have questions.

"Then let's go — take your weapons, and get ready to run."

When everyone had gone out into the driveway, he turned to me.

"We're going to run as follows: you in the front, me in the back, and the weaklings in the middle. A little faster than medium pace. When we pass house number twenty-seven, you can start to gradually speed up and head towards gate number five. Jog to a clearing outside the gates, and we'll do some combat training there."

"Do you think they'll listen to you after that show you put on?"

"No," said Theophane, smirking. "They won't last long, but you'll knock the dust out of them before long, and I'll help. That'll be enough for a short while."

"I haven't fought any mages yet," I noticed tensely.

"What about winged demons?" said Theophane with surprise. "Yesterday you killed a winged Anthro. That thing was at roughly the same level as they are. Just try not to expose yourself — worst comes to worst, use your Spirit Shield."

"Got it." I nodded.

Cunning Theophane! Besides the obvious advantages of this agreement, he'd managed to get me some not-very-skilled mages as sparring partners, free of charge. Now I'd know what I might be up against when fighting mages. Look who was the real Avtiukian!

Jogging came easily to the teens — it was clear that they devoted a decent amount of time to athletics. Stanislav somehow got into the lead position and ran along right behind me. A couple times, he tried to "accidentally" step on my heel — he probably hadn't forgiven Theophane for what he'd said. But I sensed his intentions in time, and whenever he did that I moved my feet faster, flung them out backwards, and "accidentally" hit his shins with the tough heels of my boots a few times. That made him let out wheezy yelps, swear, and attempt to repeat his nasty trick with obvious anger.

"It's not a good idea to run so close to me," I

commented on the situation definitively. “I could accidentally hurt you.”

When I got tired of this, I hinted that his jokes might earn him a smack from my saber hilt in the spot that was most dear to any man.

A blurry movement of my saber in Stanislav’s direct vicinity clearly demonstrated to him that his family jewels were in danger. After that he finally stopped messing around.

We jogged out past the city limits, kept going for another mile or two, and then turned into the woods. There was a fairly large clearing there that someone had fitted out like a target range, with a few benches conveniently fixed to the ground around the perimeter.

Luckily for us, the place was available today.

“Couple minutes to warm up, and then we’ll start,” announced Theophane when we switched to walking. “Let’s see what you can do.”

The rich kids, of course, weren’t even thinking about listening to his words. They started discussing the “unhinged grandpa” and his “weird student.”

“Time’s up,” said Theophane. “Stand in single file.”

The teens made faces, but they got into a formation sort of like that.

“You — ” Theophane jabbed a finger at a tall, muscular guy. “ — why do you have a staff now when you fought with a sword yesterday?”

“Because my staff got broken in two,” he said,

frowning. “I had to take a wounded demon’s sword to defend myself with.”

“Ooh, turns out a demon got wounded,” laughed Theophane, glancing at me. “By the entire group! What heroes!”

“I’m just...” the guy tried to say, but Theophane interrupted him.

“You’re just a good-for-nothing weakling who let a demon ruin your specialty weapon!”

The guy tried to say something else, but Theophane interrupted him again.

“You think you’re not a weakling?”

“I’m not a weakling!” bellowed the guy without even thinking about it.

“Well, let’s see.” Theophane glanced him over skeptically. “You and Ivan — in the center.”

I went to my place and started to pump myself up with spiritual energy.

“I have to fight a kid?” said the guy, to his credit. “Even if he is a warrior — isn’t there too big of a difference in our skill levels and ranks? It’s dishonorable.”

“Hah, well, we’ll see,” Theophane barked at him sharply. “Go!”

Dodging a spell I didn’t recognize that was hurtling in my direction, I quickly got closer to my opponent and — catching him in the middle of an exhale — hit him right in his “little sunshine.”

My spiritual energy-infused body had become several times stronger, quicker, and more powerful, so — not expecting that kind of speed and power from a child — my opponent got thrown back and couldn't move, trying to inhale at least a little bit.

Here was the strange part — he'd seen yesterday who'd killed almost all those demons, so why didn't he take me seriously?

"Yes, you're on very different skill levels," said Theophane scathingly.

The girls ran to their friend lying on the ground and started trying to help him.

"Next." Theophane pointed to the short, frail guy.

After Theophane called "Go," the second guy started rapidly bombarding me with spells, not letting me get within striking distance and hoping to finish the fight quickly — which didn't exactly work out for him, because I wasn't that artless. I sped up sharply, made a couple of quick jumps in various directions, and finally got close enough to land a hit that shattered a barely visible light blue film.

A shield, I realized! My next hit, with the help of a lot of spiritual energy, ended up being the last one for my opponent in this duel.

"This one's a little better." Theophane scratched his head. "Next."

Stanislav actually turned out to be not as bad as I thought he would be. He cast spells at me at maximum speed, and at one point he unexpectedly used a wide-range spell. I did a high jump with the help of my Shiki-Cho, and voluntarily throwing down a Spirit Shield beneath my feet allowed me to escape the bounds of the dangerous area.

Disappointed by his lack of success, Stanislav didn't switch to his shield in time, and with a couple of painful blows he fell to the ground.

I was bewildered.

I didn't understand this at all! Mages were more powerful and dangerous than warriors! Why was I able to deal with these guys so easily? I got the feeling they didn't know what to expect from an opponent wielding spiritual energy — or could they not believe that I was able to wield it?

"Let's give you a little bit of a chance," said Theophane to the remaining teens. "Two of you against him alone."

The girls, angered by the beating I'd given their friends, glared at me threateningly. They stood in fighting stances, held out their staffs in front of them, and without waiting for the "Go" command started showering me with a whole bunch of spells. Cross my heart, I had to admit that from a magical standpoint the girls turned out to be a little better than the guys. In addition, they were very dexterous and quick, which helped them evade a few of my strikes.

A few times, I didn't manage to dodge their spells, but my Spirit Shield defended me nicely — I perfected it more and more with each spell I tanked, and the final time I managed to ward off two strikes simultaneously.

"I've got him!" yelled Stanislav, who'd come to his senses. My leg fell into a hole and got pinned down by dirt on all sides.

That jerk! Crawling in here to be the third man? What was I supposed to do?

My Spirit Shield wasn't able to defend me from everything, and I took a small burn to the left arm.

I yelped slightly from the unexpected and intense pain, which kicked my brain into gear. I directed a Power Whirlwind at my leg, with which I freed it from its dirt prison and managed to get myself out of the line of fire.

I sped up sharply, stood between the girls, and repeated the move I'd used at Abraham's target range. The two of them had thrown themselves towards me and weren't expecting such a dirty trick. Yelping, they started to close their eyes as the dust, dirt, and other debris got into them.

After that, it was easy to deal with them.

When the dust and debris settled, I was already standing serenely behind Theophane's back.

However, this outward serenity was difficult for me — the center of this nasty pain was throbbing in my arm, and I was aching inside from overloading my spiritual energy system. I'd given it my all for the second day in a row, and I shouldn't be doing that.

Theophane looked pleased. As he should! I'd

proven that I had a better foundation than teenagers from noble families who'd already finished school, and that was probably the first "A+" in his work as a teacher.

"What a sorry spectacle," he said with a wry expression. "Now you can see your true level of skill." I hoped I wouldn't have to listen to any more arguments or get into any more unnecessary fights.

Chapter 13

OUR FIRST JOINT MISSION in the Wasteland happened the next day. It started off very tensely. We hadn't even been walking for ten minutes after getting past the customs point when a big group of demons attacked us. It was worth noting that it was in the exact same place as where we'd met the young nobles.

I saw the demons coming well in advance and gave Theophane our prearranged signal, but when he saw it, he shook his head at me. He most likely wanted to wait for the teens to step in and give a report on how close we were to the enemy's position. But that didn't happen. They'd all let their guards down and were acting like they were on a stroll — smiling, casting around carefree glances, and chatting intermittently.

They probably thought that since we were

taking their money, we were supposed to monitor the area, and their only task was to kill enemies. Well, someone was probably going to be in big trouble!

We drew closer and closer to where the ambush was waiting. The teens weren't showing any signs of worry, and Theophane didn't give the signal to prepare for battle. So after some consideration, I decided to draw my saber from its sheath so I could warn the teens about the nearby enemies that way.

Noticing my quick movement and hearing the sound of the saber being removed from the sheath, they immediately tensed up and turned their heads, not knowing where the danger was lurking.

At that moment, it all began. Seeing that we'd stopped, the demons decided to attack. Theophane, as if he'd appeared out of thin air in front of the teens, beat back a spear flying towards them and barked: "Shields!" Then he jumped back.

Our mages lost their heads — they didn't understand what had just happened, but that simple and clear command told them what they needed to do next.

"SHIELDS!" Theophane barked again at the girls, who didn't understand what was happening at all. It seemed to get through to them the second time. "No sleeping on the job! Keep eyes on all sides and rely only on yourselves! Don't anticipate me saving you! I'm not mommy and daddy! If you die, that's the road you take! It's every man for himself!"

"You're supposed to protect us!" cried Stanislav. "If you don't, my father will have your hide!"

"I don't give a damn!" Theophane started to laugh. "I have one goal — to make you regret your foolish behavior! And if you kick it in the process, it won't be a problem! Your father has other children! So he told me. That goes for all of you!"

The conversation didn't get on too well after those words, most likely because the fairly big group of demons trying to get at us interfered.

In the heat of the fight, the teens proved not to be as bad as they'd seemed at first. After they got past their confusion and realized that this would be no easy excursion, and that Theophane not only wasn't going to help them but had also led them right to the demons, they focused and started bitterly shooting spells at the demons.

"Fight with precision! You're wasting too much energy on one pathetic spell!" shouted an infuriated Theophane in Stanislav's ear. "Less glamour, more results! And don't you dare lose your pace! Move faster with your staff."

The other teens got the same treatment.

"What are you, drunk? You can't hit a gigantic Nocer?" he shouted furiously at Vladimir, the tall and muscular guy who'd taken me on first during the duels. "Aim better! Sakes alive, what a sniper! Hit its leg! Its wounded leg! Take away its ability to move! And then finish it off!" The third guy was likewise chewed out.

Even the girls got it.

"What's the matter, girlies, never seen blood before? Are you sure you're nobility? Or little peasant girls getting their first periods? Huh?"

Damn! Theophane was merciless — he wasn't shy about talking to anyone like that. Did he want to make them angry?

Even though I didn't like it when Theophane used this kind of teaching method, he was clearly getting the point across. The group's effectiveness immediately got several times better.

Especially with the girls. They stopped being squeamish about blood, and their fury- and rage-fueled spells literally ripped the nearby demons to shreds.

Theophane didn't fail to notice this.

"Don't waste so much energy on weak, ordinary demons! This won't be your last fight today, and you'll need your energy yet!"

He had a satisfied smile on his face — he seemed pleased with how the fight was turning out.

I saw two spears fly right at Stanislav; he stopped one with his shield, and I had to beat back the other one. Thankfully, I was standing pretty close to him.

"I don't need your help!" he roared.

Then there would be a spear sticking out of your stomach right now! I thought, not saying anything. In the meantime, the demons had stopped rushing into this without thinking and were now attacking more intelligently. If this went on any longer, they could hurt someone, or even kill someone!

Theophane had most likely considered that very thing, because he commanded:

"Forward! Attack! Before it picks you off one by one like kittens at a target range!"

I threw myself forward first, giving them an example to follow, then immediately put up my Spirit Shield voluntarily to stop the fire spells hurtling towards me. I infused my muscles with spiritual energy, sped up, and burst through the demons' formation while dealing out light, spiritual energy-filled blows.

These teenagers needed to see my true worth — otherwise, it seemed like they'd already forgotten who dragged them through the mud yesterday!

There weren't many demons left, so we killed them very quickly.

"Well, better than nothing," said Theophane scornfully. In a tone indicating he wouldn't tolerate objections, he added, "Now take your knives and double-check them, because I'm not sure you finished off all of them."

"Double-check?" asked Xenia.

Theophane looked at me.

Understanding what I needed to do, I drew my knife and quickly thrust it into the nearest demon's chin. It convulsed a few times, making the teens jump back, then died.

"We need to finish off the wounded and not-quite-dead demons," I explained to the teens after my demonstration. "No one wants a body part getting ripped off in the middle of the corpse dissection phase, do they?"

"Di... ssec... tion?" said Vladimir.

"Yeah, you saw what we were doing after the last fight, and you know that's exactly what gets used for most potion ingredients."

"It's one thing to know it and see it," he said, turning green, "and quite another to do it yourself. Besides, I have money, and I don't want to do it."

"What are you standing around chatting for?" said Theophane angrily, and started putting pressure on them by force of will. "I told you! Draw your knives and get going! If you're scared, you can start by hitting them with spells from a distance! Just remember, after this we're continuing our peculiar crusade against the folly of the youth! And you're going to need energy."

"How dare you speak to us like this?" fumed Stanislav. "We're noble heirs! And you're just some kind of..."

A light slap to the face knocked him off his feet.

He would've tried to get up, but he got another slap.

The third time, he tried to attack Theophane from the ground. His staff got knocked out of his hands. Stanislav got to his feet on his own and then was once again thrown to the ground with another humiliating slap.

"That's what you are! Not a noble heir!" spat Theophane. "A piece of garbage, incapable of even defending yourself! Do you see what a high sense of self-importance leads to? Do you see?"

He looked each of the teenagers in the eyes in turn, but no one dared to hold eye contact for longer than a few seconds.

Theophane looked scornfully at Stanislav.

"What are your trinkets worth if you yourself aren't capable of anything? Do you think that because you preened like a peacock while you got dressed, and put on all those rings, people would respect you? People look at you like a stupid, attention-deprived child trying to stand out like this.

"Remember this!" Theophane finished. "You can tell real nobility when you see them! They have nothing to prove to anyone! And believe me, I've seen many worthy people in my time!"

He turned to Stanislav again.

"You think I just humiliated you in front of your friends?" he asked. "And you're probably hoping you can get revenge, right? Then know that no one is guilty of making you roll around on the ground like a beaten dog but yourself and your vile tongue. Try to attack me, and I'll show you something more horrifying than ordinary slaps!"

"Theophane," I said to him as a harsh, oppressive silence hung over us. "We need to do our double-check. We're going to have demons starting to run away soon."

"Excellent suggestion," he said to me, and added to the others: "Draw your weapons and get moving!"

"I'm not going near them!" cried Eugenia, the girl who'd hated Marissa's house so much. She jumped a few paces back from the nearest corpse. Thrusting her staff out in front of her, she declared: "And no one can make me!"

She was looking around with wild horror.

She was the first to throw herself at Stanislav and show off, but when there was a job to be done, then "no one could make her." Although, of course, she was a girl — we had to treat her with understanding.

Theophane said to me:

"Help her."

Nodding, I approached Eugenia, took her by the hand, and said as softly as possible:

"Let's go, I'll be there to support you."

"No!" she cried, once again trying to jump back, but I held onto her hand firmly so she wouldn't manage it.

"Come with me, and I'll support you," I repeated to her more harshly.

"No!" she cried again, pointing her staff in my direction. "I'll fire if you don't let me go."

"Sure, try it!" I said, frowning. To be honest, I was tired of all the fuss.

That and the irritation that had overtaken me

were probably why I called on the ice inside myself again. I admit I hadn't done it in quite some time, for some reason it hadn't been necessary. As it turned out, I wasn't doing it for nothing, otherwise I would have realized that my level of spiritual energy had grown because of my constant training with Shiki-Cho, and that I'd tempered my will pretty well. Which led to a surprising effect!

Thick waves of piercing cold radiated from me like ripples on the water.

The teens froze, deciding not to move.

"Ivan, there's no need to get so worked up," said Theophane dryly, but with obvious notes of satisfaction in his voice. "She was just joking, right?"

Eugenia didn't answer.

"Right?" he said more forcefully. He walked up to her and lightly touched her shoulder.

"I don't know," she said in a quiet and somehow lost-sounding voice, looking around us with empty eyes. "I'm scared."

"Ivan will work with you precisely so that you'll be less scared. Understood?"

She didn't respond.

"Understood?" Theophane shook her shoulder again.

"Understood," said Eugenia quietly.

What we did next I can describe with only two words: filthy and disgusting. And believe me, it had nothing to do with the demon corpses. Well, almost nothing...

As it turned out, all of our valiant noble heirs were anxious about corpses being dissected before their eyes, and if they worked on it themselves, their levels of anxiety rose repeatedly. I couldn't blame them for it — I'd been exactly like that hardly very long ago. But, despite that, being in a company of vomiting people was extremely unpleasant, and the numerous noises accompanying that shared activity raised the level of unpleasantness to an even higher degree.

When the teens finally finished dissecting the carcasses, they were all smeared with clotted blood.

"You couldn't have been any tidier?" said Theophane, glaring at them. "Why are you such a mess? It's vile to look at! Good thing none of you soiled yourselves! And you're nobility, for heaven's sake! The noble class has gotten shallow! So shallow..."

Thanks to that "subtle" psychological gambit, the teens happily forgot about the demons, the blood, and their own weakness, and other very strong negative emotions flashed across their furious faces.

"What'd you stop for?" said Theophane with a nasty smirk, then pointed to me. "A little boy is behaving more suitably than magic academy graduates."

He was silent for a while, then finished harshly:

"I want you to understand, when you look at

him, what useless weaklings you are! To clearly sense your own weaknesses, see the new horizons you need to strive for, and want to work and evolve! To become at least slightly aware that your achievements are still very few, and that you're making nothing of yourselves! And if you don't start working on self-improvement, you'll remain just as useless!"

While Theophane spoke, a kind of aura of strength and power radiated from him. The teens were silent and didn't dare to say anything in response.

I figured they'd remember those words, and this day, for a long time.

"I'm watching carefully to see if you've gotten anything out of today's experience." Theophane paused for a bit. "Our first lesson is finished, let's go on to the second. Get back into walking formation, pull yourselves together, and prepare to move. Let me remind you that you're not on a casual walk, so keep a careful eye out on all sides and don't miss an attack like you did the first time. All right?" he finished. "Let's see if you're really noble heirs capable of learning new and important things, or if you're just a herd of pregnant moose with overly high self-esteem."

Our tasks were a lot more fun from that point on.

Theophane's words did a great job putting the teens in a bad mood; they were ready to cut any demon they laid eyes on to ribbons, and to prove to this loathsome geezer that they weren't as weak as he thought.

Casually and without exerting ourselves at all, we killed several groups of demons — Theophane and I didn't even have to step into the fight. It seemed like they were now a completely different group of mages — just went to show what motivation and the proper approach to teaching could mean.

Despite this, Theophane had some critiques: "Your hits aren't precise," "You're wasting too much energy on that spell," and so on.

The spoils, the precious ingredients, didn't present any particular problems either — the teens worked fairly quickly and neatly, even if they made faces the whole time.

A few times I caught extremely unpleasant glances being directed at me.

Why did Theophane use me as an example? I thought, irritated. It could lead to conflict, which I really didn't want. After those duels in the clearing, they didn't really like me. After he'd compared them to me, it was even worse. That and they knew perfectly well not to tangle with Theophane as a rule, which meant they were projecting all their negative feelings onto me — I was clearly smaller and weaker than him, so in theory my face was punchable. Well, I'd like to see them try...

The next several groups of demons didn't pose us any real problems either. The teens were still angry and focused.

"All right, let's gather the ingredients and go back," Theophane ordered once he noticed the mages were starting to look a little bushed. According to his plan, they needed to return home with some strength in reserve, think about everything that had happened, and prepare for a good day's work tomorrow.

While they worked on dissecting, I took a look at our surroundings. I suddenly saw a strange apparition.

"Theophane," I called to him, since I hadn't had time to go far from our stopping point yet. "Something's clearly casting an illusion on me, and the Eyes of the Wolf aren't helping!"

I did the tech a few times, infused my eyes with a lot of spiritual energy, but no — nothing changed.

"No, that's clearly not an apparition," said Xenia slowly.

And indeed, it was something to be surprised at.

Through the Wastelands, with the lightly swaying gait of a drunk and at the same time boundlessly happy person on an unburdened stroll, walked a bearded old man. He was wearing simple linen pants and a shirt of the same material with patterns embroidered on it in red and blue. His legs were securely protected by high, sturdy boots, on his head was a straw hat I knew well, and he wore a wide, nice-looking belt around the waist of the shirt.

In his hands was a jug of wine, and I could see a rustic wicker basket on his shoulder.

His quiet voice, as he sang a gleeful song, was also very familiar to me.

"Oh, my little bottle is so empty —
I've been drinking since the morning light.
Still, my little daydreams always tempt me —
Wish my bottle had no end in sight..."

Yes, you guessed it, the drunkard with the wobbly walk strolling his way through the Wastelands was the smiling old man Taras.

What could he be doing here? I thought in bewilderment. It was really dangerous here!

"It's your juicehead neighbor!" Stanislav noticed with surprise. "What is he, suicidal? Wandering around alone here?"

Theophane cleared his throat expressively at that remark.

"Sorry, I meant your Avtiukian neighbor," Stanislav quickly corrected himself.

I glanced at Theophane, who quietly shrugged.

"Where'd he go?" asked Vladimir, puzzled.

I looked around. Indeed, I saw no sign of old man Taras in the area.

Very, very strange.

"What was that?" I asked Theophane.

"Everyone earns their keep however they can," said Theophane instead of answering.

If you think I understood what you meant by

that, you're sorely mistaken, I thought.

We got back to the customs point surprisingly fast, but we ran into two small groups of demons that preferred not to get into a fight.

"There really are a lot of them in this area," I noticed thoughtfully. "Seems like there should be fewer of them in theory — we didn't see this many in the last area. Seems like they're getting smarter too — they're not attacking big groups anymore."

"Yes," said Theophane thoughtfully. "There are indeed a lot of lesser demons in this area. We'll have to tell them at customs that something strange is going on here."

A couple of cars waiting for their charges met us in the parking lot of the customs point.

The mages and warriors of the nobility looked with wide eyes on the blood-soaked teenagers. They'd probably never seen them in such extravagant attire.

"I expect you back tomorrow at the same time," said Theophane to the teens, then let them go home to rest.

"Covered in blood, big deal," I heard Stanislav say casually. "We tore whole groups of them to shreds..."

What a braggart! I wondered if he'd tell anyone that he puked under a tree or that Theophane tore him a new one? Probably not, I figured...

* * *

The whole ride home, I tried to figure out what old man Taras had been doing in the Wastelands, why he'd been alone, and how he'd vanished so suddenly. Theophane was silent, ignoring my questions, so I decided to find out for myself.

Once I'd gotten myself back together, I headed off to Taras and Marissa's house. I found the man I was looking for in a cozy wicker gazebo in his house's yard. There was a jug of wine and a plate of sliced apples in front of him.

"Good evening," I greeted him.

"And a lovely evening to you, Ivan," said Taras with a smile, beckoning me over. "Sit down, have an apple slice, help yourself to what the good Lord has given us."

I sat and eagerly helped myself to some fruit.

"You here on business, or just because?" Taras asked.

"On business," I said decisively, trying not to beat around the bush. I laid out my curiosities right away. "We were in the Wastelands today, and we saw one entertaining character. At first I thought it was just some kind of hallucination, and there was some kind of advanced demonic magic affecting me, but it turned out that wasn't it. Because there's no such thing as mass hallucinations. Right?"

Taras scratched his beard thoughtfully.

"Eh, so that's why you stopped over," he said. "I can see right away that you're no ordinary boy."

He poured some wine into his glass, downed another helping, and said, "You're right, there's no such thing as mass hallucinations."

"So," I said, lowering my voice, "you really do go to the Wasteland? Alone? Does Marissa know about this?"

Taras raised a finger to his lips pointedly.

"Shhh, don't blurt out things like that in front of her — she'll kill me."

"I'll take it to my grave," I reassured him.

"If that's the case, then I can tell you — yes, I do. I collect herbs and other little trinkets."

"You're not afraid of the demons?" I said, surprised. "If they notice you, you'll be in big trouble! If I can be honest, you don't seem like a strong fighter."

Taras started to laugh.

"Say that again," he brushed me off. "*You don't seem like a strong fighter!*" He repeated my sentence and laughed. "I don't even look much like a weak fighter."

"Then what's your secret? You were walking along like you were on a stroll for pleasure."

"You're right — the demons would have to notice me first. But if they don't notice me, I won't have any problems."

Was it possible he had an amulet like the one I'd seen on Godimir? Something like that would cost a fortune!

"I see," I said thoughtfully, and asked for the sake of curiosity: "How's the haul? Did you find a lot of stuff?"

He winked and smiled.

"Do you like blueberries?"

"Blueberries?" I repeated thoughtfully, then nodded right away. "Who doesn't?"

Taras reached under the bench and, like a magician, produced the wooden basket I already knew well. It was full of little paper cups with big, ripe bluish-black berries in them.

My mouth watered immediately.

"Just promise you won't tell Marissa where I got the berries," he said quietly.

"You can buy them for cheap," I replied just as quietly, taking a big cup.

"No." He shook his head. "But I'm simply begging you — "

"I swear, I'll take it to my grave," I repeated quietly. "Thank you for the hospitality, and for answering my questions. "Tasty!" I tried one of the berries.

"Of course," said Taras. "In the Wastelands they're especially big and tasty, and no one collects them except me — everyone's preoccupied with more valuable plants."

"Now where did you run off to, you old coot?" A displeased Marissa came out of the house. "Oh, Ivan, what are you doing here?" She saw me.

"I asked him to come," said Taras. "I wanted to treat him to some blueberries — you blind, or what? Can't you see them?"

"So!" said Marissa, taking the towel off her

shoulder and putting her hands on her hips. "Drunk again, you old ass?"

Taras's expression changed sharply. He left the gazebo and started to follow her slowly.

"What do you mean, old?" he asked unexpectedly.

"So you don't mind 'ass?'"

"An ass is a sturdy beast with a good work ethic," said Taras, laughing.

"Not in front of the kid!" fumed Marissa, brandishing her towel at him. "Or you can get out of here, you cursed Avtiukian!"

"Don't be so hard on me!" he said, tugging at his beard belligerently. "I didn't mean anything by it! I was joking! What are you at my throat for?"

"I think I'll go," I said quietly, withdrawing very quickly.

I get it! I thought. *An ass is indeed a sturdy beast with a good work ethic.*

* * *

I honestly had to admit, these days of combined lessons were becoming more than a little bit of a burden even for me. Since Theophane had been given all of two weeks to achieve some kind of results, of which he was naturally seeing very few, he decided not to skip even a single day of training with the teenagers. To this end, he specially shortened the lessons in the Wasteland to a few hours and was watching to make sure the teens didn't overwork themselves and get tired.

However, despite him taking these measures, the fatigue had a tendency to build up. After ten days, when he sensed his students' mental fatigue, he decided to give them one free day.

"No problem, they'll rest for just a day, and in the remaining four days everything will run like clockwork!" he said as he was driving our car. "The skills that I've built up in them need to go from conscious to subconscious, so that they won't even think about what they're doing and how to do it — they'll start to use the experience they've gained instinctively."

"What?" I couldn't decipher his gibberish the first time, since I was thinking about my long-awaited relaxation. "I didn't understand any of that."

"Don't worry about it," he brushed me off. "I was just thinking out loud."

The training had actually helped me — by a long shot — to understand what mages really were, the range of spells they could have at their disposal, and how to adapt to spell attacks.

One other thing that had added to my fatigue was that the local demons in that part of the Wasteland were getting stronger and stronger every day. This, of course, could be seen in the level of resistance they showed us.

For example, those Dwarf Saws' fire spells had now become two or even three times more powerful. The Spirit Shield I had to use because of that took up a lot of my energy.

I couldn't be disappointed that Theophane's unwilling students were making surprisingly rapid progress. Whether because he was constantly mocking and needling them with his reproachful and caustic critiques in every fight, or because having bloody fights to the death and killing tons of enemies ages and hardens you, all five of them without exception were showing outstanding results.

Their spells were getting more precise, economical, and deadly on top of that. The constant danger was teaching them to use detection spells easily and be vigilant.

Despite that, the teens were still making small mistakes anyway, for which they got scolded plenty by Theophane. There was nothing surprising about that, of course, since to get something truly worthy out of this the teens would have to keep up this routine diligently for at least a couple months, and not a paltry two weeks.

Almost every fight and every day's wrap-up ended with Theophane holding me up as a good example, making the teens grind their teeth in annoyance and anger. I understood — they'd become a lot stronger, and their teacher was still using some little kid as the gold standard. I couldn't help being anxious about it — I was getting the sense that Theophane was pitting the young mages against me. I wasn't sure about the others, but Stanislav and Eugenia were clearly annoyed.

The only thing I had to be happy about during that time was the delicious lunches Marissa cooked. Her blueberry dumplings were superb.

After the day off, the teens changed. It became clear that they really hadn't needed the rest, but they'd made somewhat irrational use of their free time: my "favorite" couple had come up with ideas on how to teach me a lesson.

"Where's Theophane?" asked Stanislav as soon as I came out of the house.

My wristwatch told me it was nine o'clock in the morning, so I was surprised they were here this early. We'd agreed on eleven.

Stanislav and Eugenia were already in the driveway.

"Good morning," I said, even though no one had said it to me. "Theophane said that he wouldn't be here in the morning. He asked you to arrive a little later."

"Perfect," said Stanislav. "In that case, he won't bother us." He paused for a bit and added, "I challenge you to a fight!"

"A fight?" I was taken aback. "Where's this coming from?"

"From you thinking too much of yourself," said Stanislav, pointing a type of magic staff I'd never seen before at me.

"When did I have time for that?" I asked, a little irritated. "The two of us especially haven't talked much — I only do what Theophane tells me."

"Oh, yeah?" said Eugenia indignantly. "You telling me you didn't browbeat me during our first lesson in the woods? Or did Theophane help you do that?"

"I wanted to help you, and I did," I answered her, then turned to Stanislav. "As far as I remember, I had your back a few times!"

I didn't feel like fighting them. We still had to spend a few days going to the Wasteland together. What was I supposed to do post-infighting? Expect to get hit not only by demons, but by them too?

"We didn't need your help! I had it handled!" cried Stanislav hysterically.

"So did I!" Eugenia jabbed a finger at me angrily. "You think you're really tough? Well, let's see now how tough you are!"

With those words, she quickly drew another staff I didn't recognize and cast a lightning spell at me.

I had to admit, I'd never seen a trick like that in her arsenal. Or, to be honest, in any of the others'. However, despite my mild surprise, the instincts I'd gained in the Wastelands didn't let me down.

The spell turned out to be so powerful that only my second Spirit Shield cut it off.

Eugenia's second strike was much more cunning and refined. It hit not me, but the ground next to me. When I remembered that the ground also conducted electricity, it was already too late

— an arc of electricity reached me mid-jump, and I screamed loudly.

It hit me really hard — a spasm locked my body into place, and my vision went dark. I was even thrown back a dozen feet or so. As if a horse had kicked me.

"Do you get the lesson?" she cried, angry and happy at the same time. "Do you get it? Just like I did?"

I tried to stand and ended up collapsing.

A ghostly light shone from the staff in Stanislav's hands, which he used to prevent me from moving.

He looked down at me scornfully with a victorious grin.

"Now do you understand who's truly powerful? Mages! And you, you pathetic peasant, will have to spend the rest of your life fiddling around with warrior techs." He turned to Eugenia. "Blast him again to make sure he understood properly."

My attempts to fill my body with spiritual energy were useless, and the weak shield I put up was mercilessly shattered. I got a second stroke of lightning to the chest.

My body was immobilized by painful convulsions.

"What the — are you totally out of your minds?" I heard Xenia's furious voice. "You just wanted to challenge him to a fight! A practice duel! And what am I seeing here? Two mages attacking a little boy!"

"We're well within our rights!" replied Stanislav angrily. "This commoner didn't speak to us like he should have. He needs to be taught a lesson!"

"And he never agreed to just a practice fight! So it's his own fault!" added Eugenia.

"Maybe that's because you brought family heirlooms to that practice fight?" said Xenia scornfully, and added harshly, "Leave him be, or this won't end well for you."

"Don't even think about it!" said Stanislav. "You're really supporting this filthy degenerate instead of us?"

I lay on the ground and tried to recover my breath from the last lightning strike. I was immeasurably grateful to Xenia for her support, and for the slight breathing room her words gave me. The darkness in my eyes brought on by the strike sent me involuntarily into the internal world, and I found myself standing before a much bigger slab of ice.

Little by little, a flame of cold fury flared up in my chest. And what was really strange was that it wasn't the attack itself making me angry — rather, it was the fact that those two considered themselves above me.

How dared they talk to me like that? Who gave them that right? Who was the real noble heir here? Who was a simple viscount, and who was a future prince? I, a Morozov, heir to one of the oldest bloodlines, was supposed to consider them above me?

Spiritual energy filled my body, followed in turn by a Power Whirlwind that easily snapped Stanislav's magical fetters holding me to the ground.

A few quick rebounds, three shattered shields, and I easily escaped the strokes of lightning.

It was like a spiritual energy-infused arm was coming out of my chest. I made it a few times bigger and swept the mages off their feet, planting them against the side of the house.

That same invisible arm tore the staffs out of their hands and landed them next to me.

"Give it back!" cried Eugenia, jumping after her staff, and got punched by a strong, Shiki-Cho-infused fist right in her "little sunshine."

Her scream emptied her lungs of air, and she tried to breathe frantically.

Perfect. Let her feel the same way I did after that low blow of hers!

Stanislav threw himself at me but got stopped at a distance by the invisible arm. Like one of the bad guys in *Star Wars*, I grabbed him by the throat and started to choke him, slowly lifting him upwards.

I had to admit I didn't know how I managed it — my strengthened will, my strong desires, and my constant training were probably doing their job.

Stanislav thrashed around in the air, trying to breathe, but he couldn't. His attempts to cast spells at me weren't particularly successful either — with him suspended mid-air without a staff, they didn't seem dangerous at all.

This new tech sucked the spiritual energy out of me like a vacuum cleaner, so despite my great desire to keep strangling this ungrateful creature a little longer, I let him go.

"Without a staff, you can't even cast weak spells," I remarked coldly. "What a sorry spectacle," I spat.

My new "limb" had spent far too much of my energy, so I was barely staying on my feet, but I tried not to look it.

"Thank you so much for your help and support. You're very different from these losers," I said, looking at Xenia. "You have a noble heart."

She gave me a strange look and nodded silently.

After standing in front of my face-down enemies for a little while longer, I finally gathered my strength and went inside so I could lie on my bed for a bit and recover my strength. I had no desire to remain in their company.

As I passed by the mirror, I noticed that my eyes were glowing with some kind of ghostly blue light.

* * *

The last days of joint lessons were torture for everyone involved.

It was unpleasant for me to be near those two losers, so I had to constantly keep my shield up behind my back, which I made a show of doing.

It was unpleasant for those two to deal with my scornful glances and the rest of their friends' displeasure. It was even more unpleasant for them to go without my help in fights. Stanislav got his first serious injury because of it.

When he indignantly stammered that I was OBLIGATED to defend him, he immediately got a clip to the ear from my energy-arm and the reply that when he and Eugenia had attacked me so unfairly, they'd screamed to the whole city that they didn't need my help. Besides, I wasn't obligated to do anything for anybody.

My new tech turned out to be incredibly useful, but it took a whole lot of energy out of me. When he saw the energy-arm, Theophane said that its use wasn't popular due to its high energy consumption, and hardly anyone practiced it.

Theophane demanded that I stop letting the loser get beat up and defend everyone, and I was forced to obey him. I could still argue with him in everyday life, which I was definitely planning to do later, but in the Wastelands he wouldn't tolerate disturbances from anyone.

He, incidentally, was also not in a very good mood, or at least he didn't seem like it. I made him angry by saying that a mentor who pitted other people against me didn't deserve any respect or esteem. Although, maybe it was more about how I stopped talking to him.

Despite only having two weeks, he accomplished a lot. He managed to make the teens grow up a little, think about the actions they'd taken, and reflect on who they were, what they made of themselves, what they wanted out of life, and how they were going to achieve it. He showed them that they weren't as strong as they themselves would like, and he put the desire to evolve further — even after our training ended — into their teenage heads.

An awareness of one's own weakness and the strength of one's potential enemies could provoke that desire in anyone. Up till this moment, the teens had earnestly believed that they were prepared to a high degree, not realizing until the end that they didn't just need to possess knowledge — they had to know how to use it.

For my least favorite couple, one motivation towards further development would of course be the understanding that there was a specific person out there in the world that they hated, but who — despite his age and his practice of nothing but warriors' arts — was much stronger than them for some reason.

Maybe that wouldn't have played such a vital role if Theophane hadn't constantly harped on about it. I'd become to them like a red flag to a bull. I was sure they'd improve not just to make themselves stronger, but also to become stronger than me and get revenge for their humiliation.

From a magical standpoint, the teens had also gotten a lot better — they'd become much more serious opponents than they'd been at our first meet-up.

The speed, precision, energy conservation, and power of their spells had grown, although before the start of the lessons each of them had had problems with a few of those things.

Well, and the most important thing was that in my humble opinion, they'd learned how to kill, and that was sometimes much more important than the power of the spells they were casting.

Our parting was very simple.

After the final lesson, Theophane announced that the two-week preparatory course under his guidance was over, and gave each of them an envelope.

"Here are my observations on each of you. I've named your strong and weak points, and I've indicated which aspects you've improved in and which you need to keep working on."

Stanislav would've wanted to throw out his envelope, but Theophane added:

"I think it will be of interest to you to learn what's inside, since your parents have already received similar envelopes."

"We'll meet again," Stanislav and Eugenia hissed at me without saying goodbye.

My goodbyes with the rest of them were

unexpectedly warm. They even left me their phone numbers so we could keep in touch.

"Hang in there while you're here with your monster, and try not to die during his next lesson! I'm going to worry about you!" Vladimir whispered in my ear, and we laughed.

It was nice that at least someone didn't think badly of me.

"So how did you manage to make them agree to these lessons?" I asked Theophane once all the cars had driven off.

"By chance," he replied. "Once they knew that there was a readily available 'Knight'-rank warrior in front of them, they threw themselves at the opportunity. I just needed to give them a little push."

Chapter 14

THE IDEA THAT I'D HAVE to go to school soon made me depressed. On the one hand, I wanted to get a basic knowledge of this world so I could get closure on the many questions that had arisen as I'd studied it.

On the other hand, however, I had no desire to spend half my days in the company of children. What would I talk about with them? Perhaps, of course, I'd find common interests to discuss, but I might just as well not.

At one point I asked Theophane if he could hire private tutors. It actually wouldn't be as expensive as it seemed at a first glance. And the quality of my education might be better by a long shot — one had to agree that it was easier for a teacher to teach one student than ten or twenty at the same time, and I also wouldn't be able to loaf around in that kind of situation.

Theophane, however, pointed out my low level of sociability and my lack of the simplest knowledge about life in contemporary society, and he insisted on the school option.

I frowned and got indignant. I explained that in my scenario he and I would have more time left for training and Wasteland excursions. But Theophane was still adamant.

To ease my apprehension, he added that I'd been making a lot of good progress in this time, and that my young body needed rest from the constant, irregular growth of my skills and abilities. He also added that school wouldn't be quite that simple, and it was vitally important for me to study there.

Once I realized I couldn't change Theophane's mind, I — so that I wouldn't gain a reputation as an ignoramus in my new environment — made him take me to a bookstore and buy the textbooks I needed in advance for independent study.

"Right, then," said Theophane thoughtfully, looking at his phone screen. "Nemiga Street, building three."

"That's it, we're here," I said, pointing to a neat plaque with the street name and address number.

Theophane tucked his phone into his pants pocket and confidently pushed open the sturdy oak door.

"Good morning, can I help you?" asked the

bookseller as soon as the door closed behind us.

He was a sturdy middle-aged man with a rough-looking beard and a wide, friendly smile.

He was sitting to the right of the door at a small counter piled with novels and apparently reading something.

I saw *The Inhuman* written in yellow on the spine of the book, which he picked up as he rose from his chair and greeted us.

"Yes," said Theophane in response to his question. "We'd like to buy textbooks for school."

"Then you've come to the right place!" said the bookseller with a smile. "Gennady's has the best books in the city, all the more so school textbooks. What grade are you buying textbooks for, by the way?"

Theophane froze and looked at me uncertainly, then looked at the bookseller, then back at me.

"Fifth?" he asked and answered.

The bookseller directed a nonverbal question at me.

"Fifth," I said confidently.

Good thing we sorted that out before I went to school!

"Would you like to buy new or used?" the bookseller asked next.

"What? You can buy books used?" I was surprised for some reason.

"Of course." He gave me a funny look, probably wondering which backwoods rock I'd been living under. "After the end of the school year, you don't need them anymore, so you can return them to the bookstore and get a refund. Not a full refund," he added quickly, noticing that I intended to ask that clarifying question. "I'd even say not much of one at all, but still, you get something."

Aha, I thought, nodding thoughtfully — he wasn't just telling us about the very small refund for no reason. He was probably buying used books really cheap, upselling them, and getting a little additional income. Something about his little workaday scheme seemed very familiar to me.

"You're not an Avtiukian, by any chance?" I asked, not expecting it myself.

"No," said the bookseller, embarrassed for some reason. "I'm from a different ethnic group.

He didn't seem like he was lying, I thought, but he was still a crafty one.

"Textbooks," Theophane reminded him, interrupting our discussion. "New."

"Ah! Yes indeed!" The bookseller shot us an infectious smile and disappeared into the back room, the entry to which was right behind him.

On the back of his blue t-shirt was written in bright yellow letters: *Book Garden.*

Hmm, I thought, remembering that I'd seen something like that written above the shop's front door. That was most likely the name of the establishment.

The bookseller reappeared carrying a small bundle of seven books tied with gray string.

"Would you like to look at them?" he asked.

"Of course." I nodded confidently.

Judging by the number of books, this whole thing didn't seem as bad as I'd thought at first. There were only six school subjects — I didn't remember exactly, but I was pretty sure we'd studied a lot more in my fifth-grade class on Earth.

Math, history, language arts, literature, geography, and technology.

"And what school will the boy be attending?" Gennady asked — his nametag with his name and picture was lying lonely on the edge of the counter, informing me of his name.

"Why do you need that information?" Theophane frowned.

"What do you mean?" said Gennady, surprised. "So I can give you textbooks for any additional subjects."

"What additional subjects?" I began to suspect the worst. "These textbooks don't cover all the subjects?"

"These are just the basics." Gennady confirmed my worst fears. "Required for all the schools in the country. Each school's administration designates additional subjects and textbooks."

"Understood," said Theophane, nodding. "He's going to the Imperial Academy."

"The *Imperial Academy?*" Gennady emphasized it strangely for some reason and gave us another once-over. "Then you'll need a few more books."

He dove into the back again, and to my enormous relief, he only brought back three books, one of which I knew very well. Well, not me — Ivan.

The Velvet Book — a special reference book that listed all the noble families of the Empire and gave a short history of what was notable about them. The second book was called *Etiquette: Year Five*, and the third was *Demonology: Year One.*

"Why is the etiquette book year five but the demonology book is only year one?" I decided to clear up my lack of understanding.

"Because etiquette is studied starting in first grade at the Imperial Academy, but demonology doesn't start until fifth. It's believed that learning about demons and their peculiarities could have a negative impact on children's psyches, so those studies begin a bit later."

"In that case," I said thoughtfully, "I'll need the other four etiquette textbooks for the first four years of school — we can get those used — and one big, complete encyclopedia of etiquette. If you have something like that, of course."

"We do! Gennady's has everything!" said Gennady confidently.

"Why do you need an encyclopedia like that?" asked Theophane after Gennady left. "As far as I remember, I taught you etiquette."

"Yes, you did, but not everything I might need by a long shot. Besides, I at least need to know how much the other students know. I want to be the best, not the worst."

Theophane gave me a satisfied nod — that kind of explanation really spoke to him.

While Gennady searched for the books we needed, I opened the math textbook and selectively read a few paragraphs.

It seemed like it wasn't too complicated — I remembered Ivan studying some similar stuff with private tutors — but "seemed" was the key word. I'd definitely have to refresh this knowledge.

"I need to get the textbooks for the earlier grades," I said after thinking a bit.

"Why?" Theophane was genuinely surprised.

"Because my tutors may have taught me well, but there's a lot I already don't remember, and there are probably a couple of topics I never studied at all."

I started reading one of the paragraphs.

"Lesson three: points, line segments, rays, and lines."

"So what?" said Theophane.

"So I can explain in my own words what those things are, but I wouldn't be able to give a teacher the official definition! That means we need to buy those books — I need to memorize everything in the time I have left before the school year starts."

"In theory, unneeded books can be returned here, for a refund..." said Theophane thoughtfully.

"For a small refund!" we heard from the back.

"We get it already!" I grinned and asked

Theophane quietly: "Are you sure he's not an Avtiukian?"

"He's not." Theophane shook his head. "He's from another nation renowned for their cleverness."

I bought a couple general-purpose notebooks and the writing utensils I needed at the bookstore, and then we went home with clean consciences after leaving the smiley bookseller with a good sum of money.

I'd have to work hard in the time I had left before the start of the school year and get to know the basic concepts taught in elementary school, otherwise I might — for example — be told to solve a problem using some guy named Ferbenbrücher's method or whatever, and I'd disgrace myself in front of the class when it turned out to be utterly elementary.

No, I really didn't want to embarrass myself over trifles like that.

"Can you manage that?" asked Theophane, looking askance at the back seat crammed with books.

"What else do I have to do?" I shrugged. "Nothing but this."

* * *

The days, which had already been passing pretty fast, now seemed to grow even shorter and fly by almost imperceptibly.

Every morning, according to my schedule, I did some light drills. Right after that was my first proper training session (sparring with Theophane) or occasionally a lesson on developing my spiritual body. Once I'd finished the physical exercise, I switched to working through and writing summaries of topics from various academic disciplines.

The elementary-school stuff was fairly simple, so I didn't have much of a problem with my independent mastery of those subjects, even more so because there was a lot of crossover between my earthly knowledge and what Ivan knew. After lunch was my second battle skills training session — more sparring with bladed weapons, with the use of other types, of course. Or a fight using whatever improvised resources were available — anything that came to Theophane's mind.

Next came more meditation, and since I never had almost any strength left for anything after that, my textbook studies continued. At the end of the day, another sparring session with sabers awaited me — this time a light one, and then some extended work on the spiritual side.

Once every three or four days, Theophane and I visited the Wasteland and methodically cut down the demon population over the course of a few hours. During these visits, I had to take on the dirty work while Theophane acted like he'd come there on a pleasant walk, and only from time to time did he help me beat back the strongest monsters.

I noticed the demons attacking us were becoming stronger and smarter with every encounter. I'd even say they were making developments or something...

Small groups of Dwarf Saws that we encountered along the way didn't even think of attacking us now — on the contrary, despite there being groups of winged demons among them, they tried to hide. Large forces tried to attack us and win, but they didn't mindlessly throw themselves into fights either. Instead, they went about it more intelligently: they set up ambushes or tried to use the element of surprise.

It got to the point where demons of one type started using the other types' weapons. I wasn't used to seeing a Nocer using an Anthro's saber, or a tailless Dwarf Saw using a makeshift club.

"There's nothing surprising about that," said Theophane in response to my questions. "Demons can also get stronger and — let's put it this way — evolve. You already know yourself that up until now we've essentially only run into the weak demons in the first-circle region."

"The first circle?" I said, hearing the unfamiliar term. "You didn't tell me about anything like that earlier."

"Because I didn't need to at the time," he replied. "Your head's so swollen from all the new information you're constantly looking up, analyzing, and fitting into your own worldview. I didn't want to overload you with non-topical information, but now that you're asking questions it means you're ready for new knowledge."

I nodded.

"If you look at the trunk of a tree that's been chopped down, you can see that it's divided into circles. That's roughly what a Wasteland looks like from above. Of course, the circles aren't visible, but our scholars have proven that they're there. The circle closest to human territory is known as the first. That's where the weakest demons and the least mutated plants are. If we were to go a little further, we'd reach the second circle, where the demons are stronger and smarter than in the first. If we went just a little further, we'd reach the third circle. Accordingly, the demons of the third circle are stronger than the demons of the second."

"So what you're saying is the demons attacking us now are most likely from the second circle?"

"I think they're from the third," Theophane corrected me. "Or they're clearly aspiring to that level of strength. They need to be wiped out in a timely manner, or else they'll become a serious problem even for mid-level warriors and mages."

"Very strange." I scratched my head. "If your theory is right and the demons are just making advances right now, and they're not holding the source of that higher power, then we need to find out what's letting them get so much stronger so quickly."

"You're right. That's precisely our main task right now: to learn why the demons are getting more powerful. The authorities are already working on it and looking for the reason. There are a few theories on the cause, but there haven't been any certain results yet."

Long story short, I spent a lot of time working on myself, trying to get good results out of that short time period. There was one beautiful moment when the soft-hearted Marissa, who couldn't bear to see this "child torture," kicked us out of the house and said that "the boy needs a break, or else he'll look all sorts of vampirish."

So that we wouldn't think of returning, she took it upon herself to do some general cleaning. Theophane and I pondered her words and decided to agree to an unplanned break.

For sure, a break wouldn't hurt.

"You've been slaving away with all your might for two weeks," said Theophane. "You really do need to take a break. Oh, and as far as I know, the Kuznetsovs have left the city, so there's nothing more to fear."

With those words, he handed me thirty thalers.

"Give me a ride to the city park," I requested, taking the money. "I don't feel like taking public transit."

Now that I had a day off, I could relax, and maybe I'd see Godimir again. Otherwise, I'd promised to come back and then vanished. That was no good.

I stayed at the park for a few hours and had some difficulty shaking off Theophane, but I didn't see my new friend until I was getting ready to leave for home.

"Psst, Ivan!" I heard a quiet, happy voice from behind a tree.

"Hi!" I said, turning around. I noticed a blurry silhouette, which after a bit took the form of the boy I knew. "I thought you'd never come."

"I was the one thinking *you'd* never come!" he said, a little offended. "I've managed to get out here every Sunday, and you haven't been here."

"I've been busy." I shrugged. "There's some kind of market near here, I passed it on the road. I'd be interested to stop by and see what they have there. Do you want to join me?"

"Let's go!" said Godimir. "I'm really getting tired of this park already."

"Me too," I agreed, nodding.

"How did it go with the little Kuznetsov girl?" I decided to ask. "I hope she didn't rat you out to your dad."

"No." He smiled with relief. "But when no one could hear us, she said, 'I'll never tell anyone about you or Ivan.'"

That put me in a cold sweat.

"She said that?" I asked. "Or Ivan?"

"Yes," Godimir replied, then asked curiously, "Which noble family are you from?"

So now it was my turn for uncomfortable

questions.

"Where did you get the idea that I'm from the nobility?" I had to ask. "I'm a commoner."

"Oh, come on," laughed Godimir. "As if your background isn't obvious! How about this — you tell me your family's name, and I'll tell you mine."

"I'm very curious, of course, but I have nothing to answer, so better yet, let's not do that."

"Are you sure?" he said.

"More than anything."

"Then I don't understand what secret Maria Kuznetsov was talking about, and why she wasn't going to tell anyone about you."

"I don't either."

"Okay." Godimir frowned. "If you don't want to talk, it must mean there's an important reason. I won't pry."

To my great disappointment, I never found out what the local Sunday market was all about, because most of the vendors had already left their stations and only a few enthusiasts were left. We walked around, and I bought us two big crepes with ham, cheese, and mayo and a tumbler of kvass.

After I'd been walking for hours, they went down real nicely.

While we were eating our crepes, I noticed a straw hat and embroidered outfit I recognized.

Old man Taras was a vendor here? Weird that I hadn't noticed him right away.

He was standing at one of the tidy counters

and selling blueberries; next to him, of course, was the wine bottle I knew so well.

Seeing that I'd noticed him, he waved at me, and I said hello in response.

Godimir told me about how his older brother was getting on his nerves, and on September first he'd finally be going to middle school.

"Middle school?" I repeated. "Fifth grade, by any chance?"

"Yes," he said, nodding. "I got through the first four levels of elementary school at home, with hired tutors, on my own. Believe me, it's very boring. I hope I'll find a lot of friends at school."

"Yeah, I get it," I said, laughing — Ivan's education had been exactly the same. "I think you'll have a better time there."

Incidentally, the local school system made me happy.

Instead of eleven years, here you only had to go to school for nine. Four years in elementary school, three in middle school, and two in high school.

While we were talking, some unpleasant types started hanging around near the sellers' booths. Bald, muscular guys with faces that hardly glittered with intellect. They started walking up and down the aisles and pestering people.

"What's with these jerks?" Godimir knitted his brows. "How dare they behave this way, and where's security?"

"Look! It's an Avtiukian!" said one of the guys

loudly, jabbing a finger towards old man Taras. “What are you doing here, bumpkin — swindling people?”

“What are *you* kiddos doing?” said Taras, smiling drunkenly. “How can you say that! You can buy the best blueberries here. I picked them myself!”

“Buy?” One of them smirked insolently. “Why don’t you give them to us?”

“No,” said Taras, still smiling. “Fair price for my berries, half a thaler. You won’t find them cheaper anywhere.”

“That’s a fair price? Why don’t you let us try them anyway?” asked one of the guys. He tried to grab Taras by the collar, but Taras tottered drunkenly right at that moment, and the young guy’s hand somehow grabbed nothing but air. The guy tried again, but once again he didn’t manage it.

For the first time, I saw how alcohol could save people from bodily injury — usually it was the opposite.

“Hah!” laughed Taras when his knees buckled, and he sat down on a bench. The guy tried a third time to grab him, with no results. “Please don’t hug me, I have a wife, I don’t swing that way.”

Despite the seriousness of the situation, I couldn’t help laughing, and neither could everyone around us. The guy went red, flew into a rage, and raised his hand, but he didn’t have a chance to strike.

I appeared next to him and tugged politely at his sleeve.

"What do you want, small fry?" he exploded.

"Can you tell me how to get to the library?" I asked with the tone of a studious little fellow.

"The what?" The guy froze, not expecting a question like that.

"The library — where you go to read books," I said.

"What do you mean, books?" the guy raged.

"You know, books. The paper kind." I kept making fun of him. "With cardboard covers and pages inside, and there are a bunch of different letters in them too."

At that moment, security showed up and headed straight in our direction, so the group of rude guys got out of there, throwing Taras dirty looks.

"Thanks, kid," said Taras, smirking. "Quick thinking — you dashingly scared them off without your fists. Ain't for nothing you spend all day reading those books."

"I didn't feel like fighting," I admitted. "Marissa said I had to relax today, so it was better to do what she told me."

"Right you are," said Taras, nodding. "Any fool can wave his fists, but not just anyone knows how to use his head."

He took two big paper cups of blueberries and offered them to me.

"Take these, and treat your friend."

"My friend?" I said, surprised, and turned to Godimir.

"Yes, yes, I'm talking about him."

"Thanks," I said, taking the cups.

"Hey, give me one!" said Godimir, laughing. "I thought you were jumping in to fight, but you asked about the library — I thought I was going to die laughing. He was looking at you like you were an idiot."

"So did your amulet stop working or what?" I asked quietly.

"No." He checked on it. "Why?"

"Because even the old guy at the counter can see you now."

"Are you serious?" He stared at me distrustfully.

"More than anything. I was surprised too. I thought you dropped the disguise yourself."

"You know what, let's get out of here," said Godimir. "There's something about this I don't like — so many people being able to see me. Maybe the amulet really is going to stop working?"

* * *

The Imperial Academy was a small campus in the middle of the city walled off by a tall wrought-iron fence.

"Come on, let's go," said Theophane to me, heading for the main entrance to the campus.

There was a small, tidy building next to the elaborate gates — the entry checkpoint.

A sturdy man in black pants and a short-sleeved white shirt came out of it.

"Good morning, how can I help you?"

"My name is Theophane Elizarov. I have an appointment with the vice-director of academic affairs."

The man got out some kind of folder and leafed through it.

"All right," he said, letting us onto the campus. "Follow me."

The Imperial Academy was pretty imposing-looking — from the expensive fence and the tidy campus to the big two-story red-brick building with a black roof.

In the center of the building's foyer was an enormous marble staircase covered in red carpet. The foyer itself was decorated with ornamentally carved columns, wall moldings, and big paintings.

However, we didn't have a chance to examine the decor for long. The man turned into one of the hallways and led us to a large oak door.

"Hello," a nice-looking young secretary greeted us sweetly. "You're expected."

The vice-director was a well-groomed, elderly woman in a refined dark gray suit.

She greeted us warmly and asked us to have a seat.

"I've been appraised of your situation," she said, getting right down to business. "This young man studied for four years at home, but now you've decided to give him the best education you can, and you want him to enroll in the fifth grade."

"That's right." Theophane seemed pleased with her straightforwardness — it was clear that he really didn't want to stay too long.

"Then I have to warn you in advance that this is not an easy school. Children primarily from noble lineages or other wealthy families of the region study here. Thus, we have special educational requirements and rules of conduct.

"This young man — " She cast a stern glance at me. " — must not only study well, but also know behavioral norms and rules of etiquette."

"Without a doubt," Theophane agreed.

"Excellent." The vice-director nodded. "If you have no objections, we'll test Ivan's level of knowledge."

She placed three pages of questions in front of me.

The characteristics of parallel lines are... I read the question and looked over the answer choices. Hmm, just an ordinary test. Nothing too complicated.

I took a pen and quickly got to work, trying to be attentive and not mess up on trivial points.

A good half of the questions were about etiquette, so I was glad that I'd studied the textbooks I needed in advance. At least I didn't have to be embarrassed now.

The vice-director took the test back,

examined it quickly, and looked at me warmly.

"Great job," she praised me, then turned to Theophane. "This young man's teachers earned their pay. Just leave your documents here, and we'll get him registered."

Theophane handed her a gray folder with everything she needed, and she in turn gave him a light blue envelope.

"Here's the number of the account the tuition should be transferred to," she explained. "We'll be expecting you on the first of September, the first day of the school year."

With that, our meeting was complete, and we took our leave of each other and went back to the car.

"A real temple of knowledge," said Theophane with enthusiasm, closing the car door.

"Except it's too luxurious," I said regretfully. "It's hard on the eyes."

"If only you knew." Theophane smirked. "You're still young."

"Can we afford for me to go here?" I decided to ask just in case.

"We can," Theophane replied. "But we'll have to work even harder, because I put a large portion of the money we made from teaching the noble kids into your bank account."

My bank account — that was good. He'd done the right thing. I needed to prepare in advance for my adult life and accumulate resources, since I had the ability. It would really come in handy in the future.

* * *

To be able to handle the Morozov family's money, George Temnikov had to undergo a complicated ritual at the First Imperial Aristocratic Bank.

This bank wholly and entirely belonged to the imperial family, and it was there that the country's most influential families' money was kept.

Hmm... clearly, that's why the imperial authority is so strong, thought George, not for the first time.

This complicated ritual required ten powerful mages provided by the bank. Mages with ranks no lower than a bachelor's degree took their places routinely and, at the agreed-upon signal, started to work the magic.

George was dressed simply in a long linen shirt over his naked body. This was no coincidence. Clothing made from any other material could interfere with the flow of energy circulating through the ritual area.

At a certain point, as George stood at the very center of the ritual star, he could physically feel the energy starting to fill the space around him.

Standing on cold stone with bare feet wasn't the most pleasant ordeal, but he just had to wait. It would all begin soon.

Directly in front of George was a large, ancient wooden chest bolted with strips of iron, and in front of the chest stood an empty wooden bowl and a clay jug of spring water. A bronze knife, tarnished black with time, was also nearby.

All of these things were laid neatly on a linen towel embroidered in red. One might think it was an ordinary towel with runes embroidered on it, but it wasn't at all...

Once the energy had filled up the space inside the star, runes began to glow on the towel, the jug, the bowl, the knife, and even the chest with a ghostly bright blue light.

Hmm. At first they looked like they were only on the towel, thought George.

At a certain point he realized it was time. He poured a bit of water from the jug into the bowl, picked up the knife, and cut his hand. The water was stained red and then started to shimmer with the ghostly light.

Dense fog poured out of the bowl in thick streams, and it started to rise above the floor and fill every bit of open space.

George took a step forward, lifted the bowl, and set it on a special ledge on the lid of the chest.

The mechanism clicked, the lid was flung aside, and a stream of energy poured forth from the chest.

In another moment, George found himself standing in snow up to his ankles with an unbelievably cold wind blowing around his body.

The ritual star vanished, as did the decor of the hall. It was like George had been transported to the far north. He saw the moon and glittering yellow stars in the sky.

Little by little the wind started to grow stronger.

What's happening? Where am I? thought George anxiously. He'd never heard of anything like this happening before.

Suddenly an aura of darkness cloaked him, and it made him feel much warmer.

George peered into the open chest, where he noticed a splinter of ice suspended in the air giving off incredible cold.

He got down on one knee, stretched out his cut hand, and squeezed it. A few drops of scarlet blood landed on the edges of the ice shard, then disappeared as if they'd never been there.

It seemed to George that someone incredibly ancient was watching him intently now.

O darkness that knows not the cold, there is yet Hope for the line of Morozov! he unexpectedly heard resounding in his head, and everything changed abruptly.

George once again found himself in the center of the ten-point star with mages standing at each point. Only now many of them were showing signs of magical exhaustion and had blood flowing from their noses.

Healers came into the hall and started efficiently giving them the help they needed.

George ran his hand over his face. No blood.

Well, that was good.

"How do you feel?" asked his father, a bit tensely and with some notes of concern in his voice that George wasn't used to hearing, once George had left the bounds of the ritual area.

"Fine," George replied dryly, then asked, "Is it just me, or did something go wrong?"

"Something went very wrong," replied an old man wearing the regalia of a professor of magic, and announced: "The ritual has revealed that the house of Morozov has another heir."

* * *

The time I had left before school flew by in an instant. Our constant excursions and battles in the Wasteland, my studies of various academic subject outlines, and my increased workouts took up all of my free time.

At the same time, we tried to figure out the reason for the demons getting stronger in that one part of the Wasteland, as our study of other areas had shown that the demons there still had the same level of strength as before.

Theophane was right. We weren't the only ones who'd noticed this trend — so had the authorities and the free hunters. The customs point was full of people, and we started running frequently into other groups of hunters in the Wastelands — and even seeing skirmishes between them.

We often came across reinforced patrols of

soldiers and representatives of mages' leagues, fussing over some kind of devices and trying to determine what precisely was the source of the anomaly.

On one of the last days of the summer, we'd gone to the Wasteland as usual. We'd walked to the side away from the customs point so as not to run into other groups of hunters, then gone as deep as we could and found ourselves somewhere in the third circle.

The demons there were truly much stronger than the ones from the preceding circles. They were smarter and more skillful. We started to come across types of demons I wasn't familiar with.

I was already used to fighting, I knew my own strengths and weaknesses, I understood what to expect from my enemies, and thus I was fighting pretty skillfully. I was constantly weighing my options — how to wipe out the most enemies with the least energy in the shortest time — and so I was making constant progress.

"These ones were a little too smart," I said to Theophane as I bandaged up deep abrasions on my shoulder and arm.

For the first time, I'd just been attacked by a demon fighting with two swords at once. Quite frankly, if I didn't have my new "Star-Wars-villain" tech, I wouldn't have known what to do about it.

Theophane nodded.

"They've gotten even more powerful," he said thoughtfully. "Let's collect everything valuable and get out of here. My intuition is telling me that we could find something even more powerful here."

I nodded understandingly.

In truth, I couldn't handle such strong enemies yet. It wasn't worth the risk.

While we dissected the demons, I got the feeling that something was watching us, and then I heard a suspicious noise.

"Something's approaching us from behind," I said quietly to Theophane, not letting my voice get too loud.

"Yes, there is," he replied tensely, glancing around. "Group of five humans. They'll get to us soon. They clearly heard the sounds of battle and decided to come and see who's throwing a party over here."

"It seems to me like something else is watching us, but I can't figure out from where."

Theophane didn't have a chance to respond, because a few people walked up to us.

"You're not a bad fighter, old man," said one of the men, looking at the demon corpses. "You even killed the dual-wielder."

"What do you want?" said Theophane sullenly without pleasantries.

"Hah!" one of the others laughed. "Grandpa gets it."

"We want you to share the loot. You can kill something else for yourself later. How's that?"

"You're not worried I'll tell the customs people about your disgraceful behavior?" asked

Theophane. "If not, you've set yourselves up nicely here. Rob people without even killing demons."

"Oh, you're not going to be telling anyone," said one of them.

"Dead guys don't talk much." Another one winked at us.

I sensed that something was approaching us from behind, and I stood behind Theophane, but nothing showed itself yet. Somehow I knew that there were a couple somethings.

Theophane turned his head back, then looked at the men and said:

"I think I'm starting to understand why the demons are all becoming stronger."

"Yeah? Why?" I asked, looking around attentively.

"Because these weasels are attacking people, robbing them, and leaving them wounded at the mercy of the beasts — and the demons, fittingly, are doing rituals to become more powerful."

"Such a clever grandpa," said the group leader, smiling. "But that's not it at all."

Out of the woods came two enemies, and I swallowed from the surprise as my mouth became sticky with saliva.

There were two demons. Their upper halves looked like humans, their bottom halves like snakes, and they had the heads of cobras.

Naga, I realized instantly.

"Because the demons reward us for bringing them people as useless as you — there's nothing to take from you," laughed one of the men, noticing the reinforcements.

Theophane, in response, also unexpectedly let out a vicious laugh.

He pulled off his shirt, and a whole bunch of different kinds of scars became visible on his bare, muscular torso. Practically every inch of his body was covered in them.

I was standing with my back to Theophane, afraid to get distracted from the new enemies even for a moment, so I couldn't really watch what was going on. And I was very surprised at this turn of events — I'd never seen all those scars on Theophane before.

"I've already been put on a demon's ritual altar," said Theophane. "Once, very long ago. So you, you swine, can expect an excruciating death."

The smiling man didn't have a chance to react in time, and the hand holding his sword fell to the ground.

He screamed, and Theophane started fighting with what turned out to be a pretty strong warrior.

"Demons take you all!" I cursed, angry they'd set us up like this, and dodged sharply to the side to avoid a spell.

I'd rather be fighting the humans while Theophane fought the demons, I thought with irritation.

One of the demons was holding a long, elaborately carved staff that went all the way to the ground. That was the one that had shot the spell at me, and the second one was twirling a twisting scythe — a bladed weapon with a long shaft and a scythe blade mounted on it vertically.

"*Hssss*, a human whelp, *hssssss*," said the one with the staff. "Tender morsel, *hsssss!* Tasty, *hssssss!*"

My stomach turned when I heard that — it was the first time I'd heard demons speak, which meant big trouble.

The demon with the twisting scythe was waiting for exactly that moment. It appeared next to me unbelievably fast and struck at me. My body had filled with spiritual energy from fear, and that miraculously allowed me to avoid injury.

The demon spread its arms, and a hood appeared behind its back, like a cobra. It fixed two bright, hypnotic eyes on me.

Put down your weapon! Surrender! I heard the command in my own head and jumped back.

"No!" I bellowed in response, and threw myself at the demon, trying to break off the hypnosis attack.

My initial plan worked — I interrupted the terrifying attack in an instant — but the demon turned out to be much faster and more skilled than me.

Somehow, I didn't know how, I took a hit between the eyes from the back end of the twisting scythe. Blood gushed from my forehead. I fell on my back and started to sink into unconsciousness.

Just before my mind became clouded by dark fog, I saw someone's blurry figure attacking the demons as they celebrated their victory.

Epilogue

"AND NOW, BOYS AND GIRLS, I'm happy to present another new classmate to you — Ivan Yegorovich Frost."

I walked into the classroom and stood next to the teacher. A really nice suit had been made to order for me — dark blue pants, a snow-white shirt, a narrow tie, and a dark red school jacket with the Imperial Academy coat of arms over my heart. It was the school uniform, so I didn't look any different from the other students. The only serious difference was the huge but barely noticeable, almost healed, yellowish-bluish-greenish bruise around my eye.

I greeted my classmates briefly, as etiquette dictated.

"Please sit." The teacher pointed to one of the empty desks at the back of the classroom.

Yes, here each student sat at a separate desk, which I couldn't say I was unhappy about. I really didn't feel like sharing one of those long desks with someone and having to get to know them.

The teacher then presented a few more new students to the class, after which she began the introductory lesson.

I was a little disappointed. For some reason I'd thought that Godimir would be in my class, since he was from a noble family and was and was also planning to start school this year.

And where would a member of a noble family go to school other than an imperial institution? Clearly, he'd been enrolled in some other class...

"You've completed your first four years of schooling in elementary school. You are now in middle school — you're fifth-graders. These three years will go by like it's nothing..." the teacher pontificated.

She told us about the curriculum, the work we'd be doing, our new teachers for various subjects, and of course the essays.

There was one interesting part of her speech.

"Starting this year, you may participate in national competitions and represent our school." After she said that, several children stealthily shot each other happy looks and smiled.

After the bell rang, informing us that the lesson was over, the teacher announced that it was break time and left the room.

The children immediately started talking

amongst themselves and casting curious glances at the new kids.

One of the boys, who looked very intelligent, got up from his desk and approached the group of new students.

“For some reason, I don’t remember your names from the Velvet Book,” he said, giving us an insolent look.

I noticed a number of kids in the room knitting their brows, but no one said anything to him.

“What do you think, wimp?” he said, walking straight up to my desk.

Well, hello, school! I sighed internally, realizing that he was right, and that my bruise was what would start my first fight at school.

End of Book One

Thank you for reading *Living Ice!*
If you like what you've read, check out other sci-fi, fantasy and LitRPG novels published by Magic Dome Books:

NEW RELEASES!

Gakko Academy
a portal progression fantasy adventure series by Evgeny Alexeev

War Eternal
a military space adventure LitRPG series by Yuri Vinokuroff

The Hunter's Code
a LitRPG series by Yuri Vinokuroff & Oleg Sapphire

I Will Be Emperor
a space adventure progression fantasy series by Yuri Vinokuroff & Oleg Sapphire

An Ideal World for a Sociopath
a LitRPG series by Oleg Sapphire

The Healer's Way
a LitRPG series by Oleg Sapphire & Alexey Kovtunov

A Shelter in Spacetime
a LitRPG series by Dmitry Dornichev

Kill or Die
a LitRPG series by Alex Toxic

Living Ice
a portal progression alternative history series by Dmitry Sheleg

Crossroads of Oblivion
a portal progression fantasy adventure series by Dem Mikhailov

Reality Benders
a LitRPG series by Michael Atamanov

The Dark Herbalist
a LitRPG series by Michael Atamanov

Perimeter Defense
a LitRPG series by Michael Atamanov

League of Losers
a LitRPG series by Michael Atamanov

Chaos' Game
a LitRPG series by Alexey Svadkovsky

The Way of the Shaman
a LitRPG series by Vasily Mahanenko

The Alchemist
a LitRPG series by Vasily Mahanenko

Dark Paladin
a LitRPG series by Vasily Mahanenko

Galactogon
a LitRPG series by Vasily Mahanenko

Invasion
a LitRPG series by Vasily Mahanenko

World of the Changed
a LitRPG series by Vasily Mahanenko

The Bear Clan
a LitRPG series by Vasily Mahanenko

Starting Point
a LitRPG series by Vasily Mahanenko

The Bard from Barliona
a LitRPG series
by Eugenia Dmitrieva and Vasily Mahanenko

Condemned
(Lord Valevsky: Last of The Line)
a Progression Fantasy series
by Vasily Mahanenko

Loner
a LitRPG series by Alex Kosh

A Buccaneer's Due
a LitRPG series by Igor Knox

A Student Wants to Live
a LitRPG series by Boris Romanovsky

The Goldenblood Heir
a LitRPG series by Boris Romanovsky

Level Up
a LitRPG series by Dan Sugralinov

Level Up: The Knockout
a LitRPG series by Dan Sugralinov and Max Lagno

Adam Online
a LitRPG Series by Max Lagno

World 99
a LitRPG series by Dan Sugralinov

Disgardium
a LitRPG series by Dan Sugralinov

Nullform
a RealRPG Series by Dem Mikhailov

Clan Dominance: The Sleepless Ones
a LitRPG series by Dem Mikhailov

Heroes of the Final Frontier
a LitRPG series by Dem Mikhailov

The Crow Cycle
a LitRPG series by Dem Mikhailov

Interworld Network
a LitRPG series by Dmitry Bilik

Rogue Merchant
a LitRPG series by Roman Prokofiev

Project Stellar
a LitRPG series by Roman Prokofiev

In the System
a LitRPG series by Petr Zhgulyov

The Crow Cycle
a LitRPG series by Dem Mikhailov

Unfrozen
a LitRPG series by Anton Tekshin

The Neuro
a LitRPG series by Andrei Livadny

Phantom Server
a LitRPG series by Andrei Livadny

Respawn Trials
a LitRPG series by Andrei Livadny

The Expansion (The History of the Galaxy)
a Space Exploration Saga by A. Livadny

The Range
a LitRPG series by Yuri Ulengov

Point Apocalypse
a near-future action thriller by Alex Bobl

Moskau
a dystopian thriller by G. Zotov

El Diablo
a supernatural thriller by G.Zotov

Mirror World
a LitRPG series by Alexey Osadchuk

Underdog
a LitRPG series by Alexey Osadchuk

Last Life
a Progression Fantasy series by Alexey Osadchuk

Alpha Rome
a LitRPG series by Ros Per

An NPC's Path
a LitRPG series by Pavel Kornev

Fantasia
a LitRPG series by Simon Vale

The Sublime Electricity
a steampunk series by Pavel Kornev

Small Unit Tactics
a LitRPG series by Alexander Romanov

Black Centurion
a LitRPG standalone by Alexander Romanov

Rorkh
A LitRPG Series by Vova Bo

Thunder Rumbles Twice
A Wuxia Series by V. Kriptonov & M. Bachurova

Citadel World
a sci fi series by Kir Lukovkin

You're in Game!
LitRPG Stories from Our Bestselling Authors

You're in Game-2!
More LitRPG stories set in your favorite worlds

The Fairy Code
a Romantic Fantasy series by Kaitlyn Weiss

***The Charmed* Fjords**
a Romantic Fantasy series by Marina Surzhevskaya

More books and series are coming out soon!

In order to have new books of the series translated faster, we need your help and support! Please consider leaving a review or spread the word by recommending *Living Ice* to your friends and posting the link on social media. The more people buy the book, the sooner we'll be able to make new translations available.

Thank you!

Till next time!